"Watch out, here comes the transvestite killer thriller. An absolutely shocking comedy" Peter Tatchell

"Somer h   r round
its haunt   e search

for the elusive killer whose murder rate is accelerating... a highly recommended read" *Aesthetica*

"A twilight world of online and real-world extremism that's murkier than the lighting in any transvestite nightclub. A delightful confection" *Time Out*

"A camp comedic thriller... amusing high-adrenalin romp" *The Times*

"Istanbul's Miss Marple – although he prefers leather catsuits to tweed skirts" *Daily Telegraph*

"[A] stylish pulp thriller... *The Prophet Murders* gives the crime genre a naughty, original facelift" Tina Jackson, *Metro*

"Surprising and entertaining... this eye-opener of a crime novel is not to be missed" Joan Smith, *Sunday Times*

"Superior mysteries" Maureen Freely, *Guardian*

The
Kiss Murder

✤

MEHMET MURAT SOMER

Translated by Kenneth Dakan

A complete catalogue record for this book can
be obtained from the British Library on request

First published as *Buse Cinayeti* in 2003 by Iletisim Yayinlari

First published in 2009 by Serpent's Tail,
an imprint of Profile Books Ltd
3A Exmouth House
Pine Street
London EC1R 0JH
website: www.serpentstail.com

ISBN 978 1 84668 693 1

Printed in Great Britain by CPI Bookmarque, Croydon, CR0 4TD

10 9 8 7 6 5 4 3 2 1

This book is printed on FSC certified paper

Acknowledgments

Thanks for everything Mr. Ros, Barba Ros . . .

Chapter 1

✢

$\mathcal{H}$eading for the bathroom, I switched the channel on the television to a game show, just to listen. Like all such programs, it's aimed squarely at the unrepentantly ignorant, but that doesn't mean I don't enjoy getting most of the questions right. In fact, some of the girls at the club even egg me on to become a contestant.

"Wouldn't it be great?" they speculate. "You'd really sock it to them."

"*Ayol!* As if they'd let someone like me on their show," I always respond. That shuts them up.

I finished shaving before the first round of questions was over. Next it was time for my makeup. When I'm in high spirits, this process can last for ages. Otherwise, it's over in less than a couple of minutes. It was a hot night, so the club wouldn't fill up until late. I had plenty of time.

With the right makeup, I'm transformed into a glamorous star of Hollywood's golden age. My all-time favorite is Audrey Hepburn, that boyish beauty.

Perfect, once again. I blew myself a big kiss in the mirror. After dressing in a slinky leopard-print dress, semi-transparent and dripping with sequins, I phoned the stand for a taxi. Hüseyin arrived. He's one of those characters who addresses me with a respectful *abi*, or "elder brother," by day, but salivates at the sight of me by night. As I emerged from the apartment building, he grinned at me like a fawning dog, as always. The moment I entered the cab he switched off the light. At least he's a well-trained dog.

"The club?"

As if I would be going anywhere else at this hour.

"Yes."

I abhor small talk.

We drove off. His eyes were on me, rather than the road. Not content with glimpses in the rearview mirror, he insolently turned to steal glances at me over his shoulder. Now, if he were my type, no problem. But not with that baby face. I like my men manly.

"It's steamy out, isn't it?"

"Hmmm . . ."

"Everything's sticking to me. I'm in the car all day long . . . Like a sun-dried sausage. But dripping wet."

Once again, I was subjected to the sight of a groveling hound.

"But you work nights, don't you?"

"I get all sticky at night, too."

"Take lots of cold showers, then."

"You think there's a shower at the taxi stand? . . . Could I come to your place? We'll cool off . . . Together . . ."

"Don't be impertinent."

"Okay, *abi* . . . Just trying my luck. No big deal."

Over time, as the neighborhood has got to know me better, their attitude has changed. The guys at the taxi stand, too, suddenly saw me in a new light when I managed to teach a neighborhood creep a lesson, employing my formidable skills in Thai kickboxing and aikido, dressed all the while in the tiniest of miniskirts. The public thrashing of a guy twice my size gained me quite a bit of respect.

As I got out of the taxi in front of the club, Hüseyin asked, "Should I pick you up when you finish?"

If there'd been even the remotest chance of his turning out to be another John Holmes, I'd have entertained the idea. But there were none of the telltale signs. Neither his nose nor his fingers showed any promising length.

"No," I said. "There's no telling when I'll get out of here. Don't bother waiting."

Our bodyguard, Cüneyt, met me at the door. I've always suspected that he uses an alias: somehow he seems more like a Mehmet Ali. Whatever his real name is, he's one of those pumpers of iron. One night, when the club was empty, and only at the girls' insistence, I arranged a little aikido demonstration. Apparently his back ached for a week. And I'd held back, only intending to put on a show! It's so typical. Those gym bunnies often turn out to be paper tigers. And the steroids mean they're not much fun in the sack, either.

The club was crowded tonight. Praise the Lord; we are very much in vogue. I won't deny that I deserve some of the credit. After all, I'm the one who introduced a novel management approach, and a new set of rules and regulations.

Because I own a legal, if tiny, share of the club, the girls treat me as their boss. Their high regard for me is the result not only of my stake, but due to the fact that I hold down a day job. In other words, I am not dependent, as they are, on the payments collected from club customers.

Serap made a beeline for me, turning down the noisy music in order to speak:

"*Abla,* my boy's here again . . . Should I go off with him?"

"For free again?"

"But you know I've got a soft spot for him."

"He's taking advantage of you. At this rate you won't even make the rent this month."

"I'll work later."

"Doesn't he stay with you all night?"

"*Ayol*, are you kidding? . . . He lives with his family. He's got to be home by midnight. Or deal with his big brother."

I smiled to myself. I know those censorious big brothers. They're the sort who get up to things, or at least imagine getting up to things, that would make even my hair stand on end.

The sight of a pair of eyes glowing with longing made me change my mind about trying to talk some sense into her.

"It's up to you, sweetie, but take care not to let yourself go too much," I warned.

"I'm as gone as I'll ever get," was the reply.

"So off you go, then."

Serap raced toward her sweetheart, a dry, dark, skinny slip of a nineteen-year-old, who was shorter than her and would have good reason to fear an older brother. Even as she ran, Serap did not neglect her trademark waggle of the hips. From what she says, the boy's tackle warrants a second look, although that's certainly not the impression he makes on first sight. Well, I suppose it's never really clear who's sporting what.

Leaving my drink on the bar, I pushed through the crowd toward the dance floor. Various girls greeted and kissed me as I passed. When I emerged on the floor, DJ Osman played my favorite track, the Weather Girls' "It's Raining Men," and I started dancing. Buse approached me, her pallor obvious even in the darkness. Makeup does have its limitations. Acting like she was dancing, Buse came right up to me.

"Can we talk?" she said.

Placing an arm around her shoulders, I led Buse off the dance floor. In response to the quizzical look Osman threw me from the DJ booth, I gestured, *Later.*

"What is it?"

"Can we go upstairs? It's too noisy here. I don't want to shout."

The girls often tell me their problems, consulting me on

every subject under the sun, employing me as everything from financial advisor to agony aunt.

We went to the office on the top floor. It's a low-ceilinged mezzanine, with a small window looking out over the interior of the club. It's cluttered. Crammed into the room are a huge desk, a safe in the corner, two old armchairs, stocks of toilet paper and napkins, and crates of alcohol. I perched on the edge of a crate of wine. Buse sank into the only empty armchair. She fixed her eyes on me, as though expecting an explanation of some sort. I waited for a few moments, doing my best to understand. Had I forgotten anything? No, I hadn't.

"What's going on, *ayol*?" I finally demanded. "What's with the questioning eyes? You're the one who wanted to talk."

She continued staring intently, silent. Like she was sizing me up. She was clearly wondering whether or not to spill the beans.

"I'm terrified," she began. "Absolutely petrified . . ."

I looked at her inquiringly. Thinking it best, I also allowed a sympathetic smile to settle into the corners of my mouth.

"I don't know where to start. I'm so confused."

"Just start talking. Tell me anything you like," I encouraged.

She stared down at the floor, still silent. I began counting the stocks of *rakı*: nine crates, all fully wrapped in plastic.

"I'm so frightened . . ."

"That much is clear, sweetie," I said. "But why?"

I waited for her to continue. Still not a peep. I began counting the boxes of white wine: five in all; less than I'd expected. There do seem to be a lot of white wine drinkers these days. We're flying through the stock.

"I'm in possession of certain documents."

Buse was still looking at the floor. Carefully choosing each word, she slowly continued, "They concern an important person. A prominent person. If it ever got out, all hell would break loose. It'd be the biggest scandal ever."

My interest was piqued, despite myself.

"Years ago... I was with someone, someone who's very important now. And it wasn't just a one-night stand. It was more like a relationship. It lasted for a long time. There are photos of us, together, at various times, in different places. And the notes he wrote me. I say notes, but one of them is more like a letter. Handwritten and signed. I mean, a proper letter. It spells out everything."

There was another long period of silence. I'd become more curious, but I still lacked the patience to wait for more. I moved on to the red wine. Only two cases. What concerned me most was the beer: only sixteen cases and four kegs left.

"Someone knows I have the photos and letters."

The girls tend to be chatterboxes. They tell everyone everything, particularly if they bed a celebrity, however minor. Every last detail. Inevitably, the lover is straight, but just couldn't resist yours truly. In fact, he's fallen head over heels. Of course, these little tales are designed to advertise the beauty and singularity of the narrator—not all of them are true. Even I occasionally stretch the truth.

But the Buse I knew never indulged in these ego-inflating exercises. In fact, when I thought about it, I realized how little I did know about her. Her real name was Fevzi. She was from Istanbul. She lived alone in Teşvikiye. She had a cat. She was a bit older than the others, I'd guess close to forty.

When our sort passes forty, those with money shut themselves up in their homes; those without resources end up in third-rate music halls or back in the countryside, rubbing shoulders with "the people." Every province in the land has a licensed kebab hall that employs our girls. Those exiled to the country come to Istanbul once a year to shop, exhibit themselves, and lie pitifully about how fabulously contented they are.

Anyway, Buse started having silicone injections about ten

years ago. Then she began spraying herself liberally with L'Eau d'Issey.

"I would never betray a relationship. I never have. When it's over, it's over."

Once again, she fell silent. This time, she lifted her eyes to the wall. Her unseeing eyes scanned the management license and tax report affixed there, and I began to read it as well.

"It was very private and special in any case. And it still is. Very personal."

Buse focused her eyes onto the management license and fell into a sort of reverie. Although she said not a word, she was clearly on a virtual journey, reliving that relationship of which she'd said so little. I began toying with a bit of adhesive that had come loose on the tabletop. I lifted it with a fake fingernail, then allowed it to fall. I didn't keep track of how many times I did this, but it took a while before Buse spoke again.

"It's got complicated. I told someone about it. I was high. I don't remember exactly what I said, but it must have been too much. Then someone else found out about the documents, and now they want me to hand them over."

"Why?" I asked.

"For blackmail, I suppose."

"Who are they?"

"I don't know. First they left a message on my answering machine. I didn't give it much thought. I didn't do what they asked . . . Then they broke into my house. Last night, while I was here at the club. They went through all of my things but didn't find anything."

"Could it have been a burglar?"

"I thought that at first, but it wasn't. They didn't touch the money I had lying around. The stereo was still there. None of my jewels were missing. But the apartment had been turned upside down. I spent all day today cleaning up."

"So where did you hide them? Why couldn't they find them?"

"They're at my mother's," she replied.

"I don't understand."

Most of the girls have no contact with their families. They're mostly outcasts.

"At my mother's. In my old bedroom. I sometimes stay there."

"I see."

"I'm afraid they'll find her house, too. She's old, never goes out."

The words rushed out of her. Our conversation had picked up speed.

"If she never leaves her house, there shouldn't be a problem."

"Unfortunately, there is. My mother's blind."

Now I got the picture. My eyes widened.

"So she doesn't know about you."

"Of course, she knows all about me," Buse said. "The blind see with their hands. She didn't get it for quite a while, but the breasts, and then later the hair. She may be blind, but she's not stupid."

The door opened and Hasan poked his head inside. In the nick of time. The last thing I needed tonight was more of Buse and her paranoia.

"So you're here," he noted.

It was easy to see that Buse couldn't stand Hasan. Because of that, Hasan also seemed uneasy. Buse was not a favorite of his, either.

"Sorry to disturb you. I just wanted to let you know that a group claiming to be friends of yours has arrived," he announced. "Group" meant that it was a mixed party of men and women.

"They're asking for you. Are you going to come down?"

My employees address me with the formal *"siz."* I enjoy it. I turned to look at Buse, who had already risen to her feet.

"I don't want to give you any headaches. Forget it," she murmured. "Whatever happens, happens."

I followed Hasan down the staircase, reluctantly adding, "We'll chat later. If you want to, stop by my place when you leave the club. It's up to you."

"Maybe," she said. She sounded drained. I let her pass me on the stairs.

We went down one by one, Hasan leading the way, followed by Buse and myself. Hasan's jeans had slipped below his hips, exposing a bit of cleavage. I suspect he's a bit light on his feet, he just isn't aware of it yet. He's been working at the club for nearly a full year and he's on good terms with all the girls, but hasn't slept with any of them—or a real girl for that matter. Not that we've heard of, anyway. Isn't that a bit odd?

Then I inspected Buse's bottom. She was unbelievably elegant as she descended the stairs. As the narrow male bottom shifted inside her tight leather miniskirt, the lights played incredible tricks. I realized I'd never really given her buns a second look. They stuck out like the two halves of an apple, eminently pinchable.

She hadn't explained who it was she feared so much, or why. But just talking about it seemed to have soothed her. Then she was lost in the crowd.

Chapter 2

❖

$\mathcal{H}$asan's "group" consisted of Belkıs, the proprietor of a boutique in Nişantaşı, her husband Ferruh, the lyricist Suat, a man in advertising, and a lady journalist whose name I promptly forgot. It was the first I'd seen of the latter two. The advertising man was Ahmet, and he seemed to be a bit of a pansy. But all would be clear soon enough. I sat at their table. Assuming his most professional air, Hasan awaited our orders.

Despite his familiarity with Belkıs, Ferruh, and Suat, Hasan kept his distance, in deference to the strangers. Otherwise, he would have been arm in arm with Suat, excitedly exchanging the latest gossip.

A real macho man, Suat crossed her legs, lit her cigarette, and ordered a *rakı*. She was a lesbian of the extremist school. Many men appear positively feminine in comparison. Ferruh ordered a whiskey with lots of ice. The rest wanted white wine. Based on his choice of white wine, Ahmet revealed himself as almost certainly gay. Real men with money order hard liquor, the others settle for beer. What is the allure of wimpy white wine?

The club grew more crowded. It seemed the admission charge incited more people to come out.

While enjoying myself with Belkıs and the others, I completely forgot about Buse. Belkıs's shop is a bit démodé, but the occasional garment is just right for me, and at a good price.

That is to say, we enjoy a special friendship. I sometimes find it hard to believe that her husband, Ferruh, is a financial advisor. He always strikes me as being a bit constipated. The jewelry he affects plays a large part in my disbelief: on his right wrist, a thick bracelet on which his name is written in diamanté; on his left wrist, a watch with a gold strap. Unfortunately, not a Rolex. Even less pleasant to the eye, three bejeweled golden rings on his hairy fingers. Isn't that reason enough to explain my repulsion?

Suat's real name is Ayşen; Suat is actually her surname. Having become famous under the name Suat, and with a decidedly more masculine appearance than you'd expect from an Ayşen, she now uses only that name. Suat ridicules men at all opportunities, and the fact that not a single male hand has touched her is a source of great pride. According to her categorization, the highest ranks of people consist exclusively of lesbians, followed by nonlesbian women, girls like us, gays, bisexuals and, finally, at the very bottom of the heap, straight men. She has not yet managed to write decent lyrics for a male singer. For them, she writes only the silliest tripe, depicting the most foolish of emotional states. All of her hits—and their number is considerable—are written for female singers unable or unwilling to return her passionate feelings. For a time, Suat was tailed like a shadow by a freckled, red-haired singer who helped Suat quite a bit in making a name for herself in the market. But the day the singer addressed Suat in a loud voice, in front of everyone as "Ayşen," it was over. The event was splashed across the front pages of the entertainment press.

This was her first appearance at the club in quite a while. She didn't clasp me in a bear hug and pat my bottom, as was her habit, and I took this as a positive sign. But there was no saying what she would do after her fifth glass of *rakı*.

Latent Ahmet, the gentleman in advertising, was the picture of refinement as he took tiny sips of his white wine. His unease manifested itself in chain-smoking. Being in a place like this, with people he knew, was more than he could handle. He looked around enviously, inwardly sighing at the sight of the boys dancing with our girls. It was a foregone conclusion that I'd see him arrive at the club on his own one day, prepared to let his hair down when there were no acquaintances around.

The lady journalist, whose name I had missed, looked around curiously. It may have been her first exposure to our culture. She threw stealthy glances my way from time to time, but permitted herself no eye contact. I used my bass range, out of spite. When she looked my way, I smiled sweetly. After answering their questions, I took my leave. I'd finished half my drink, in any case. As I said, there's a lot to do on a busy night.

When I rose from the table, Buse took a seat next to Belkıs and her husband, both of whom she knew. From what I remembered, the three had engaged in some sort of ménage à trois once upon a time. Buse had described the encounter as less than successful, with all three unable to overcome a fit of giggles. When Ferruh and Belkıs began quarreling, Buse took off.

I began focusing on other things. There were any number of men of different ages and types, and the girls, my girls, so attractive and so very grateful for my attentiveness. And then there are those who occasionally cause trouble. I will not have in my club girls who become drunkenly abrasive. Such girls, and the men who get out of hand jockeying for a favorite, are not permitted to pass through these doors a second time. Even Alain Delon would be barred under such circumstances. It's terribly old-fashioned, I know, but the word "man" instantly conjures up images of Alain Delon. And his youth! I inherited at least some of this admiration for Alain from my mother, who was a big fan. When she was pregnant with me she would constantly look at his photographs, hoping I'd grow up to look like him. After I was born, she continued looking at his photos. As my interest in men developed, we looked at them together. She took me to all his films. We'd sigh in unison as we watched.

Time flies when there is such a heavy flow of customers. Greet so-and-so, chat with him or her, etc. Next thing you know, it's morning. We're open until dawn's early light. On weekends, few girls are left unclaimed as the last of the customers straggle out. In fact, some of them even manage several engagements throughout the course of the night, returning to the club after each one. This was one of those nights. I glanced over the bills —great turnover, yet again—and left. I could feel my beard growing out beneath my foundation. I got into a taxi Cüneyt had arranged, and immediately removed my high heels, massaging my feet all the way home. It's not easy, moving with deerlike grace from table to table for eight hours while weighed down with four-pound shoes. The taxi driver was a familiar face. An elderly, gentlemanly man. He knows where I live; we seldom chat. And he never has change. Naturally, that was the case this morning, too. I wasn't about to pay twice the normal amount, so I told him he could pick up the money at the club in the evening.

I entered my home barefoot. I would be taking a shower before bed in any case. I might even decide to drink something warm—my new favorite was fennel tea. It soothes and cleanses. I know, because I'm constantly reading up on what is good for what.

Chapter 3

❖

A shower was just what the doctor ordered—standing under the steady flow for a long period of time has a hypnotic effect. It relaxes you completely. The amount of makeup flowing off my face in the shower has always startled me. It seems like next to nothing as it's being applied.

I examined my body in the mirror—a favorite pastime. I'm one of those slender, lightly muscled types said to have a swimmer's build. My body has not been altered in the slightest by plastic surgery or silicone injections. Breastless women are not uncommon. The size and firmness of my nipples is more than enough for most. What's the need for silicone? My legs are waxed, my arms in their natural state, my bosom the site of a bouquet of chest hair. That hair remains untouched unless I am required to wear a provocative outfit. Fortunately, my mat of hair is lightly colored. And there are times when a glimpse of chest hair in a plunging neckline has a special allure all its own. I applied lotion to my entire body. The result was a pleasant sensation of coolness, slipperiness, and hair standing sweetly on end.

There's nothing I enjoy more in the morning than wandering aimlessly from room to room, before the papers are delivered. A large mug in hand—acquired for a small fortune from Casa Club—I drifted with my fennel tea. The morning light in my home is stunning—a pale gold. Long horizontal beams line the narrow corridor. Strange shadows. It gives me peace.

The shop boy was late, as usual. It was nearly seven a.m. That's another of my obsessions. I cannot sleep without having read the daily papers.

The bell rang repeatedly. It couldn't be the shop boy intruding on my little paradise. He never rings the bell, merely slips the papers under the door and leaves. I raced toward the door, ready to confront the intruder. Naturally, I glanced through the peephole first: In front was Hüseyin, the taxi driver; behind him stood Buse, looking thoroughly haunted. I flung the door open.

"What on earth has happened?"

Hüseyin jumped in before Buse had a chance to answer.

"Your friend went to the club. I saw her walk in. She was looking for you, so I brought her right over."

He spoke in one breath. I resented the use of the familiar *sen*, in place of *siz*. Besides, what business did he have trolling through the narrow street in front of our club?

Speaking in a voice not her own, Buse asked, "May I come in?"

Of course she could. I stepped aside to let her. Hüseyin made to go in after her, but I barred his way.

"And where do you think you're going, *ayol*?"

"I just thought something terrible might have happened. Maybe you'd need help ... So you wouldn't want to be on your own ..." He hemmed and hawed. On his face, I noticed the familiar hungry look. Once rejected, he should know better than to insist.

"We will be fine!" I said. "There's no need. We'll handle it."

The bold expression remained on his face. He clearly imagined himself to be the Istanbul version of Brad Pitt. I prepared to shut the door in his face, but he grabbed it.

"If you need anything, I'll be at the taxi rank. Don't hesitate to call if you need help." And that grin again. He gestured toward the room. "I don't understand what happened. But it's nothing good."

"All right, it's a deal. I'll call if necessary. Now go. Thanks for bringing her over."

I tried once again to close the door. He held it open.

"Don't be tiresome," I warned.

"Uh," he began, "who's going to pay the fare?"

It was natural for Buse to have forgotten, in her state. I must have looked blank for a moment.

"I can pick it up from the club," he offered. "That is, if you haven't got it on you . . ."

"How much?" I asked.

"I didn't check the meter. You know, whatever you pay every night."

I paid him slightly more than the appropriate amount.

"All right, then?" I asked. The hopeful gleam in his eye faded, then was fully extinguished. He turned around aimlessly. I shut the door and went to Buse's side.

She had sunk into an armchair and was staring into space, eyes open wide.

"Would you like something to drink?"

"Please." I waited for her to name something. Tea, coffee, cola, water, alcohol . . . Nothing.

"What can I get you?"

She looked at me with the expression of a quiz show contestant attempting to answer a difficult question. I tried again.

"What would you like to drink?"

She paused. The question was a difficult one, and she was determined to drag it out. She resumed staring blankly. She seemed drugged. Some of the girls indulge, most only occasionally. As for me, never.

I am extremely patient, but it is a virtue best not strained. Especially early in the morning.

"I'm drinking fennel tea. I'll make you some."

"Fine."

As I prepared the tea, I reviewed what she had told me the previous night. Maybe there was something to her story. I added a bit of cold water to the mug so she'd be able to drink it immediately without burning her mouth. Then I returned to her side.

We sat in silence for a while. I noted her strange appearance, her makeup mussed, her stubble catching the morning light. She was a true hybrid of Fevzi and Buse. She lifted her head and looked at me intently. I returned the look with my most sympathetic smile. I'm an accomplished listener, and have learned quite a bit as a result. Unfortunately, I'm not at my best in the morning just as I am preparing for bed.

Eventually—yes, finally—she began.

"I'm terrified," she began again, just like in the club. "I didn't know where to go, who to turn to. So I came here. I'm sorry. Believe me, I'm at the end of my rope."

"You were right to come to me."

What else could I say? I was tired. I looked at her inquiringly, waiting for her to explain, so we could go to bed.

"They came to the house," she said. "When I got home I almost bumped into them. There were three people. They'd gone inside. They were waiting for me."

I could ask how later. First I'd need a general sense of what had happened.

"When I realized they were in there, I shut the door right away. Then locked it and ran. Thank God the key was still in the hole."

"Good . . . you did well," I congratulated her. "So who were they?"

"I don't know," she said. "I didn't see them, just heard them."

"How do you know what they were after?"

"Two nights in a row!" she exclaimed. "The night before,

they'd searched the house. They couldn't find anything, so they came back to catch me."

"And what if they've followed you?"

"The front door is pretty solid," she said. "They were locked in. It would take them at least an hour to open a steel door like that. I took three separate taxis, and I'm sure no one was following me."

She continued staring. Considering what she'd been through, she was incredibly calm. She spoke in robotic tones. Calmly and slowly.

"I didn't really have a chance to think . . ." she said. "My nerves were wrecked. I took something to calm down, then I decided to come to you. My head was swimming."

It'd be impossible to get more out of her if she'd taken something.

"If you like, let's go to bed," I suggested. "Get some sleep. Calm down a bit. We'll talk again when we get up."

"Fine," she said.

I led her to the guest room. She got into bed without removing her makeup, just taking time to slip out of her clothes. She was, of course, wearing the tiniest of G-strings.

Chapter 4

❖

Sleep did me good. I awoke shortly after noon, with light filling the room as I pulled back the heavy curtains. I immediately opened the window: fresh air. No matter what the summer temperature is outside, the garden behind my building is always cool and moist. I adore this garden, filled with fruit trees and hydrangeas.

The closed door of the guest room reminded me of Buse; I made my way as quietly as possible to the bathroom. She must be asleep. The cool water was refreshing, and I was flooded with the excitement of a new day. Then I prepared coffee for two in the kitchen. The first bitter swallow takes my breath away, then stimulates me.

I went inside to choose some soothing music. I decided on Bach's BWV 1060 double concertos. It's a particularly appropriate piece for sunny days. I don't even remember how many different versions of it I've got. There's nothing like having good music close at hand. My favorite is the synthesized version as played by the Pekinel sisters and jazz musician Bob James, and also the authentic harpsichord played by Hogwood and Rousset. Christopher Hogwood and Christophe Rousset are both gay, another plus.

I went to the guest room to wake up Buse. Tapping on the door, I peeked in: the room was empty. The bed had been made. I instinctively called out her name. Listening carefully, I waited for a reply from any part of the house. Nothing. I scurried through the flat, calling Buse's name. My home is spacious, but no Dolmabahçe Palace. I quickly checked every corner: Not a trace of Buse! She was gone.

Dumping her untouched coffee into the sink, I settled into my favorite chair with mine. I wanted to evaluate the situation calmly. Accompanied now by Handel, I began to think: Someone—or as many as three people—was after Buse, whose real name was Fevzi. Actually, it wasn't she they wanted, but the photographs and letters in her possession. The documents involved someone of importance who had once had a romantic adventure with Buse/Fevzi. She claimed they would make perfect blackmail material. The photos and letters were in the "teenage girl's" old bedroom back at her blind mother's house. Buse's home had been ransacked. What's more, three men had lain in wait for her there.

Considering how easy it had been to locate Buse and her home, it would be easy enough for them to find the club too. Maybe tonight, or perhaps tomorrow . . . they would most certainly show up at some point. That particular fact was of great personal interest to me.

Buse had come to my house after hers was broken into. As you might imagine, our girls are no strangers to criminal activities. They endure minor theft and physical attacks on an almost daily basis. So they're not easily spooked. However, Buse/Fevzi was in a state of shock. Unsure of what was really happening and why, she had been unable to tell me much. Now she'd disappeared. Full stop.

That was all I knew. It was now up to me to decide whether or not to become further involved. The choices before me were:

(A) Wait and see. Wait for Buse/Fevzi to contact me when she needed me.

(B) Assume some degree of responsibility for Buse/Fevzi, who is, after all, a part-time employee at the club I run. Act preemptively, therefore, by attempting to find and protect her.

(C) Get to the root of the problem in order to resolve it. I'm not really sure what that means.

(D) Find the photographs and letters. Act as some sort of intermediary, surrendering them as painlessly as possible, destroying them, or selling them to the highest bidder for the benefit of Buse.

There were, no doubt, dozens of other possible courses of action. But these were all that I thought were worth considering.

I jumped at the sound of the ringing phone. It might be Buse, wanting to explain why she'd left without a word.

It was Hasan.

"Good morning," he said. "I hope I haven't woken you."

"No. I was up."

"Good," he said. "Is Buse still there?"

"No. She was gone when I got up this morning."

"Hasn't she called?"

"Not yet."

It suddenly struck me. How did Hasan know that Buse had stayed with me?

"How do you know she was here?" I asked.

"After you left, while I was closing the club, she came up to me. I sent her off with that taxi driver of yours, Hüseyin, who was still here. Perhaps Cüneyt hadn't told him you'd left and he was waiting for you."

This explanation seemed plausible.

"I was worried," he continued. "She didn't look well."

"You're right about that," I agreed.

"So what's wrong? What happened?"

"It's a private matter."

"I see," he said. "Well, I just wondered."

"Look," I warned him, "you're a little too curious. You know what they say, it's either pricks or prying. Dicks or curiosity are the root of all troubles."

"Well, I prefer the second," Hasan said. "No dicks for me, thanks . . . They're all yours."

Either he didn't know what he was missing or he was pretending.

We hung up.

Immediately afterward, the phone rang again. Assuming Hasan had something he'd forgotten to say, I picked up right away.

My "Hello" must have sounded a little brusque.

"The line was busy. I hope I haven't woken you up . . ."

At first I didn't recognize the voice on the other end. Then it introduced itself: Belkıs's husband, Ferruh. I get on well with Belkıs, but it was very strange for Ferruh to be ringing me. Especially in the morning.

He asked how I was, and thanked me for my hospitality the previous night. Although he didn't sound at all convincing, he claimed to have enjoyed himself greatly.

I rarely talk to Ferruh outside the club, but I could tell he was speaking more hesitantly than usual. There was enough space between each sentence—even between each word—for a commercial break.

"Belkıs sends her best," he said.

I thanked him again and sent her my greetings. That's odd, I thought; Belkıs would normally be at the boutique by this time.

First it was Hasan who had given me pause for thought; the fact that he knew so much, and was so eager to learn more. Ferruh's call raised my suspicions even further. Why now, of all times?

I decided on number one in my list of possible courses of action: To wait and see.

It was actually the most difficult alternative, because my mind had begun racing. It would be extremely nerve-wracking to just sit and do nothing. I'd have to restrict all thoughts on the subject to a corner of my mind and go about my daily business. After all, I have claimed patience as one of my many virtues.

Luckily, I had plenty to keep me occupied. I went to my study and looked through my appointment book. Just as I'd remembered, I had a meeting at four-thirty with a company called Wish & Fire.

My day job is in technology support. I develop security systems for computers in order to protect them from hackers. It pays quite well, and I can arrange work around my schedule, which offers me a great deal of freedom. What's more, I'm still only second-tier, in professional terms; that is, I haven't yet made a name for myself. Those unable to afford the big names come to me. That means a large pool of potential clients to choose from.

I also have an office at one of the companies that offers these services. On my door there's a sign that says CONSULTANT. I go there occasionally, when I feel like it. Otherwise, I work from home. When large companies want to meet with me, it usually means rewarding work is on offer. My job is by no means easy. Hackers are constantly developing more effective methods, and it's becoming increasingly difficult to keep up with them.

When I go to meetings, I think it's best to dress a bit unconventionally. Clients tend to associate quirky clothes with better-quality service. The last thing they expect is for me to arrive looking like a banker. I selected a shirt in a fashionable shade of saffron. In that, paired with white slacks, I was sufficiently radiant.

I arrived early for the appointment. All went as I'd anticipated: Their computer systems had been crashed twice, just for "fun." They needed my help to prevent future attacks. On and on they went about the vital flow of information, their overseas connections and their sensitivity to such problems. I took copious notes and commented freely on each point they brought up. When it comes to business meetings, I consider myself head of the company; Ali, my business partner, merely shoots slightly bewildered glances at me from time to time. And that's exactly what he did now. I winked, taking care that no one else saw.

When the meeting was over I told Ali I'd have to have a good look at the company's systems to determine the best course of action. I suggested deciding on a fee only after I had done so. Although this was incomprehensible to his mercantile mind, Ali nodded in agreement.

"You know best. You're the expert," he said. He was right.

I went home without wasting any more time. Once there, I got onto the Internet to research Wish & Fire, visiting both their local and international websites. I even covertly entered their system to gather some more data. It was easy enough to do. The global computer system had been established in the typically naïve manner of Canadians. Security precautions were virtually nonexistent. I estimated my task would take about ten to twelve days, and a fee of $20,000 would be adequate. International companies are incredibly tight, so I doubted we would get more.

When I was satisfied, I rang Ali. He was somewhere noisy, but when the subject is money, he somehow manages to hear every word. He listened eagerly.

After I hung up with Ali, all I really wanted to do was laze in front of the television for a bit, then make myself dinner. As I was surfing through the channels, the doorbell rang.

It was Hüseyin from the taxi stand.

"*Efendim?*" I inquired. I managed an admirably rough tone, albeit somewhere in the upper register.

"Uh," he said, "what happened to your friend? Is she all right? She was in such bad shape this morning. I was worried about her."

"She's fine," I informed him crisply. "Most kind of you to inquire."

It seemed like everyone was worried about Buse.

"You were going to call if you needed anything . . ."

"I didn't."

My tone was sufficiently stinging, but he kept standing there, apparently reluctant to leave. What he wanted was perfectly clear, but he lacked the courage.

"Yes?" I asked.

"I'll drop by to pick you up whenever you're ready. I promised to take you to the club, you know."

He attempted a lady-killer sneer.

"It's still early," I noted. "I'll call the stand. Don't bother to wait."

"What do you mean?" he protested. "What could be better than waiting for you?"

"Well, wait, then! It's up to you. You're your own man."

"But when will you be going out?"

"I'm not sure. When I'm good and ready, I suppose. Good evening."

I shut the door.

I was getting annoyed with Hüseyin's attentions. And what was he doing in front of the club so early in the morning? If he'd really been following me, he'd have known I don't stay there that late. And what was with all the interest in Buse? He'd only met her once. I figured it was all just an excuse to talk to me.

As usual at this hour, I clicked from channel to channel,

looking for something decent to watch. Nothing was on, so I switched off the set. Off I went to the kitchen to make myself something appetizing. I'm not involved with anyone at the moment, so all my meals are prepared for one. Even if it takes me twice as long to prepare a meal as to consume it, I find cooking calms me down.

Chapter 5

❖

J ate with gusto, then loaded the dishwasher. There was still no sign of Buse. If something major had happened, surely I'd have heard. It was still too early to go to the club, so I decided to get online. I could try out some new software and also check out the dreamy men on some porn sites. It wasn't like I had the opportunity to meet such men in my daily life. And it provided a feast for my eyes, an anatomy lesson, and some general knowledge.

I opened John Pruitt's site. There were new photos I'd never seen before. He is one of the few men able to turn me on with a mere photograph. I mean, I normally much prefer them in the flesh. Unlike so many others, I am no addict to erotic soft-core or hard-core pictures. In order to fully appreciate a man, I need him to look at me, to move. I need to get a sense of his scent. But that John Pruitt... those looks, those lips, those hands... perfect. He's head and shoulders above the rest, a superstar model for Colt Studio, and renowned for years in gay circles.

While downloading the photos, I simultaneously glanced at the new protective software on offer, but there was nothing ground-breaking. That's the advantage of belonging to Internet groups devoted to the subject. It enables me to keep up on the latest technology.

Just as I was preparing to enjoy a little heart-to-heart with John Pruitt, the doorbell rang. Spotting Hüseyin through the peephole, I flew into a rage. I flung the door open. The slightest false move, and I'd flatten the dog. Enough is enough!

"What is it?" I demanded. "What are you after?"

"Excuse me," he said. The grin was gone. "I rang, but the phone wasn't connected. Were you watching TV?"

"I was," I said.

"Fine, then . . ." He turned to leave, but wished to add something else, and was unable to.

"Stop harassing me," I said. "You've got me all wrong."

He blushed, unable to meet my eye.

"N-no, you got it wrong," he stuttered.

"No, I haven't! There's been no misunderstanding. Get your act together or else. I'm warning you. And stop addressing me as *sen*. Your customers are to be addressed as *siz*."

"Look," he pleaded, "I was watching TV at the stand. Your friend's been murdered. I just came up to say I'm sorry. We're neighbors, after all. I think I have the right."

Buse! Fevzi! Or whatever her name was. Now it was my turn to blush.

I let Hüseyin in and he related what he'd seen on the news. His eyes remained downcast. He'd immediately recognized the girl in the news report as the one he'd brought to my house in the morning, so he'd listened carefully. A transvestite had apparently quarreled with a customer, according to the news account. The perpetrator had not been apprehended. It may have been a case of self-defense. Her head had been split open. They even showed it on the screen.

He ended with, "So her real name was Fevzi," and looked up at me. Actually, he has lovely eyes, full of meaning. But it's still hopeless. I'm not sure how I looked at him, but he rose to his feet. "I'd better get going," he said. "If you need anything, call me."

He'd remembered the *siz*. Though he had tacked it on at the last minute, it was progress of some kind.

"Okay? I'll do whatever I can to help."

And that look again: two rows of bright, white, healthy teeth gleaming at me.

I appreciate determined people. But not when they're determined to hit on me.

In my driest voice, I thanked him as I accompanied him to the door. Things were getting out of hand. An innocent love affair had become material for blackmail, then a threat, then the motive for a gruesome murder. As always, the police would relegate the "transvestite file" to a dusty drawer. In fact, there was bound to be much more to all this than meets the eye.

I suddenly remembered the letters and photographs. The motive for the crime! Hidden at the home of Fevzi's blind mother! Any moment now they might find her. Another innocent victim to the slaughter. I had to find her before they did. She needed protection, and I needed to prevent them from finding the documents.

I made up my mind instantly. Once again, I would have to get involved.

Chapter 6

✤

$\mathcal{I}$ don't know where the girls from the club live, or at least not many of them. Nor do I recall the exact addresses of those I have visited. I don't even know most of their real names. It was therefore nothing out of the ordinary for me not to have the slightest idea of the exact whereabouts of the house of the dead transvestite's mother. Her surname must have been mentioned on the news report that Hüseyin saw, but the story was almost certainly not important enough to be covered once more on the evening news. I could find out from the coroner's office or the police. But that would take time, something that was in short supply. I had to find this elderly lady as soon as possible, and take possession of those letters and photographs.

I tried to remember which of the girls Buse had been close to. Due to her advanced age, most of them had kept their distance. Not to mention that she was under the impression that she was made of finer stuff. As a transvestite, she was an odd duck. While most of the girls dressed in evening gowns or sexy outfits, Buse/Fevzi went in for more ladylike costumes. Once she had even arrived at the club in a tailor-made, pale pink, classic Chanel suit. If her alter ego wasn't Catherine Deneuve, it was at least Sabine Azéma. I'd seen the latter more than a few times in outfits like that, sipping tea on the terrace of the Etap Marmara Hotel. While wearing a tad too much makeup, and something of a coquette, she did manage to stand out as her own woman.

I called Hasan at the club. If nothing else, we had Buse's body to think about. If we didn't claim it and the family refused to do so—as is so often the case—Buse would end up as a cadaver at some medical college. What, exactly, aspiring surgeons would do with it was another question. Anatomy lessons from the dissection of a decidedly male body, complete with pert breasts and loads of silicone in its cheekbones and lips? The times, they are indeed a-changing.

Hasan had seen the news, but couldn't remember Buse's surname, either. "Who would she hang out with?" I asked. He thought for awhile, running through a list of the names of all the girls he knew, then returning to the top of the list. He finally settled on one of the older girls, Sofya.

"You mean the Sofya I know?" I asked. "Didn't she retire ages ago?"

"That's right," he confirmed. "She doesn't get out much anymore. She leads a quiet life." He paused. "At least I think she does."

"How am I supposed to find her?"

"She still lives in Çatalçeşme."

"Hasan, get to the point. Do you know exactly where she lives or not?"

"I've been there once. I'm not sure I can remember."

"A simple yes or no will do."

I do not, and cannot under any circumstances, tolerate shilly-shallying.

He thought for a moment. The seriousness of my tone apparently forced him to answer with a gulped "Yes." Congratulations, Hasan. Then he added:

"But you know she can't stand you. She'd tear me to pieces if I brought you to her house."

"I know," was my crisp reply.

It was all such a bore. Yes, I must admit that we were

divided into various factions. Not every girl is overflowing with humanist tendencies and the capacity for fast friendships. Enmity is not unknown. It is, in fact, common.

"She absolutely hates you. She's never forgiven you for coming between her and her friend Sinan. There's no way she'll ever help you, you of all people."

While I expect Hasan to be frank with me, siding with Sofya was really going too far. My employee, supporting Sofya! This was absurd.

"Look here, Hasan, don't push me. She won't be helping me. This is serious. I've got to reach Buse's mother. It's a matter of life or death."

"Why?" he asked.

I paused, then decided he had every reason to ask me that question. Buse/Fevzi had never been a favorite of mine, was not someone with whom I'd spent any time. The interest I was now showing far exceeded that demanded by my role of employer.

I briefly summarized the situation. He listened, breathless.

"So, it's in her mother's house?" he asked incredulously.

His question was normal enough. Possessions of such a highly personal nature are not usually left with one's parents.

"Buse's mother is blind," I added.

"Ah, now I understand," he said.

"Now go call that desiccated hag Sofya and get the address of Buse's mother, if she knows it. Also, be sure to find out her last name. Then call me the minute you're done."

"But I don't know her phone number," Hasan said. "Only where her house is."

Another fly in the ointment. I tried to put my thoughts in order.

"Look," I suggested, "put Şükrü in charge of the club. I'll pick you up and we'll go to Sofya's together. You talk to her while I wait in the car."

I hung up before he had a chance to answer.

Next, I called for a taxi. Naturally, Hüseyin showed up.

"You can't be going to the club at this time. Where to?"

"To the club," I replied sharply.

His fleeting look of bewilderment pleased me no end. His self-confidence had been badly shaken, the insolent expression replaced with one of surprise. Then, of course, I had to tell him where we were actually going. I thought I detected a sudden gleam of excitement in his eyes. But images seen in rearview mirrors can be misleading, so I paid it no mind.

After picking up Hasan, then crisscrossing for some twenty minutes through the one-way streets of Suadiye and Çatalçeşme, above and below the railway tracks, and along the coast, we stopped in front of a tall apartment building. "This is it," said Hasan. We parked. Hasan got out. Hüseyin and I waited in the taxi. You could cut the tension with a knife. Hüseyin appeared to be working up the courage to say something, but would then change his mind. I avoided his glance in the mirror. It was your standard French film: a man, a woman, and a quandary. Well, not exactly, but somewhere along those lines. He finally cracked.

"Do you want me turn on some music?"

"Whatever you like," was my brief reply.

"What would you like?"

The question was a loaded one. I toyed with, *Anything but you.* But now was not the time.

Instead, I settled for, "Something light. I need to think."

"You mean slow, or classical?"

I raised an eyebrow. Our taxi stand drivers invariably play either arabesque or Turkish pop.

"It doesn't matter, just make it something light."

"I know you listen to classical music. I saw the CDs at your house," Hüseyin revealed.

He had once again resorted to the familiar *sen,* and I started
to correct him, then held my tongue. Just as I began to wonder
what was taking Hasan so long, the door opened and he got in.

"So?"

"I guess she's not at home," Hasan replied.

He sat there without a word.

Thanks to Hasan, we'd wasted a whole hour. And time was,
as they say, of the essence. At this rate, someone was likely to
get hold of Buse's mother, and the photos and the letters, before
I did. We'd traveled all the way to the Asian shore for nothing.

I had no time to sort through alternative courses of action.
"To the coroner's," I ordered Hüseyin. "We'll drop you off," I
told Hasan.

Hüseyin began forming his own interpretation of events,
based on what he'd overheard.

"We're looking for the mother of the friend I brought to your
house this morning, aren't we?" he asked.

"No," I said. "We're going to the coroner's office to learn any
details we can about Fevzi's—that is, Buse's—death."

The three of us fell silent for the rest of the trip. When
Hasan stepped out of the taxi, I said to him, "Let's do whatever
is needed for the funeral."

"Don't worry," he said, slamming the door, doing his best to
look responsible and mature.

We proceeded to Çapa.

Hüseyin broke the silence: "Well, he calls you *sen,*" followed
by a glance over his shoulder.

He had apparently comprehended my sensitivity over the
use of *sen,* and had taken it to heart. That was good.

"Yes, but we've known each other for five years."

Silence.

"But why do you get so cross when I say *sen*? You call me *sen.*
I don't have a problem with it."

I considered whether or not to embark on a long monologue. Were I to let it slide, he'd misunderstand. Were I to try to explain, he'd misunderstand.

"Whatever. Don't worry about it."

We arrived at Çapa.

The entrance to the morgue was an unusually colorful sight, thanks to our girls. They were as loud as they were vibrant. Some were decked out in costumes, others were in civilian clothes. News, particularly bad news, travels swiftly in our circle. I've always believed that the system of communications goes beyond mere telephones. It could even be a form of telepathy, but I have yet to fully comprehend what exactly it is and how it works. Nor did I have any intention of dwelling on it. It was enough to see that, whatever it was, it was running smoothly.

I looked for Gönül, who regularly haunts the morgue. She's a large girl, badly dressed and quite ugly, but with a saucy tongue and bold manners. More important, though, I had heard that she was somehow related to Buse.

Most of the girls were here in the name of solidarity. There was an unbelievably united front against all enemies of transvestites and the police who failed to be of assistance to girls like us. I wondered how many of them had known Buse personally. Most of the girls were from a world unfamiliar to me—that is to say, they were the girls of Aksaray, Laleli, and the motorway. I pressed my way through to the middle of the crowd. Intent on extracting any shred of possibly useful information, I began questioning one and all.

Fury boiled in the eyes of some. They were prepared to take any form of action in order to demonstrate their rage. I quickly realized that most not only didn't know Fevzi/Buse, they weren't even aware of what exactly had happened. All they knew was that a transvestite had been murdered. One of them!

This meant action was required. I had growing doubts about their reliability as sources of hard information.

I approached one of them.

"My condolences. Did you know her?" I asked.

She sniffed, eyes running with mascara. An unmistakably baritone voice, altered through habit into a falsetto, demanded to know, in a thick Eastern accent, why I was asking. "She's dead. They killed her. Isn't that enough?"

"I knew her well," I said. "We hung out at the same club." There was no need to mention that I owned a stake in the club, or that the girls looked up to me as their boss.

"Hmm . . ." was her reaction. She sniffed again. I waited, sensing a possible breakthrough. She knew something.

In my most affected voice, I continued, "I adored Buse. We were such good friends."

She stopped sniffing and looked me up and down. All she saw was someone dressed as a man, and lacking even a single piece of jewelry. I looked far too masculine to have been a bosom buddy of Buse's.

Determined to put her right, I mincingly added, "Don't pay any mind to my clothes right now. I'm one of you. Like Buse."

She continued scrutinizing me. Cutting me off, she demanded to know, "Are you one of the girls, or just a fag?"

Well, I never!

"Oh, I'm completely different by night. I dressed like this for the funeral."

Suddenly the graceless Gönül materialized, spouting unintelligible cries.

"Ay, *ablam*," she said as she embraced me. "There's nothing in the world like a loyal friend."

I was enfolded in a stifling bear hug. She reeked of fake Joop.

"Gönül, *abla*, do you know this person?"

"Ay, of course I do," said Gönül, introducing us.

I took Gönül by the arm and led her off.

"Did you know her?" I asked.

"Her real name was Fevzi."

"I know," I said. "And she had a mother ... I wonder if anyone's informed her."

"You mean Sabiha Hanim?" That was it! The name of the blind lady. "How do I know?"

"There's no point in waiting around here. Let's go check on her. She may need us. She can't see, after all. At least, that's what Fevzi said."

"What's with calling her Fevzi? Her name was Buse," scolded Gönül.

Moments ago, it had been Gönül who for no reason had introduced the name Fevzi into the conversation. There's no predicting what our girls will do or say, and Gönül is the most erratic of them all. She was glaring at me.

"Of course I know she was called Buse. I only said Fevzi because you had," I explained.

"Well, don't. It's disrespect toward the deceased."

I had grown used to Gönül's attempt to sound refined, which she tried to achieve by replacing all her *a*'s with *e*'s. But it still took a brief moment to figure out what she was saying.

The final syllable of each word was drawn out, singsong. The end of each sentence was marked by the lifting of a single shoulder, toward which she would rotate her head. The head toss was accompanied by what she believed to be a highly significant stare, delivered through narrowed eyes toward the raised shoulder. Upon hearing my voice, she would once again look directly at me, and the shoulder would sink back down. Undoubtedly, the move had been rehearsed repeatedly in front of the mirror for an appreciative audience of one. There is also no doubt that it worked its magic among the louts at less sophisticated beer houses.

"Fine, then," I said. "Now let's go to Sabiha Hanım's house. I just can't remember where it is . . ."

"What does everyone want with that poor blind woman? Just a few minutes ago there was a bunch of ruffians here asking where she lived." Alarm. Alarm! Red alert! So I wasn't the only person who'd come here to extract information.

"What did you tell them?"

"They didn't ask me," she said. "I suppose I wasn't their type. They talked to everyone but me. It wasn't so crowded then. Just look around now though, this place is crawling with trannies. It's wonderful, isn't it?"

I feigned interest and had a look around. She was right. The crowd was swelling. The news had spread from ear to ear, from cell phone to cell phone. And all who heard had come.

"It's still early, you know," Gönül continued. "That means no customers, empty bars, families still in command of the streets. The girls had nothing better to do. Now look at them! They're about to break into the morgue. You'd think the undertaker had killed Buse!" she said with a rueful grin.

"But who were those men, and why were they looking for Sabiha Hanım?"

Gönül let loose a luxurious, low laugh, her head turned toward the raised shoulder.

I smiled sweetly. She observed me out of the corner of her eye. Then she tossed her mane of hair and focused her attention on me once again.

"They must have been cops or something. Why else would those thugs want to see Sabiha?"

"So where did they go?" I asked.

"How am I supposed to know, *ayol*! And what's with all the questions? What's your problem anyway? You're not some kind of spy, are you? All I get is a whole load of questions every time I see you."

"*Ayol,* the things you come up with," I said. "And we've known each other all this time."

"For as long as I've known you, you've been pestering me with questions. 'What do you know? What have you heard?' It's like some kind of Judgment Day examination."

"Don't be such a child," I reprimanded her. "If I can't even count on you, what will the others be like? You know me, I've always had an inquiring mind."

"I can't say I think much of know-it-alls or busybodies. They rub me the wrong way."

"*Ayol,* here I am trying to help this poor lady. Buse's mother, Sabiha Hanim, could be in terrible danger. Whoever killed the daughter could go after the mother next. I can't tell you all my suspicions right now. Buse came to my house last night—well, this morning. She said her house had been broken into. She was terrified."

Gönül's eyes widened with fear and curiosity. She nearly pierced my eardrum with a shriek that echoed through the entire district.

"Who broke into Buse's house?"

All heads turned in our direction. The low murmuring suddenly stopped. Ears pricked, the crowd gave us their full attention. Gönül lowered her voice to a whisper.

"Who were they?" she repeated.

"I don't know," I admitted. "I'm trying to find out. I need help. I don't know what to do. And all you do is tell me I give you the creeps."

"Well, it's true. I got all funny," she said. "Once I get that way, that's it. The end. *Finito.* Even if I were in the sack—with Kadir İnanır, no less—that's it. Off I go. Speaking of Kadir, I'm just wild about him. I think he gets better with age. If he gave me a sign I'd be his on the spot. I'd put on a head scarf and nestle at his feet. I mean, I'd be his love slave for life, *ayol.*"

Gönül's stream of consciousness *nouveau roman,* in the manner of Nathalie Sarraute, had me reeling. I immediately revised my rather low opinion of her intellect. I tried, and failed, to suppress an appreciative smile.

"It's not possible to talk here. Would you like to go and have a chat over tea? I could really use your help."

She was eyeing the crowd, which was still growing. She seemed reluctant to miss the show—perhaps she thought she might even seize a leading role in it. But I had no time for such indecision. Grabbing her arm, I said, "March. I'll explain everything."

Chapter 7

❖

$\mathcal{T}$he moment we got into the taxi I told Gönül as much as she needed to know. In the front seat, Hüseyin listened silently, and was therefore fully briefed as well. In fact, he even went so far as to interrupt near the end to tell Gönül how he had spotted a panicked Buse in front of the club while looking for me, and then brought her to my house. Then he added, in his most injured-male tone, that I had refused his offers of help, or even to allow him to come inside. The consolation he sought was forthcoming. Gönül Ablam sprang to his defense:

"A dependable young man like this. He wouldn't be able to help? Of course he'd have been of use. I mean, really."

Hüseyin basked in the praise. Gönül's commendation was apparently interpreted as giving him the right to make further claims on me.

"Now, that's more like it!" he exclaimed. I was subjected to a lascivious wink.

Hüseyin would require a sound thrashing once we were through with our business. Right in the middle of the neighborhood, from pavement to pavement, somersaulting through the air.

All traces of urgency and sense of our real mission erased from her mind, Gönül focused exclusively on Hüseyin.

"Where are you from?"

"Istanbul," said Hüseyin. "The whole family's from Istanbul, on both sides."

"Istanbulians are so refined. There's nothing they like more than a bit of ladylike friskiness in bed."

I wondered just what methods of comparison Gönül had used to arrive at this arbitrary conclusion.

Gönül turned to me. "He's such a lion of a man, *ayol*. His heat alone would be enough for any girl. Real men have no time for coyness. They don't wait around. Oh, no. Someone else snaps them up!"

Judging from the trademark sideways simpering, Gönül liked what she saw of Hüseyin. She was declaring that unless I pounced on him, he was fair game.

"These summer nights are hot enough," I said. "I have trouble tolerating my own skin, sometimes."

Hüseyin wasn't going to let that go by.

"We'll cool you off," he said with a leer, the grinning dog-face making a reappearance.

The insolence! I had really had enough. Heedless of the fact that we were hurtling down Vatan Caddesi, I inflicted a sharp chop on the back of his lower neck, near his left ear. He must have seen lightning. A strange croak erupted from his mouth. But—and I really had to hand it to him—he continued driving as though nothing had happened.

"That's really shameful," he said. "Ever since last night, I've given up my job to ferry you around, and look what I get in return. It was a joke! I understand. You said I'm not your type. Okay, fine. But we've been in the car together for three hours, and you haven't spoken once to me the whole time. That's okay, too. But at least don't hurt me! What's the big deal? So I like you, so what?"

"He's right," Gönül said. "Those dark eyes. Those eyebrows. He's young. He's handsome. A hunk of a man."

"Okay, okay, I apologize. You can see how wound up I am.

We've got to hurry. I just lost my temper when you started drooling at me."

Under the mistaken illusion that we'd become fast friends, Gönül gave me a playful pinch, as though to say, *Good for you*. I deplore that sort of behavior, but I forced a smile. Now she poked me, as though to say, *Keep going*.

"Tell us exactly where we're going so Hüseyin can get us there as soon as possible," was my only response.

Staring at me foolishly, and clearly miffed that the fun and games had come to an end, Gönül said, "But you were the one who invited me. I thought we were going to have a drink somewhere. It's not up to me to tell Hüseyin where to go."

Hüseyin seized the opportunity. "Come on, *abla*; let's go to the house of Buse Hanım's mother, whatever her name was."

"Who are you calling 'big sister'?" retorted Gönül, ready to lash out at Hüseyin.

"Her name is Sabiha," I interrupted.

"But it's so far away!" Gönül whined. "Can we at least have something to eat first? I haven't even had dinner. I was too distraught to think of myself. Just ran right out of the house."

She cast an appraising eye at her shoulder, as though it were the first time they'd met.

"And my clothes are all wrong. Look at these old worn-out shoes."

Hüseyin continued driving in a circle between Vatan Caddesi and Millet Caddesi.

I grasped her hand, squeezing firmly but gently. "Look, we've got to hurry, or something terrible could happen to that nice old lady. Afterward, I promise we'll all go out to eat."

"But won't it be awfully late by then?"

A good number of Gönül's brain cells are obviously in a state of indolence.

"What do you mean, 'late'? The Etap is open past midnight, until two in the morning."

"But they won't let me in there."

"We'll go anywhere you like. Now come on, tell us the address."

I squeezed her hand. This time, it hurt. Her eyes widened as she realized the seriousness of the situation.

"Ay! That smarts, girlfriend. Okay, fine. Take the next right. Toward Kocamustafapaşa."

We shot across three lanes of traffic, barely managing to make our turn. Winding our way through a series of increasingly narrow roads, in ten minutes we reached it. There was a sharp tang of smoke in the air. Daytime balcony barbecue parties had created a stench.

We parked in front of a run-down, sixties-style, four-story apartment building. The cramped hallway smelled of bleach and urine. Gönül giggled, as though the odor were somehow cause for hilarity. It's a scientifically proven fact that our brain cells are dying with each passing second, but Gönül was miles ahead in that particular race. That much was certain.

Each floor contained three flats. The corridor walls had been painted milky brown up to shoulder-height, and the paint was peeling.

Emboldened by Gönül's attentions, and now considering himself a full-fledged partner, Hüseyin followed us, a respectful few steps behind. If I put my mind to it, I am able to walk with minimal wiggling of the hips. I had no intention of treating Hüseyin to the sight of a swaying bottom. With a determined— even manly—gait, I led the way. In any case, even I would find it difficult to shimmy in trainers.

We rang the bell of the only flat whose entryway was not cluttered with rows of unpolished shoes. No one had removed shoes in front of Sabiha's door. There were no visitors offering their condolences. We waited, then rang the bell again. And resumed waiting once more. Meanwhile, one of the doors behind the mountains of shoes opened slightly, and a five-year-old girl with badly cut curly hair poked out her head. She looked at us intently. We stared back.

The smell of cooking wafted out from the partly open door.

Hüseyin smiled uncomfortably. I reached over and gave the door a sharp rap. Perhaps the blind lady was also a bit hard of hearing. She may have gone to bed. Or she could be watching TV and unable to hear the bell. I stopped for a moment to ponder whether or not blind people watch TV.

Interpreting Hüseyin's smile as an offer of friendship, the girl spoke.

"She's not home." Bashful, the little head withdrew into the apartment. The door closed. If a child knew Sabiha was not at home, her parents may well have known where she was. We moved to the door and rang the bell. It opened instantly. Before us stood a stout woman of about thirty. Red-cheeked and cheery -looking, she was nothing like her daughter. Her eyes traveled from me to Hüseyin, then to Gönül.

"May I help you?"

"We were looking for Sabiha Hanım. Your daughter just told us she wasn't at home. We thought you might know where she is."

"I don't know," she replied, still looking at us, the same smile plastered across her considerable face.

"I—I mean, we—are friends of her son's, Fevzi," I explained. "We really must see her."

"You mean her girl Fevzi." Her smile became slightly mocking. "He became a woman. By the name of Buse. We were good playmates as kids."

"So you were Buse's childhood friend? How nice."

Did she have any idea Buse was dead? And was I really the person who should be informing her?

"Sabiha Hanım doesn't really get out much. If she does, it's to visit us, or the neighbor upstairs. That's it. The rest are all tenants. We're the old-timers. This flat belonged to my mother, and my husband came to live here with us." Mercy. We'd known each other for all of five minutes and I was already drowning in unnecessary details.

"Why don't you go upstairs and check on flat number seven? If she's not there, come on over. I've just made a pot of fresh tea, and we've got some ice-cold watermelon. We can all enjoy it together."

I thanked her and set off for the top floor. As we approached the landing her voice rang out from below, "I'm expecting you. Do come."

The door to flat seven was slightly ajar. I rang the bell nevertheless. A television blared from inside, but no one came to the door. "Good evening," I called as I pushed open the door and entered. The others followed me in. I can smell danger, and a strong whiff of it hit me as I stood near the doorway. The flat was dark, illuminated only by the flickering light of the TV. I carefully made my way to the source of the racket. There, in the middle of the dark room filled with old armchairs, I saw her. Even in the gloom, there was no mistaking the round hole in the middle of her forehead. Her head was tilted back, lifeless.

Chapter 8

❖

$\mathcal{I}$t would seem an obvious case of murder. Elderly ladies are not generally found slumped in armchairs with bullet holes in the center of their foreheads.

"Is she dead?" Hüseyin asked. I nodded yes. Gönül bellowed in a decidedly masculine fashion.

"They found her, too," I said.

"We're in deep shit now," sighed Hüseyin. He was white as a sheet.

We had two choices: inform the police or scram. Simply running away seemed the less intelligent of the two. The robust lady downstairs had seen us. And I had touched a few things since we'd entered the flat, so some of the fingerprints would belong to us. It did cross my mind that the police didn't always bother with things like fingerprints, but caution was still advisable. And what was there to be afraid of? We had every reason to be there. We had come to pay our condolences to the mother of a dead friend. Unable to find her at home, we'd checked at the upstairs neighbor's and been greeted by a corpse.

Against my will, I found myself listening to the game show still blaring on the TV set. The question was: the most common intrusive igneous rock type is: (A) granite; (B) rhyolite; (C) basalt; (D) andesite. It was easy enough to whittle down the right answer to (A) granite. After all, it's the only intrusive rock on the list. Of course, the contestant was clueless.

Gönül's voice brought me back to my senses and the present situation:

"*Abla,* who is this woman?"

But wasn't it Sabiha Hanım? Perhaps not. There was no way for me to know. I turned to Gönül, my face a question mark. She provided a swift answer.

"This isn't Sabiha."

The contestant had eliminated two of the possible answers. Rhyolite and andesite were erased from the screen. I devised my own set of possible answers to the question confronting me: (A) This was an unrelated murder; (B) We were face to face with a serial murderer prepared to eradicate all who crossed his path; (C) This woman, whoever she was, had mistakenly been killed in place of Sabiha Hanım; (D) Why on earth were those letters and photographs worth killing for? The response deserving of immediate elimination was, of course, (D).

Hüseyin placed a hand on my shoulder. "Maybe we'd better get out of here."

I politely, but firmly, removed the overly familiar appendage. "No way," I said.

In a clear voice, for their benefit, I summarized the situation: Getting the police involved would mean being escorted to the police station and spending the rest of the night there; Gönül would most likely be roughed up, and have a visit to the state venereal clinic arranged for her; there was no telling what exactly would happen to Hüseyin.

The contestant insisted on "basalt" and was promptly eliminated.

The corpse was not yet cold. The time of death was fairly recent. Who was behind this? Were the blackmail materials so damning that they justified these cold-blooded killings? How was I supposed to find out his identity? Where was the real

Sabiha Hanım? What, if anything, had happened to the letters and photographs?

It was safe to assume that Sabiha Hanım was still alive. I ran through the list of alternatives once again. Finally, I decided to consult the studio audience:

"Look," I began, "if this woman is not Sabiha Hanım, we still have to find her—that is, we still have to find Buse's letters and photographs."

"First let's get out of here. I don't like cops," said Gönül.

She had a point. Neither do I. And I suspected Hüseyin wasn't partial to them, either. Taxi drivers are such easy pickings for the cops, real whipping boys when it comes to issuing tickets and general bullying.

"Well then, let's remove all signs we've been here and clear the hell out!"

I had to hand it to Hüseyin; perhaps he wasn't so dim after all.

After we had restored the scene to its original state, we slowly pulled the door nearly shut, as it had been when we'd arrived. It was like a film being played backward. In order to pull off the pretense that we had never set eyes on the freshly killed corpse, to be able to say we had not seen, heard, or learned a thing, we had to first make an appearance at the home of Mrs. Robust. Only then would it be wise to flee the scene. Truly, the last thing we needed was a compulsory visit to the local precinct, followed by an interrogation at police headquarters at the homicide desk.

I silently considered the possibility of forcing our way into Sabiha Hanım's flat, conducting a thorough search of Fevzi's old bedroom and finding the photographs. I suppressed the urge, stopping instead in front of the collection of shoes, where I rang the bell. The door immediately opened. It seemed at least one of the inhabitants of this flat was stationed in front of the door at all times.

This time, it was the man of the house. He was the type of man who wears a tie even at home, a sight seldom seen these days. His collar was even buttoned down. Like his wife, the husband, too, had a cheery demeanor. He reacted as though he had been expecting, and was now receiving, dear old friends.

"Welcome . . . Do come in."

The apple-cheeked wife had no doubt told her husband all about us. He was primed to greet us.

"I'm afraid we can't, but thank you so much," I politely refused. "We were looking for Sabiha Hanım. Your wife suggested we check on flat seven."

Perhaps afraid I would say too much, Hüseyin interrupted. "No one was at home. We rang, but no one answered the door."

The smile froze on the husband's face. He looked surprised.

"That's strange. It's impossible. Hamiyet Hanım doesn't ever close her door. She's hard of hearing. She always leaves it open in case she doesn't hear the bell. Just give it a push and go right in."

Trouble had announced its imminent arrival. Now he would decide to accompany us upstairs to show us that the door was indeed open a crack, the corpse would be discovered, and we would all end up at the police station. No, I couldn't let that happen.

With a swift fluid movement, he removed the imitation leather house slippers from his white-stockinged feet, slipping into a pair of shoes waiting in front of the door. Hüseyin grabbed his arms.

"*Aman,* dear *abi,* don't trouble yourself—"

"Ah, what do you mean, 'trouble'? It's just one floor up." He shouted into the house, "Aynur, I'm showing our guests to Hamiyet Hanım's. I'll be right back."

Before he'd finished speaking, the small girl appeared between his legs, taking his hand. If it weren't for me and

Hüseyin directly in front of him, blocking the way, and Gönül, a brick wall of reinforcement just behind us, that agile man of the house would long since have bounded to the floor above.

Hüseyin stroked the head of the girl, who still retained her father's hand and was saucily casting flirtatious looks in Hüseyin's direction.

"*Maşallah*, aren't you a little sweetheart? What's your name?"

Suddenly shy, she retreated behind Daddy's legs.

"Go on, Sevgi, tell him your name."

I was overwhelmed with the desire to forget all I'd seen and get as far away as possible. I detest middle-class families. I'd striven all my life to put as much distance as possible between myself and them. They're suffocating. And here I was, on the verge of getting hopelessly entangled with one of them.

"I think it's best we leave now," was all I said.

Gönül had already turned, prepared to make an escape down the stairs. I extended a hand to the man in the tie. At that moment, a cheery voice rang out from the smiley, red-cheeked woman.

"*Vallahi*, you can't leave! I won't hear of it. I've got the teapot all ready."

"We really can't. Another time, perhaps."

The tie leaped backward into his slippers, and began tugging at my arm.

"Come in, come in . . . We'll have a cup of tea. Then you can go. And you never know, Sabiha Hanım may arrive while you're here."

There was a certain logic in what he'd just said. That is, if Sabiha wasn't dead, or being held hostage somewhere.

"The car's in a no-parking zone. They'll tow it away. We really can't stay any longer."

It was Hüseyin's best effort. "They won't tow it . . . they can't.

It's never happened on our street," he said immediately. Gönül's face fell further. We added our shoes to the collection in front of the door. Gönül leaned forward to whisper, "They'll be on to me, won't they?"

Of course they would. Even he-men camping it up in drag comedies were more convincing as women than Gönül.

"I expect so. They'll at least suspect something," I told her.

"Then I'm not coming in."

That was enough whispering in front of the door. I grabbed her arm and shoved her inside. "Don't talk, and maybe they won't get it."

Chapter 9

❖

$\mathcal{E}$ven if I had instructed Gönül to talk nonstop, she couldn't have been more of a chatterbox. From the moment we settled onto the tacky fabrics shrouding the sofa and armchairs, Gönül appointed herself group spokeswoman. The increasingly warmer weather; the likelihood of another earthquake in Istanbul, and the probable epicenter and magnitude of the natural disaster, were it to occur; how to select the juiciest watermelons; which soccer team should recruit which players for the upcoming season; how a pinch of cinnamon and a dash of cloves transforms freshly ground coffee beans into a gourmet experience: she jumped from one unrelated subject to another.

I listened, but I was unable to forget the body upstairs. Our carelessness had resulted in our becoming stuck with this family, like we were at a theater intermission, drinking tea.

Seizing on the first silence created by our simultaneous swallowing of tea, with an Istanbul accent modeled on old Turkish films, Mrs. Full Red Cheeks inquired:

"You've turned yourself into a woman just like Fevzi, haven't you?"

At first I wasn't sure whether or not the question was addressed to me, as well as to poor Gönül, who looked terribly upset. But, I ask you, what self-respecting Turkish woman would have speculated on next year's soccer player transfers?

"My name is Gönül," she declared, as though somehow answering the question.

"So, you've had the operation, then?"

Gönül looked over at me, helpless and dumbfounded. Hüseyin was doing his best to hide behind a crystal tea glass, the kind trotted out only for company. The slim, tulip-shaped glass was nearly lost in his hand. I noted the cleanliness of his hands, his well-trimmed fingernails.

The husband detected our discomfort and graciously intervened. "Really, now, Aynur. And in front of the child . . ."

That was right! The little girl was there. Ever since we'd arrived, she'd been squatting across from Hüseyin, pining away at him with cow eyes.

"What's the big deal? These are the facts of life. Better she learn about them here at home than out in the street."

It seemed that the structure of the middle-class family, the sort I knew and despised, had undergone some serious changes in the time I'd managed to avoid it.

"But the gentlemen came here to see Sabiha Hanım."

Yes, the "gentlemen." That is, me, Hüseyin, and Gönül.

"Well . . . I suppose so . . . So how is Fevzi-girl? What an ingrate she turned out to be. She never visits us when she comes to see her mother. You'd think she'd stop by for a cup of coffee, maybe bring our daughter a chocolate bar. Don't you think so? Like I told you, we practically grew up together. I knew even back then that she'd be different. Even as a little boy, she'd wear her mother's shoes, paint her fingernails. Her mother told everyone that it was so she wouldn't bite them. At primary school . . ."

Mrs. Fat Cheeks was lost in a reverie. Had she been aware of the body just above our heads, I imagine she wouldn't have chattered on in quite the same way. Of course, she had no idea that each passing hour made a similar fate more likely for the blind lady across the hall.

We all leaped out of our seats at the sound of a bloodcurdling scream. Sevgi ran to the door; her father raced to the window. Apple Cheeks smiled apologetically, as if to say, *Is this really the time for screams, as I sit here all cozy with my eccentric guests?*

There was a banging at the door. The family led the way as we all rushed to it.

A largish female, still young enough to be plagued by pimples, stood there. Either her face had been blotched by futile skin-care remedies or . . .

"Aynur, *abla*! Aunt Hamiyet is dead! Shot! And right in the middle of the forehead!"

Ah, so the red face was the result of having seen a corpse.

"My uncle's family sent us some dried mulberries. My mother sent me along to give some to Aunt Hamiyet. But they shot her! Right in the forehead!"

There was no way of avoiding the police now. It was too late to beg leave and go. But that's exactly what we did, shameless as it was.

The man of the house was apparently a legal clerk, and suggested we not get mixed up in the affair. It was the best proposition I'd heard all day. They were pure-hearted enough not to suspect us in any way. I wanted to throw my arms around him, but his wife might have misunderstood.

As the police sirens approached the apartment building, we got into the taxi Hüseyin had parked in front of a dark, abandoned building. As we drove off, we sifted through our options.

Even if we were unable to find Sabiha Hanım, we had to get into Fevzi/Buse's old bedroom. Attempting this while the police were in control of the building would be pushing our luck. So, we eliminated that possibility.

Two elderly women murdered a floor apart in the same building could not be put down to coincidence. It was just not possible. If the killer had mistaken the lady upstairs for Sabiha Hanım, it would give us more time to find the letters and photographs. If Sabiha Hanım had fallen into their hands, that would change everything. Perhaps she had been abducted as she went upstairs to visit her neighbor. The neighbor had been killed and she had been kidnapped. If that was the case, there was nothing much we could do.

"Where are we going?" asked Hüseyin.

"Don't forget about the Etap. You promised me dinner."

It was unbelievable that Gönül was able to think of her stomach at a time like this. When I get cross, I often address the girls by their official, male names.

"Metin, it's really no time—"

"There's no way you're wriggling out of this. You promised. You high-society types always go back on your word. You've all got scorpions in your pockets."

As if things weren't tense enough, I had to deal with this.

"Fine," I said. "My treat. The two of you go and eat. I've got work to do, but I'll pay."

Hüseyin slammed on the brakes and turned around. "No way! It's too close to our neighborhood."

"What do you mean? Are you trying to say you're ashamed of Gönül?" I asked innocently. Hüseyin had no compunctions about hitting on me in public. There was no reason he couldn't be seen out with Gönül. It just required a bit of courage.

"I'm sick and tired of all of this," he said. "Go anywhere you want. Eat whatever you want. I don't care. Just leave me out of it. Got it?"

"So . . . what's got into you?" Gönül exclaimed, "What's wrong with me then? No manners, *ayol*!"

"All right . . . calm down," I said. "Gönül, sweetie, we've got a critical situation on our hands, and not much time to sort things out. You do understand, don't you?"

"I'm not stupid. What's not to understand?"

"Well then, let me treat you to a meal, but don't expect me to go with you. You can go on your own or join me another time."

The peeved expression on Gönül's face was accompanied by a pouting lower lip. "They won't let me in if I go alone."

On the one hand, I felt a pang of pity and a swelling of gay pride; on the other, I was still extremely cross with the girl.

"Well then, we'll go another day. My word is good."

"*Aman*, I know what you're doing. You're backtracking. What else do you expect from a faggot?"

Because she considered herself a full-fledged woman, the word "faggot" was, in her mind, a stinging insult.

Hüseyin lunged toward the back seat, grabbing her collar. "You better watch your mouth, mister!"

"Let her go," I said. "I can defend myself."

Collar duly released, Gönül recovered instantly. "All right, then, not tonight. But you did promise. I won't forget. Let's decide right now on the day."

I wanted to tear her to pieces, but fought back the urge. "I'll give you my number. Call me during the week, or come by the club. We'll meet there."

"But I don't go to places like Taksim and Etiler. I'm usually in Aksaray, Bağcılar . . . sometimes over in Topkapı. You know that."

"Fine. Here, take my number."

"Put down your actual number. Don't do what those men do and give me a fake one."

I laughed silently. But I jotted down the number of the club.

As she took the piece of paper, she asked, "*Abla*, what's your name anyway?"

I simply shook my head.

Gönül got out in the middle of Aksaray.

As the car proceeded toward Unkapanı, I was subjected to

Hüseyin's reproachful glances in the rearview mirror. He was looking at me as though demanding an explanation for why I'd involved Gönül. I suddenly remembered to check the taxi meter. It must be costing me a fortune. The meter wasn't on.

"The meter's been turned off."

"I never switched it on."

"Why not? You've got to make a living."

"After the way you've treated me I'm sorry I didn't turn it on. But it's too late now. Pay me what you think is fair. It's not like you want my help. We're not partners or anything. Detectives in films are real partners; they work together. We're not like that."

The suggestion that I pay whatever seemed "fair" meant one of two things: pay nothing—which would involve some other form of compensation—or estimate the actual amount and pay a bit more.

"I was just getting into it, stupid enough to think we'd be like those movie detectives. You know, like that TV series with Bruce Willis and that woman who looks a bit like you. You'd do all the fancy talking, and I . . . well, whatever . . . but you're too cold-hearted for that."

The reference to Cybill Shepherd was totally inappropriate. But I decided to win him over nonetheless.

"Forgive me . . . I'm a little confused. I didn't mean to insult you. I'm sorry if you've been offended in any way."

"You think a quick apology will settle everything. Break my heart, insult me, then offer a halfhearted apology and everything will be fine again. Nice work."

"So what do you expect me to do?"

The dog-leer was back. "Let me warm up that heart of yours."

I groaned. "You'll never learn, will you?"

We didn't talk for the rest of the way home. As I got out of the taxi, I realized I didn't have much cash on me.

"Would it be all right if I paid you tomorrow?"

"How can you even ask that? You don't have to pay me at all. But if you offer me something cool to drink I won't say no. It'd be nice of you."

I slammed the door in his face.

If he'd been anyone else I'd have let him have it by now. But there was something touching about the boy. As angry as I got, he appealed to me in some way.

Whatever the appeal was, though, it wasn't enough to overcome my reservations. I didn't give it a second thought.

Chapter 10

✥

$\mathcal{I}$ was right back to where I'd started. We'd wasted a great deal of time going to Suadiye to try to find Sofya, and had been too late to intervene at Sabiha Hanım's. Either Hasan had been unable to find Sofya's house, or she really hadn't been at home. Whichever it was, we were now dealing with a new corpse. I'd learned the location of Buse's mother's apartment, but it was now the floor below a cordoned-off crime scene, one no doubt crawling with police. Our acquaintance with the sturdy neighbors would make it that much more difficult to enter the building unnoticed.

It would be hard for the police to make a connection between the two murders. That is to say, if there was a link. Perhaps it really was a case of two unrelated homicides. But my instincts—and I do not always listen to them—told me it was no coincidence.

I pondered how events would play out in a novel or movie. The person in danger would most certainly hide the object the killers were after in the safest place possible. Suddenly bells, buzzers, even a five-engine alarm went off in my head: Buse may have hidden the letters and photographs in my house! She had arrived in the morning with Hüseyin, and may have stashed them away while I was sleeping.

I began searching the guest bedroom. I wasn't certain what exactly it was that I was looking for. I suspected it was an envelope. I had no idea of the size. It could be a range of sizes. Thickness? That wasn't clear, either. Whatever it was that I was looking for could be under the bed, behind a picture or—a favorite in films—taped to the bottom of a drawer.

The search took quite some time. I turned everything upside down. Satı Hanım would not be happy when she came to clean. As I looked for the lost documents I discovered numerous items I had thought were lost. Some were nostalgic, like my first pair of ladies' underwear; others were ridiculous, like once-treasured letters, cards, and photos.

I got tired and gave up. I'd found nothing. Apparently Buse and I did not read the same books or watch the same films. She hadn't hidden the letters and photos at my house. I gathered up all the personal items I'd found, and figured I'd sort them out later.

I pushed all thoughts of Buse out of my head as I decided to get dressed for the night. The club would be full. There was a possibility that some of the girls there would have useful information. If I was lucky, someone might even know who would be interested in the documents.

I performed the usual shower-shave-makeup ritual. There was just one difference: Try as I might to forget all about Buse, she was all I could think of. The man who had sent the letters, had the photos taken, was most definitely someone of great influence. He had taken on mythic proportions. I imagined a series of celebrities, power brokers, and politicians in romantic dalliance with Buse. First I saw them posing in romantic snapshots, then the pictures became pure porn. Buse had the most amazing missile-shaped, silicone-enhanced breasts and—so she said— quite a large penis. Joyous and hilarious images of famous faces, heaving breasts, and enormous dicks flashing through my brain, I was ready in no time. Whenever I'm preoccupied with other thoughts, especially complicated subjects like this one, I forgo my diva costumes, settling for something simple. It's probably an instinctive reaction to danger, a way of not drawing too much attention to myself.

I squeezed into a skintight, long-sleeved, flesh-colored bodysuit. Over it, I wore a long skirt, slit to the waist, and flesh -colored stockings. Flinging a honey-colored raw silk shawl around my shoulders, I was ready.

I called the stand for a taxi, requesting that Hüseyin not be sent. The last thing I needed was his flirting. In any case, they said he wasn't there.

As I went out the door the phone rang. I have an answering machine, so under normal circumstances I would have continued, knowing the caller could leave a message. But these were not normal times. I unlocked the front door and raced to the phone, just as my voice was promising to "... call back as soon as possible, *merci*."

I couldn't decide whether to lift the receiver or wait to hear who it was first. A male voice cleared its throat. And hung up without leaving a message.

Chapter 11

❖

*C*üneyt greeted me with a wolf whistle at the entrance to the club.

"Boss, you're a real knockout, like always. What a great blouse, and it matches your stockings."

Did the boy have certain tendencies, or what? Real men don't admire a lady's outfit. It's what's inside the clothes that interests them.

Despite the early hour, the club was nearly full. Advancing toward the bar, I blew kisses to the girls and our regulars. Hasan was behind the bar, next to Şükrü. When he saw me he began waving frantically. I leaned over the bar toward him.

Like a U.S. Secret Service agent revealing classified information, he hissed, "Sofya's here!"

That was strange. Here I'd been looking everywhere for her, and she'd decided, if a bit late, to come and see me. It had been years since Sofya had retired from the scene, or at least stopped frequenting clubs like ours. While no one was certain exactly what she was up to, the general consensus was that "a rich thug keeps her at home." News of her annual pilgrimage to Ibiza, Mykonos, or Mardi Gras regularly amazed our little circle. Girls she found sufficiently distinguished would be invited to her home. They'd go skipping off to the appointment, returning with wondrous tales of the elegance with which they were lavishly wined and dined. They eagerly awaited the day, month, year in which a second invitation would be granted. In short, with her money, airs, and fabulous lifestyle, Spec-tac -u-lar Sofya had attained the unattainable. She was the living embodiment of what each and every girl aspired to.

It had been some time since she'd deigned to visit the club. Furthermore, we had both allowed a tiny misunderstanding to grow into cause for major offense. Over time, our friendship had withered on the vine, like any relationship that isn't maintained and nurtured. The gossip and tales of devious self-appointed minions and intermediaries had caused further injury. We were both right on some points, wrong on others.

Considering the circumstances, it was strange indeed that Sofya had just up and come to my club.

Another strange detail was the absence of my Virgin Mary. And the fact that there was no sign of its being prepared anytime soon.

I began drumming on the bar with the two-and-a-half-inch gold fingernails I'd bought in America, as a way of making my displeasure clear. Şükrü looked at me as though to ask what was wrong.

"My drink . . . where is it?"

He apologized and hastily began mixing it. "Send it to me!" I ordered, as I made my way back through the crowd.

The girls weren't completely ignorant of what had happened. As their sources of information, they had television, Hasan, and gossip. But they had nothing new to add. When discussing Buse, they'd lower their voices, but any sad expressions disappeared in seconds. Buse was not much loved. She had no close friends. She wouldn't work in pairs, indulge in group activities, or entertain men she didn't fancy. As I said earlier, she had a set of principles and a certain classiness.

I realized too late that the man waving to me from the far

end of the bar was Ferruh, Belkıs's husband. I have trouble recognizing him when he's not with his wife.

He seemed a bit drunk. He began weaving his way toward me. I was in no shape to put up with him. With a femme fatale pivot, I headed in the opposite direction.

A crowd had gathered around Sofya's table. I joined them. The moment I appeared, the crowd parted—fell silent, even. I came eye to eye with Sofya. The tension was palpable, like a scene in a film. First, we exchanged glances. Motionless. The crowd watched, breathless. As we sized each other up, we luxuriated in the process. My God, she was stunning. A real head-turner. She wore a dark green silk spaghetti-strap blouse that brought out her eyes. The silicone could not have been displayed to better effect. As was the fashion, she had spent hours at the coiffeur to have her hair artfully mussed. Again, as was the fashion, her skin was an unearthly white, like porcelain. In short, she had stepped out of the pages of *Vogue*. As the hostess, it would be my duty to initiate conversation.

"*Merhaba*, Sofya . . . How lovely to see you here among us." I couldn't have sounded less sincere. The dryness of my voice was astonishing even to me.

"Sweetie . . ." she hissed. Her lips slightly distended, fashioned into a kiss, her teeth gleaming, she extended both arms in my direction.

Our seating units are incredibly comfortable, but rather low. After sinking into the cushions, it is no easy task to rise with one graceful movement. Sofya was a clever girl. She didn't even attempt it. Arms outstretched, she awaited me. I slowly moved toward her, bending my knees as I fell into her waiting embrace. We preserved our makeup by blowing air kisses over each other's shoulders. The encirclement ceremony was over. The tension evaporated; the crowd released its collective breath.

And applause broke out! We indulged our reverent congregation, flashing little smiles of appreciation all around.

"Condolences to us all," she said.

The trick of never fully closing her lips was one she had developed since our last meeting. No matter what she said, or where she looked, Sofya appeared to be bestowing a small kiss.

I whispered into her ear, "I would like to speak to you, when you're available . . ."

"Now!" she said, leaning her full weight into me as she rose to her feet. I was nearly knocked off balance. Sofya is an eyeful, and far from petite. She seized my hand. Like two haughty queens who have annihilated their subjects in a futile, bitter war, then decided to make peace with each other, we sauntered hand in hand to the stairs leading to my office.

"We have to speak outside. We can't talk here," she said. She had a way of giving each and every syllable its due, like an actress with the state theater.

"Why?" I asked. My voice was still dry.

"You have no idea of the danger. There is so much you don't know." During her many years in France, she'd cultivated the habit of lightly rolling her r's. No doubt she thought it was sexy.

The expression on my face must have been one of stupid admiration.

"Hasan told me everything. You came to my home. I was out. Then I found out. I was wretched. Of course. For Buse. Then, I thought, this is critical. But there is no need for panic. Or perhaps there is. It depends on your point of view. So I left my home to come here, to see you."

While garbled, it was beautifully put. And she had told me nothing. As she spoke, her eyes widened and narrowed. Each word rang with significance and hidden meaning. Even the spaces she left between the fragmented sentences were electrifying.

"What did Buse tell you?" I asked.

"It's what she told you that's important."

Just as I'd expected. We were at it again.

Reaching into a tiny handbag, a performance of the utmost sensitivity that apparently required her undivided attention, Sofya extracted a long, slender More cigarette. She lit it with an exquisite jeweled lighter, then fixed her eyes on me.

"I'm waiting. Begin."

There is nothing that infuriates me more than being subjected to the airs of the English royal family. Sofya had me right where she wanted me.

"She came to see me that morning, not you," I began.

"Exactly. Which is why you know more. Now tell me everything."

I decided against dragging things out. The surest way to get quick results was to pool what little we knew. I began to relate all that had happened. I neglected to mention the corpse of Sabiha's upstairs neighbor. She listened intently, not moving a muscle. Ash collected on the tip of her cigarette. When it had reached halfway, I stopped.

"It's even worse than I thought," she said.

She thought for a moment. Or at least pretended to. Eyes frozen to slits, she began:

"Look, the situation is more sensitive and complex than you're able to comprehend. There's so much you don't know. From what you've told me, it's begun to get dangerous. The murder makes it even more so. It means I'm at risk as well. In fact, so are you. Perhaps not yet . . . but soon."

She struck a dramatic pose, shifting slightly in her seat. Chin raised high, she blew a cloud of smoke toward the ceiling. It seemed like she was trying to tell me something. But what, I couldn't make out. I suddenly felt a bit pathetic.

"I still don't understand a thing."

"I don't expect you to." In an even more dramatic gesture, her hands fluttered gently in the air, as though to say, *None of this means anything to you; leave me alone with my troubles.* "If you'll try to be a bit patient, to understand what we're up against . . ."

How was it that she seemed to reveal so much while saying so little—and managed to humiliate me as she did it? I ran through all the times I'd felt the way I did now. Every time, Sofya was there.

"So who is the man in the photographs? What's written in the letters? Do you know that much, at least?"

Her eyes changed expression, as though to retort, *How could you possibly ask me such ridiculous questions?*

"I mean, you may have seen the photos. Or perhaps Buse told you about them."

Silence. Tension. Anticipation. Everything! She'd managed them all.

"Look," she said, once again narrowing her eyes slightly, "I know who he is. It would be a mistake for me to tell you. He's not just anyone."

"Who is it, *ayol*? The president? The prime minister? The American president?"

A plastic chortle silenced me. Like the sound a doll would make. Without so much as a facial twitch, Sofya was able to produce a wide range of sounds.

"You're so naïve."

I knew it. I was fully aware that all her efforts were aimed at confusing me. And she was succeeding.

She finished her cigarette. When she was unable to spot an ashtray upon a cursory glance to the left and right, the stub was flung to the floor and elegantly extinguished with a twist of the right ankle. She rose, gathered her long skirts, and began the descent to the club. After a few steps she turned, widened her eyes, and offered this naughty child a bit of advice:

"Blackmail. Big time. It's dangerous. Extremely dangerous. Caution is advised. Teamwork will be needed."

The eyes narrowed once again as she scrutinized me. A finger landed on the tip of my nose.

"I like you," she purred. "Despite everything," she added, after waiting a full beat. "Listen to me. Stay out of this."

She turned, and was gone.

Chapter 12

✥

$\mathcal{I}$t wasn't until later, after I'd had a few drinks, that I was able to begin processing what Sofya had said. It is impossible, the first time around, to get beyond her body language and narrative style. Sofya has mastered the art of playing the inscrutable woman.

I couldn't decide whether or not to envy her this skill. But it was food for thought.

Sofya had me absolutely stupefied. I was drained, and would be unable to carry on until closing time. To make matters worse, Belkıs's husband, Ferruh, was still at the club, eyes rolling in their sockets, too drunk to speak, but wanting to do just that. He'd taken full advantage of the discount we offer to friends.

"But it's important," he insisted. "I need to talk to you alone. You're the only one who can handle this."

He was having trouble focusing his eyes on me as he spoke. Sweaty hands pawed at my arm. Everyone knew he had a thing for our girls. Knowing how jealous Belkıs would get if he chased after them when she wasn't around, I surrendered him to Cüneyt and he was bundled into a taxi and sent home.

I needed more alcohol. I don't usually drink at the club on principle, so I went home. I'm not really a drinker, but keep a bottle of Absolut and a good selection of wine for those times when I do need a drink. Wine wouldn't do the trick. I opened the vodka.

I spread out before me the findings of my earlier search of the house. I sorted through the heap, losing myself in memories, while simultaneously losing myself in the cool lap of Absolut.

After the fifth shot, my already shattered mind was completely muddied. That was a good sign. I held a notebook I'd painstakingly prepared in middle school. I'd glued photos of beautiful women and gorgeous men on every page. They were censored versions of photos I'd cut out of a *Playgirl* I'd secretly bought. By the seventh shot, my mind was clear as crystal. The sight of the notebook conjured up the literature teacher who had given me a stinging slap across the face. I remembered her name and face, and even the khaki skirt, shiny from repeated ironing, that she always wore. I remembered the first man I slept with ... but my first evening gown: no.

I flipped through an old passport, every page of which bore a CANCELED stamp. I remembered in vivid detail every moment of my stage experience at a Parisian cabaret. I wore a wig much like Sofya's current hairstyle. My makeup was perfect; my show was a disaster. At that time, it was all the rage to lip-synch to well-known pop songs, mimicking every move of the women who made them famous. All the audience wanted was a good guffaw. But there I was in my best outfit, pursuing a career as a singer. Not surprisingly, it didn't work out.

Sofya was the real diva. She did a perfect impression of Dalida and Sylvie Vartan, two gay icons. There was a table reserved for guests who came only for her. What's more, while the rest of us had to mingle with customers when we weren't performing, encouraging them to buy us drinks, Sofya was free to hold court at her own table.

Sofya had recruited me. We met while she was holidaying in Bodrum. I was young, slender, and bold, up for anything, and eager to get as much sex as possible. Impressed by my enthusiasm, Sofya arranged a cabaret stint for me when she

returned to Paris. My stage career lasted all of five nights—
after my final performance, the club owner threw me out with a
good dressing-down. I was staying with Sofya, and the following
morning it was her turn to rebuke me.

"You've disgraced me," she began. "You've discredited Turks
everywhere. We're like ambassadors here. Just take a look at
the girls from Tunisia and Algeria. They stick together. The
Portuguese . . . As for you, not only are you unfit to represent
your country and Turkish womanhood, you don't even deserve
to be here. When I think of how I praised you. The high hopes
I had. I'd dared to imagine you would rise one day to second
billing, just below me. It didn't happen . . . it was not to be. What
a debacle."

That's right, I could still remember each and every
word of this epic and unexpectedly nationalistic rant—*ayol*,
what part of Sofya represented Turkey? The representation
of Turkish women, and me. What could be funnier? The
phrase "Turkish women" brought to mind such leading
lights as Atatürk's mother, the novelist Halide Edip, and
Miss Europe 1952, Günseli Başar. I tried to imagine myself
in their league, and I failed. And it wasn't as though they
had "stuck together" in some patriotic show of unity.

I was told to pack my bags immediately and return to Turkey
as soon as possible. I followed those instructions to the letter.

The following night, I watched for the last time as Sofya
performed onstage. She was lip-synching to Sylvia Vartan's
impersonation of a young man in "Comme un Garçon."
In other words, a man was impersonating Sylvie Vartan
impersonating a man. It was a negative of a positive of a
negative . . . or something like that. Or, a right-to-left mirror
image reflected in a second mirror, and so corrected. And it was
hilarious. The audience was in stitches. Each line was greeted

with thunderous applause. And when, at the end, Sofya's
suspenders "accidentally" gave way, revealing a glimpse of lace
panty, the hall erupted. The curtain closed. She appeared for
a curtain call, holding up her sagging trousers. She was called
back again and again, and back and forth she minced with
steps made tiny by fallen trousers, her panties now in plain
view. She saluted the crowd, raising both arms high, then,
feigning embarrassment, would clasp her crotch. Applause.
Applause. Encore after encore. As a finale, she turned around
and uncovered her derriere. On her left buttock gleamed the
scarlet imprint of a pair of lips.

Sofya was a shadowy figure even back then. During the two
weeks I spent with her, she often met with strange-looking men,
explaining them away by claiming it was "too soon" for me to
"get mixed up" with them. That didn't stop her from pairing me
off with some of these same men, earning herself a pretty penny
in the process. But she refused to tell me anything about them.

I don't know why I felt the need to dredge up all these
old memories. I felt broken and resentful. I looked back at
my younger self with tenderness and great affection, but the
memory of my earlier naïveté pained me now. Tears welled
suddenly in my eyes. I'd been so full of admiration for Sofya.
She still impressed me greatly, or should I say, dazzled and
dazed me. But I no longer felt the need to emulate her. As the
years have passed, we've grown further apart. She's refined
her particular style; and I've developed my own. And they are
miles apart.

She had succeeded in frightening me tonight, though. From
what she said, the business of the blackmail was proceeding in
a highly organized manner. Whoever they were, their motives
were less than pure. And Sofya was completely entangled. She
had even admitted to being frightened herself, which would

imply a lack of control over events. It meant she was only one of a number of players. She might even be just a pawn.

There was no way I could get anything else out of Sofya. As for the girls, they would reveal nothing about her. Especially not to me!

The vodka helped me doze off.

Chapter 13

❖

$\mathcal{J}$ woke up at an unusually early hour. As I sipped my morning coffee, I ran through the alternative courses of action for the day: (A) Wait and see; (B) Find a way to search Sabiha Hanım's house; (C) Meet with Sofya; failing that, track her down; (D) Do something completely unrelated, like tidy my messy house.

None of the options appealed. I glanced through the paper, hoping to create new ones as I read it. The Buse/Fevzi murder had received a single column of belated coverage. The accompanying photo was from her official ID card. "Fevzi" looked like a timid sort of person. I'd never seen her like that.

The murder in Kocamustafapaşa hadn't made it into the papers yet. I looked through the obituaries in any case. There was nothing of interest.

None of the girls would be up this early. For ladies of the night, a new day dawns at noon at the earliest. There was no need to begin working on the Wish & Fire account, because the contract had not yet been signed. Bitter experience had taught me not to embark on a project until I had a signed contract. In fact, only a hefty advance payment enabled me to take such companies seriously.

Remote control in hand, I flicked through the morning TV programs. The housewives in the studio audiences reminded me of Mrs. Apple Cheeks. I decided it was time for a morning visit.

Perhaps Sabiha Hanım, whose whereabouts had been a mystery the previous night, had returned.

I got a giant bar of chocolate for the chubby, demonstrative girl of the house. And one for myself, to eat on the way. For the mother, I picked up a freshly baked cake from the corner patisserie. After what had been said about Fevzi, I had no intention of going empty-handed.

Then it occurred to me that if Sabiha Hanım had returned safe and sound, it would be a nice gesture to bring her something as well. I discarded my first impulse, which was to buy flowers. No matter how fragrant, flowers could hardly be adequately appreciated by a blind person. I tried to remember if I'd ever bought a gift for a blind person before. No, I hadn't. As I ran through the list of woes suffered by the elderly—diabetes, high blood pressure, cholesterol levels, hardening of the arteries, osteoporosis and the like—I eliminated as suitable gifts sweets, chocolate, and pastries. Cologne! That was it! In the old days, cologne had been the preferred gift. On holidays in particular, bottles of cologne would be exchanged.

I stepped into the first pharmacy I saw and bought a bottle of lavender cologne. Lemon cologne makes me queasy. If I was unable to present the cologne to Sabiha Hanım—and that was highly likely—I would use it myself. I had it beautifully gift-wrapped. Then it occurred to me just how pointless the extra effort to make it look nice was.

I reached the taxi stand and jumped into the first available car, whose driver greeted me with a "Welcome, *abi*." I gave directions to Teksoy Apartments. When we arrived, I noticed that Hüseyin had parked in front of a burned-out building the night before. So that was the source of the charred smell. And I'd blamed it on balcony barbecues.

An unpleasant-looking woman living in the street-level flat had placed a pillow on the windowsill, upon which she rested her enormous bosom. She was crocheting and chatting with a neighbor across the street, who was hanging out washing on the balcony on the second floor. The subject of conversation was the pattern embroidered onto a pillowcase that had just about dried. The unpleasant woman admired it, wanted to borrow it when it was dry, so she could copy the pattern onto her own linen. I couldn't resist lifting my head to glance over at the envied piece of needlework. It was vile. There was no need to replicate it. In fact, it should be outlawed.

When they realized I was about to enter the apartment building, they looked me up and down, but they didn't say anything. I wondered what they would say behind my back, but proceeded as quickly as possible up the stairs to the first floor. The door nearest the staircase belonged to the sturdy family. Sabiha Hanım would have to wait. I hadn't bought the chocolate and cake for nothing. Although I knew the door would fly open instantly, I still rang the bell long and hard.

The door opened before I had lifted my finger from the bell. Below, a small head poked out from between a pair of thick legs; above, the mother's head poked out into the hallway. Upon seeing me, her smile seemed to fade somewhat. She must have learned the news from the TV or papers.

"*Merhaba* . . . so it's you."

"There was such a commotion when we parted last night. And I'd been unable to see dear Sabiha Hanım . . . I brought some cake, hoping we could share it with a cup of tea. And this is for your little girl . . . Take it, sweetie."

"Yes, of course you're welcome. Come in." The door opened wide. "I've lost my wits. I don't seem to know what I'm doing. I'm sure you know what's happened. About Fevzi. I couldn't believe it. Two deaths in one day. That's never happened before. It just wrecked me. I wouldn't have thought it'd upset me so much, but it sent me reeling."

She had managed to relate all this in the time it took me to put on the gold lamé slippers she'd gestured to. The choice of footwear would indicate she had certain ideas about me. I love chatty sorts, and they're especially useful if you're trying to get information about something.

We went inside and sat down. The cake remained in its wrapping on the coffee table.

"You must have known all about it last night, but you didn't tell us. I mean, about Fevzi. I wish you had—I'd have been better prepared for the news later. You must have come here to pay your condolences to Sabiha Hanım. How thoughtful of you. May Allah grant all his people a friend like you. You know what they say about friends and rainy days."

She had strong lungs. Everything was gushed out in a single breath. I listened sympathetically—there would be plenty more to come.

I locked my eyes onto hers, then slowly shifted them, landing on the package of cake. She leaped from her seat.

"Ay, pardon. I forgot the cake, didn't I? I'll put on the kettle. We can talk while the tea steeps. I've got some questions for you."

And I've got some questions for you.

The corner end table was loaded with picture frames. The most magnificent of them all framed a studio shot of a bride and groom. The photographer had enhanced the photo by superimposing pink roses. The bride wore the standard "nightingale nest" headdress, her face nestled in thousands of ruffles. That familiar beaming face also expressed a hint of pride. As she looked into the camera, she seemed to be saying, *See, I've landed a husband.* Even back then, she had filet mignon cheeks.

Right next to the wedding picture was one of a wrinkled infant, the sour-faced daughter. That same child, who followed my every move and glance, immediately remarked, "That's me," as she smiled mischievously.

Above the sideboard hung a picture in a gilt frame. Nearly everyone in the photo wore a dark suit. The man of the house was captured shaking hands with a politician. His interest in politics may well have been career-related. Civil servants who fail to join a party can find themselves exiled to a position in the countryside.

The frame was slightly off-kilter. I can't bear such things. I hesitated for only a second before rising to my feet to adjust it. Under the watchful gaze of the girl, I straightened it with my fingertips, then sat down.

There was one thing about the living room that differentiated it from most of its kind: the absence of embroidered coverings and needlework. I jotted down a point in my mental ledger. The sound of running water in the kitchen stopped and Apple Cheeks reappeared, settled down across from me, and smoothed her skirt.

"Actually, there was something I wanted to share with you. As I was preparing the tea I asked myself whether it was really necessary, but I think I'd better tell you. You know, there's been no sign of Sabiha."

Bug-eyed and staring, she awaited my reaction.

"That's strange," I mused, encouraging her to continue.

"It is, isn't it? If anything had happened I'd know. But there's not been a peep out of her. She wouldn't go anywhere without telling me. God forbid anything bad has happened to her... Where could she be? What do you think?"

I didn't answer. I contented myself with a meaningful shake of my head.

"I've got an inquiring mind. I mean, I wonder about everything. I've got to know where, and why. I'm a little like those lady detectives on TV. I always put myself in their place, try to figure out what I'd do in their shoes if there was a murder. And what do you know, here I am, faced with not one, but two murders. The case of Hamiyet Hanım upstairs is worth looking into. She's got a hopeless son. He drinks, takes drugs. He kept hitting her up for money. I suspect he did it. That's what I told the police. Who else would do it? Don't you agree?"

This was a rhetorical question. A way of transforming a monologue into a dialogue.

She was incredibly unflustered by the two murders, and sat there calmly relating her detective fantasies. She had no doubt been a big *Charlie's Angels* fan as a girl. Although Jaclyn Smith was probably her favorite, she had enough modesty to model herself on Sabrina/Kate Jackson, consoling herself by saying, *Well, she was the clever one of the three.* A more attractive woman would have set her sights on no less than Farrah Fawcett. I know I did.

"Anyway, don't let me pester you with all this nonsense. It isn't as though you even knew Hamiyet Hanım. If I didn't control myself I'd keep chatting until you shut me up. Talking about anything under the sun. You could say I'm a bit talkative. Enough about Hamiyet Hanım, we'll come back to her if necessary. Let's talk about Fevzi. Did you call her Fevzi or Buse? I couldn't break the habit of calling her Fevzi. Sometimes Fevziye, just to get a rise. I mean, when she was alive. It doesn't matter what I call her now, does it? After she became a woman she'd scold me. 'There is no Fevzi. I've buried him. I'm Buse.' It makes no difference to me, Fevzi or Buse. Whichever you prefer."

"I knew her as Buse."

"Fine, then. I'll say Buse." She turned to the little girl. "Stop sucking your thumb. Get it out of your mouth. Your big brother thinks it's such a shame, he doesn't think much of you when you do that. Go on, go back to your seat. That's a good girl. Make your mother proud. She's a good girl, isn't she, *abi*?"

The "big brother" was none other than me.

"Good girl," I said. I couldn't help thinking what a problem child she would turn out to be.

"You know the police came last night. May Hamiyet Hanım rest in peace."

As she said this, she pointed, eyes crossed, to a spot in the middle of her forehead.

"She was a bit stubborn. In fact, she was a difficult woman. I put it down to her old age. I was still upset, though. How many neighbors do I have here, after all? She was well educated. That explains her sharp tongue. She thought she knew everything, would correct everyone. Anyway . . . everyone in the building was up in arms, as you might expect. We were interrogated until dawn. My husband works at the court, so they kept it short. But they still asked even little Sevgi whether or not she'd heard the gunshot.

"I mean, really. When you think about what's on TV these days. Everyone watching a different channel, programs full of gunshots and exploding bombs. How are we supposed to know what's real and what's on TV? Anyway, my husband said they probably used a silencer."

"You've got a point."

"Not me, my husband. I didn't even take a look at the body. I just wasn't up to it. I didn't go upstairs. Was I curious? You bet. But I didn't dare. I saw my late grandmother's body, and that was enough for me. Never again, I said to myself."

"What about Sabiha Hanım?"

"Let me just get the tea."

"Can I help you?"

"No, of course not. Perhaps we should have had coffee. We could have read each other's coffee grounds. But tea goes best with cake." She grabbed the cake and headed for the kitchen. She saw right through my men's clothes. She'd had enough experience to figure me out at a glance. After all, she'd grown up with Fevzi, seen her develop over the years. Otherwise, what normal, self-respecting housewife would invite a strange man into her house the morning after they'd met, then suggest they tell each other's fortunes?

"I like you," she declared.

There was no way for her to know what was running through my mind. It must have been a coincidence.

"I appreciate your having become friends with Fevzi. She tormented me no end when we were growing up. But I always liked her. In my own way."

"But where do you think Sabiha Hanım could be?"

She glanced over at the suddenly well-behaved daughter, who sat there quietly, all ears.

"Off we go to the bedroom. You can play with your toys."

"Yahhh . . ." The little ugly face became absolutely unbearable when whining.

"Do you want the slipper?" It was instantly whisked off the mother's right foot and brandished in the air.

Eyes on the threatening slipper, the pouting face slid off the armchair accompanied by a chorus of gradually fading "Yahhhh's" of protest, and was conveyed as slowly as possible out of the room. I know the type. Instead of going to their bedroom, they invariably crouch in the hallway just outside the door, eavesdropping.

Once we were alone, Apple Cheeks adopted a secretive and all-knowing tone.

"I've got a theory: Sabiha Hanım heard the news on the TV. She then had a stroke or a heart attack. She's laid out in her flat. Where else could she be? The whole building was in an uproar last night, but not a peep from her flat. The police asked after her, but we said we didn't know a thing. They left. She's inside. Dead or paralyzed. As you know, she was blind in any case. Her heart just couldn't take it."

I failed to make the connection between blindness and a heart condition, but nevertheless. The expression on her face was one of triumphant discovery. Her eyes were shining, excitedly awaiting my approbation.

"God forbid," I said.

"Who's to say what God forbids? Just look at the state of our country."

I nodded my head in agreement, but I wasn't biting. The last thing I needed was her opinion on the general decline of our country, Istanbul's overrapid development, the general direction of our benighted land, the sad state of today's youth, politics, culture, our prospects for accession to the EU, and the troubles in the southeast. I wasn't going there.

"So, what should we do? Buse's funeral will be held today or tomorrow. Whenever the morgue turns over her body. The fact that it's a murder case means it will take a bit longer. My friends and I are handling all the arrangements. Sabiha Hanım is Buse's mother! I'm sure she would want to attend. Or she would at least want to know where Buse will be buried."

"I'd forgotten all about the funeral. I'd like to go. There must be others from the neighborhood who'd want to attend too. But I don't know that I dare to. What would I do if the media got hold of the story, showed me with a bunch of transvestites? The people here are conservative types. Forgive me for not coming."

These narrow little minds, I sighed to myself.

"Of course, you know best."

"We'll arrange a *mevlit*. You'll want to come; I'll let you know when it's held."

"Thank you." I had no intention of attending. *Mevlits* bore me. When I sit with the women, I have to wear a head scarf. When I sit with the men, they stare, then squeeze me into a corner and try to give me advice. And somehow I strongly doubted the *mevlit* would ever be held at all.

We exchanged smiles. She had something else to say, that much was clear. She just didn't know how to begin.

"Then I suppose there's nothing to do but sit around and wait. We can't really put off the funeral for more than an extra day."

She was gathering her courage. I waited patiently.

"Like I said," she continued, "I suspect the news killed poor Sabiha Hanım. My husband wouldn't talk about it. He knows best, I suppose. It'll become clear enough a week from now, when the corpse stinks to high heaven."

Her self-assurance was mind-boggling.

"So what do you suggest?"

She lowered her voice: "I happen to have a spare key. Sabiha gave it to me for emergencies. But I didn't dare go into her flat alone. I couldn't face the sight of a body. I'd go all funny."

My efforts had paid off. The stout, apple-cheeked lady had turned out to be a real diamond in the rough.

"But if you don't mind, we could go in together . . ."

Bingo. The opportunity I'd been hoping for had landed right in my lap.

Chapter 14

✣

*C*hubby Cheeks leading the way, we arrived in front of the neighbor's door in no time. My companion raised her index finger to her lips, in a *Shhh* sign. We were, after all, on a covert mission. I slowly opened and closed my eyes, to signal my assent.

Her mundane life had been enriched no end. She fully intended to live it to the hilt. The key in her hand, she glanced to her right and left, then placed it in the keyhole. I watched her, smiling to myself. She looked at me like a heroine in a film hesitating about whether or not to launch a nuclear war. I gave her a friendly pat on the shoulder, the last bit of encouragement she needed.

She turned the key. Suddenly, the door sprang open on its own. Visible through the slightly ajar door was a stern man in a lead-gray suit. He was at most thirty, but his suit made him look older. He looked at us, expressionless. The impassive face was nevertheless threatening. We stared back, dumbfounded.

"I'm the neighbor from across the hall. I've come to see Sabiha Hanım."

For the first time, her pink cheeks were pale. But though her face may have been drained of color, the strident voice still maintained a sense of authority and purpose.

The face turned to me. The blank look only made him seem more menacing. I settled on a weak grin. I didn't expect an invitation to be immediately forthcoming. Whoever this gorilla was, he was no friend. I could have flattened him with two chops, but the hand concealed behind the door most likely held a gun. There was also no way of knowing if anyone else was inside. It wasn't worth the risk.

"I called on her last night. When she didn't answer, I got worried. Maybe she needs something . . ."

Chubby Cheeks's voice was wilting under the staring eyes. She was most definitely frightened. Taking a step back, she leaned against me.

"She's resting."

Out of the immobile face came an incredibly muffled, but unmistakably countertenor, voice. Despite the obvious effort to speak as gruffly as possible, it was a reedy, comical sound. He had succeeded admirably in balancing the funny voice with an icy gaze. The door was shutting in our faces. I reached out and blocked it. For the first time, the face assumed a meaningful expression: *Who do you think you are?*

"We'd like to see her," I insisted.

"She's resting."

And the door shut. I listened carefully. Not a sound came from inside. No footsteps or voices. He was still at the door, listening to us.

We were stunned into momentary silence.

"But who is that man?" asked Apple Cheeks. "I've never seen him. I know all her relatives. He's never been here before."

That the man looked out of place in that house was undeniable. But she couldn't have expected me to answer her question.

"If you don't know him, how am I supposed to?"

She made a quick decision, and pressed the bell. Because we were being observed through the keyhole, the door opened immediately. We saw the same expressionless stare.

"I ... Excuse me, but who are you? I've never seen you before." It was exactly the sort of question you'd expect from the ever-curious Chubby Cheeks.

"A relative."

And the door shut again. We remained outside. Astonished and disappointed, we returned to her flat.

The obnoxious girl greeted us at the door. She had seen everything.

"Mummy, who was that man?"

"I'll give you such a smack! Like I know who it is. And didn't I tell you to wait inside?"

Letting loose a series of mutinous "Yahhh's," she clickety-clacked her slippered feet into the flat. We returned to the living room and sat down again. The disappointing failure to find Sabiha Hanım, to learn anything about her whereabouts, had taken its toll. We sat, deflated and silent. In our emotions and situation, Apple Cheeks and I had much in common.

"A relative. That's a lie. Definitely a lie. I'd know who he was, wouldn't I? I've seen everyone who comes and goes. And it's not like she has many relatives. There are just a few who visit. We've been neighbors for all these years. I swear that's the first time I've laid eyes on him."

I believed her.

"So he's definitely not a relative," I said.

"I wonder how Sabiha Hanim is. Now I'm getting worried."

This from the woman who only moments ago had declared the old lady paralyzed at best, dead at worst. Now she's concerned?

"So what are we going to do now?"

I wasn't thrilled with the cloying, proprietary use of the word "we."

"Should we tell the police?"

"Definitely not," I objected. "What would we tell them? That there's someone in a neighbor's house claiming to be a relative, and that they should come verify it? They wouldn't even bother coming."

"That's true . . ."

We sat thinking. Chubby Cheeks toyed with the neighbor's key. It was attached with a single ring to a plastic coffee-colored key chain.

"I may as well make some tea. It'll help us concentrate." She strode off to the kitchen, key in hand.

Events had taken a strange turn. A bodyguard of some sort had been stationed in Sabiha's house. I didn't know who he was working for, but he most certainly was not there on his own initiative. Whether Sabiha was alive or dead was no longer of critical importance. The photos and letters had been found, or were about to be. My part in all of this was over. The identity of whoever had killed Buse, and the motive for doing so, would remain a mystery. Perhaps the death of the upstairs neighbor, Hamiyet Hanım, really was unrelated.

My hostess carried in the tea tray and began serving cake, speaking all the while. I can't say she was making sense. It was more like thinking aloud. Her busy mind was spinning its wheels over the relatives and acquaintances of Sabiha Hanım and Fevzi, their exact blood connections, what they did, where they lived, and even what they looked like. I was drowning in a long list of names, places, professions, and descriptions. Her audible thoughts succeeded only in muddling up my decidedly more quiet and systematic thought process. I fixed a pleasant smile onto my face, the classic sort you see in photographs, and closed my ears.

"But you aren't even listening to me!"

She was right, if overly demanding. I hadn't been listening.

"I'm sorry, I was lost in thought."

"Well, why weren't you talking, then? Tell me what you were thinking."

If I had wanted her to know everything that was running through my head, I would have been talking, not thinking. There was no sense in trying to explain this philosophical point to her. She knew nothing about the blackmail. There was no need for her to know. I couldn't decide whether or not to tell her about the photos. Perhaps I could jog her memory; she might recall one of Fevzi's youthful adventures.

Every single one of our girls has a close female friend. They are generally of the sort referred to as "ladies": unmarried and sweet, but not at all attractive. They're reasonably well dressed and well maintained, and while not contenders in the femme fatale category, they tend to have respectable careers. A broker or bank administrator, or perhaps a deputy manager. An executive secretary, accountant. At most, an attorney or small business owner. When it comes to practical matters, to the stuff of daily life, these ladies know no rival. Their private lives, however, are disastrous at best; nonexistent at worst. Our girls confide in their lady friends. Every detail is shared, including length, girth, and position. The ladies listen transfixed, making the vicarious experiences their own. I don't believe these ladies ever have the chance to relate stirring, intense stories of their own.

Buse/Fevzi may have enjoyed such a friendship with Apple Cheeks, relating to her girlhood friend the explicit details of her most private and passionate encounters. The neighborhood girl, cheery but ugly, with repressed feelings and limited experience, would have been the ideal confidante for someone like Fevzi.

"Look," I said, "there are a few things I haven't told you. I didn't want to frighten you."

She held her breath, all ears. I summarized the events for her.

"So that's what happened. They snuffed out Sabiha, too. *Ayol*, if you'd only told me we were face to face with a killer. Now we're just sitting here. My God! Oh, my God . . ."

She clasped her hand over her mouth to suppress a scream.

"I've got to find those letters and photos," I continued. "There's no other way to find out who killed Buse. That is, if they haven't already found the photos . . ."

"I'm terrified. The killers are right next door. I've got a little girl. What if something happened to her!"

As she remembered her daughter and the potential danger, she jumped out of her chair. There was no sign of color on those cheeks; nor a hint of a smile. Even that shred of appeal was gone.

"Sevgi! Baby, come here quick! Where are you? Come here right now . . ."

The "baby" appeared and was duly clasped to her breast, shielded from harm. You'd have thought a pathological killer was in the same room.

"I've got to call my husband. And we must inform the police."

The detective adventure was rather short-lived, abandoned at the first sign of real trouble. Faced with such panic, there was nothing I could do. I decided to let matters take their course, and simply looked on as she dialed the police.

Chapter 15

❖

She was unable to reach her husband. It was the busiest time of day for the law courts. We waited together for the police to arrive. She didn't have the courage to wait alone with her baby. She frenziedly, but rhythmically, bounced her naked feet inside her slippers. I noticed that her fleshy heels were well cared for. As is always the case when waiting for something, time seemed to slow down, nearly stopping altogether. She twisted a lock of her daughter's short, curly hair. Then, once she had succeeded in tangling it into a fleecy mess, used her fingers to comb it out. As the hair was pulled tight, the small face grew increasingly tense. Just as baby reached breaking point and was preparing to bellow, the lock of hair would be released, and a pointless and proud smile would spread across her face.

I occupied myself with trying to decide what and how much to tell the police when they arrived. The involvement of the law might be useful, at least in terms of locating Sabiha Hanım. What's more, we could learn the identity of Stone Face, if he was still there.

What Chubby Cheeks would reveal to the police was an entirely different matter. I regretted having told her about the possibility of blackmail over the letters and photos, even revealing my theories about the situation. But now there was no taking it back. By remaining there with her, I would at least know exactly what she told the police, their reaction to the information, and whether or not they planned to start an investigation. Beginning with the thumb of my left hand, I began pulling back my cuticles, a finger at a time.

Finally, the doorbell rang. My hostess released her daughter's head.

"The police!" she cried out, breath rushing out as she hopped to her feet. In her mind, at least, the arrival of the police meant the end of all our troubles. She clearly believed her churned-up life would return to its former stillness and simplicity, bringing her peace of mind.

It was indeed the police. A pair of them. The short potbellied one wasn't much to look at, but his young partner was a thing of beauty. He had light brown hair, and he fastened his deep hazel eyes on me, looking me up and down. Had me sized up in a split second. The corner of his mouth curled into a half smile.

Aynur summarized events for the short, old one; the handsome Casanova and I continued giving each other the once-over. Height, weight, lips, nose, expression, hands—I couldn't detect a single flaw. His chin was strong, his nose a promise of better things to come. A tuft of chest hair peeked out from his short-sleeved, open-necked shirt. As he swallowed, his prominent Adam's apple rose and fell. His hands were large and clean. Now, if only he hadn't been wearing a uniform, I would have been ready to go. I don't like uniforms, and I have a particular distaste for those of the police.

Chubby Cheeks slowly explained everything, relishing every last detail. Her cheeks flushed with excitement, she looked like her old self.

"There's a murderer in the flat across the hall," she was saying. When she finished, the policeman turned to me. I was forced to abandon my flirting with the partner. The old one seemed to be expecting some sort of clarification.

"I came to visit Sabiha Hanım. When she wasn't at home, I came here."

I underscored the validity of my explanation by thrusting the bottle of cologne in the direction of his eye.

They asked who I was. I was more than willing to cooperate, and told the favored one my name, my telephone number, and my address, slowly spelling out each and every figure and letter.

"Her son is a friend of mine," I added. "I'm a bit worried about her."

"We'll have a look," said the potbellied one. "Would you like to register a complaint?"

I wasn't sure. Should I lodge a formal complaint or not? Ignoring the face of Apple Cheeks, whose jowls seemed to sag in astonishment, I elected not to.

We went out into the corridor together. Their radio receivers crackling nonstop, the policemen led the way to the opposite flat, where they rang the bell. Naturally, it didn't open.

They pressed the bell again. Still nothing. I had a sense of déjà vu as I recalled ringing the bell of the upstairs neighbor the previous night.

"Wait a minute, I've got a key," said Aynur as she raced back to her flat. The police and I were left on our own, exchanging glances. Potbelly really could have kept his eyes to himself. And he reeked of sweat. My guy, on the other hand, smelled of soap and aftershave lotion.

The key arrived, "We'll still have to fill out an official form," Potbelly explained.

"But she's my neighbor. She's the one who gave me the key. Just make sure it's safe; I'll open the door for you. And if anything happens, remember that my husband works at the court."

Filet Mignon Face silenced both the policemen with this

little speech. She stretched out her hand, offering Potbelly the key.

"Here you go . . ." When he hesitated, she added, "Go on, now, open it . . ."

The fact that the police didn't even bother to draw their revolvers was an indication of how seriously they took us. They'd arrived at a flat in which, over half-empty cups of tea and crumb -filled plates, a housewife and a pansy had notified them of a possible murder. If it hadn't been for the dead neighbor upstairs they probably wouldn't have bothered coming at all.

The door opened. Inside, everything was still. But a mess. Even a blind woman wouldn't have lived in such disorder. For the first time, the police looked somewhat sober. They finally raised their guns.

The one in front called out, "Police! Put up your hands!"

There was no response. Neither a human voice nor an answering gunshot.

The police searched every room. Even the contents of the refrigerator had been spilled out onto the floor. The room that must have been Buse's as a teenage boy, posters of heartthrobs still on the walls, had been ransacked. Whatever these people had been looking for, they must have found it. I couldn't have done a more thorough job myself. Some of the posters had even been torn from the wall.

Strangest of all was the absence of Sabiha Hanım, either alive or dead. If she had been killed, there would surely be some evidence of it at the scene. The two cops were busily trampling any such evidence. My guy was called Kenan. Every time he bent over the fabric of his trousers stretched even more snugly over his backside. I couldn't keep my eyes off it. A thick notebook of some kind was clearly outlined in his right back pocket. I wished it wasn't there. Still, one must make do at times like these.

When it was clear we weren't going to find anything of

interest, the four of us proceeded to look stupidly at one another. In official tones, Potbelly announced:

"There's no one here."

If he hadn't seemed quite so solemn, I'd have assumed he was going for a laugh. His sort is incapable of such irony, though. Yes, he was serious. I bit my tongue to suppress a giggle.

Aynur didn't hide her immediate reaction. "So what are we supposed to do now? Are we just going to leave?"

"What do you expect us to do?"

"*Ayol*, the flat's been turned upside down; Sabiha Hanım's missing," observed the pink-cheeked amateur detective. "I'd most certainly like to file a complaint."

"You're free to. But there's nothing more we can do right now. You can make a missing persons report."

"Oh, I see. You're saying we should sit around until they come to kill us, too."

How she had reached this conclusion was beyond me. Maybe she was privy to certain information.

"Look, ma'am," he said. Sweaty Potbelly had switched to "ma'am," a sure sign that he was feeling less tolerant. "There's nothing else we can do here. There's no sign of a murder, or a corpse. All we have is a messy house and a missing blind lady."

"But what about the body upstairs?" She began to speak in a nasal voice, and was flushed with rage and a sense of thwarted purpose.

My man intervened. "Calm down, lady . . ."

Ay! I don't think much of men who use the term "lady," either. It reeks of the lower classes. The sort who imagine romance can only end in marriage.

"I can't be calm! And I won't . . ." She was scarlet. "You're supposed to ensure our security. You can't just walk away."

"But we can't just sit here and wait . . ."

"You're absolutely right, Officer," I agreed.

I must have said something sensible. I was deaf to Filet Mignon's protests. I'm skilled at filtering out such unpleasantness. Exceptionally so. The police both agreed with me.

As we thanked the officers, I didn't fail to seize the opportunity to touch mine, grabbing his arm right at the point where his blue sleeve ended. He didn't pull back. The hair on his forearm was light-colored.

"I'll calm her down. Thank you for coming," I said. For no particular reason, I gave his arm a squeeze as I said this. He knew what I was doing. But he didn't react. The frosty thing!

There was no point in being more insistent. I released his arm. We watched as they walked down the stairs. He looked back only once. I made an instant evaluation: This was going nowhere!

I once again allowed the protests and complaints to reach my eardrums.

"This is outrageous! If they think I'm just going to wait around until the killers have picked us all off, one by one . . . !"

As the police left the building, the doors of all the flats opened, and heads of various ages and sizes poked out into the landings. They all wondered what was going on. Chubby Cheeks milked the situation for all it was worth. Like an actress who has prepared for the role of her career, she first gave a highly significant glance to each of them, then began a full rundown of events. Leaving her with her audience, I ventured into Sabiha Hanım's flat for one last look.

Chapter 16

✤

$\mathcal{I}$ wandered through Sabiha Hanım's ransacked flat, trying to put my thoughts in order. I went into Buse's bedroom and sat on the bedsprings. The mattress had been shoved onto the floor. The room had obviously been unchanged for years, and was decorated in the style of Buse's teenage years. There was even a fuzzy pink bedspread. The nightstand against the opposite wall had been used as a dressing table. Lining it were rows of nearly empty bottles of fragrance, not a single one of them aftershave lotion. All were cloyingly sweet: *siyah beyaz*; Diorella, with its Prince de Galles label; a purple bottle of Poison; L'Air du Temps de Nina Ricci, in its original Lalique bottle; YSL Rive Gauche; a square bottle of Givenchy; Samsara by Guerlain. I much prefer lighter, spicier perfumes. But then again, you wouldn't catch me dead in a Chanel suit.

The contents of the drawers of the dressing table had been spilled out onto the floor. Piled high were colorful boxer shorts, classic white briefs, lace panties, and sleeveless T-shirts with scalloped straps. A pair of flesh-colored silk boxer shorts caught my attention. I picked them up. They smelled of lavender.

I looked at the posters on the wall. They all depicted impossibly standoffish sirens and gorgeous hunks. Richard Gere featured prominently, including a bare-chested poster promoting *Breathless*. Part of it was torn off.

I didn't know what I was looking for. A photo album, journal, or diary would be quite a find. I wandered through the other rooms of the apartment, but nothing turned up. Other than a few books written in Braille, there was nothing. This was, after all, a flat inhabited until very recently by a blind woman. Perhaps written documents of all descriptions had been carted away.

What had happened to Sabiha Hanım? Where was she? Why was her flat in this state? Where were those notorious photos and letters?

I had hit a dead end. I fled the gloomy place, so lacking in color coordination of any kind.

A thoroughly rattled Chubby Cheeks subjected me to a tirade in the corridor. She was expecting me to join in.

"I'm going," I announced instead.

"Where?" she wailed. "This all happened because of you, and now you're just running away?"

Those were the words she addressed to me. Then she turned to the neighbors still watching us—watching her, would be more accurate—pointed to me and said in an even louder voice:

"That's the one, the friend of Fevzi's I told you about!"

I grabbed her by the arm and dragged her into her flat. She was so astonished she didn't resist. The moment we entered, I shut the door behind us. The bell rang immediately. We had forgotten the sniveling girl-child outside. I let her in.

"Calm down and listen up!" I ordered.

"Okay," she said. Without a trace of the dramatic pitch of only a few moments earlier, she walked into the living room and sat down. The daughter was tugged into her lap.

"I'm listening," she said. "I'm willing to listen to any explanation you may have for all of this."

I drew for her a rough outline of my main fears and concerns.

"I want you to tell me about every relationship ever mentioned by Buse," I concluded. "There may be a clue of some kind."

"All right. I'll tell you everything I remember . . . But first

I want you to know that I don't know any of them personally. She'd come and tell me about them. I may have seen a couple of them when we were in middle school, but that's it. All I know after that is what she told me. Oh, and at one point we would go to eat profiteroles at I˙nci Patisserie in Beyog˘lu, to the cinema, shopping in Nişantaşı and such. We'd point out our favorites to each other. If we liked the same man she'd tell me off, even pinch my arm. She wouldn't talk to me for two weeks just because I said I liked Richard Gere, too."

She was off and running. Meanwhile, her "baby" was being given an early and detailed version of the facts of life.

"Over time I learned to like only the ones she didn't. Ay, you can't imagine how jealous she was. Then she started wanting the ones I liked. And she'd get them in the end. I don't want you to get the wrong idea. I didn't really do anything. I'd cut out pictures of my favorite movie stars. Or admire someone from a distance. It was all talk, really. Nothing more."

The classic claim of female chastity.

"Fevzi, that is, Buse, started fooling around at a young age. I mean, we hadn't even finished middle school yet. She was off kissing other boys and such. And then, you know, she did the rest. And she would tell me exactly what she got up to."

I wasn't so certain. Our girls aren't to be taken quite so literally. What they say is often one part fairy tale, two parts John Holmes. I have never heard, for example, of a case where the boyfriend had a tiny one. That's not to say they're all lying, but reality is inescapable even in Turkey. There are such things as statistics and probability.

"Now, I suspect that there must have been certain things she kept to herself." And there were certain things Chubby Cheeks was keeping back about herself, too.

Her suspicions were justified. She knew exactly what was going through my mind, or at least some of it.

"Like what?" I asked. By commenting, I had created the illusion that she was engaged in a conversation, rather than being subjected to an interrogation. She continued:

"I mean, look at what happened. She even had a relationship with someone famous. She showed me lots of pictures, but I never saw anyone I knew. Maybe he became famous later."

"Well, where would she hide her pictures?" I asked. "I couldn't find anything in her mother's flat."

"Yeah . . . They took everything, I suppose . . ."

I'd had it. I was getting sleepy. I don't have much patience even for the girls' tall tales. A censored version of the youthful indiscretions of a middle-class housewife was more than I could bear. We wouldn't get anywhere like this.

It was noon by the time I left her. I had pushed my tolerance level to the limit. I was hungry. I declined the offer to "whip something up to eat," thanked her, and got out of there.

The neighborhood was unfamiliar to me, so I jumped into the first taxi that came along.

Chapter 17

✤

In order to relax, I was in desperate need of a quiz show. Preferably the most imbecilic kind possible. A program in which the contestants hesitated when asked what their names were. I had an unbelievably strong desire to foam at the mouth, to fly into a rage, in front of the TV.

The nostalgic items of the previous night were still piled high, a worthless heap of trash, on the sofa. The impulse to clean them up disappeared as quickly as it had arrived. Satı could take care of it when she came.

I listened to the answering machine. Ali had phoned to tell me that Wish & Fire was considering our proposal. I decided to allow them no more than a week to do so. Not a second more. If they didn't call before the allotted time was up, I would content myself with crashing their local websites, international stock systems, or even, if I could, their entire network. I despise companies that demand hours of meetings only to get cold feet over a couple of dollars.

There were no other messages of note. Ferruh had called for some reason, claiming he needed to meet me "in private." I found his persistence nauseating. He'd been on my tail since the previous night, and had phoned my home twice. Belkıs must have been preoccupied, either with shopping in Milan or gambling in Cyprus. Left on his own, Ferruh was harassing me. My friendship with Belkıs did not mean I intended to pleasure her husband—particularly without her knowledge. I ruled out the possibility of any "private" meetings.

I made myself a cup of fennel tea. Then I rang Hasan on his cell phone. I wondered how the arrangements for Buse/Fevzi's funeral were going. Everything else was a total mess; I needed to know that at least the funeral would go smoothly.

Hasan did not have good news. Because of the suspicion of murder, the morgue would not release the body. An autopsy would have to be performed, and would last for a few days. At this news, I began spewing out all my fury and frustration at poor Hasan.

At my first pause for breath, Hasan managed to get in, "But *abi*, someone else has claimed the body." I momentarily lost my voice.

"Who?" I demanded to know. "The only relative I know of is her mother. And she's blind and missing."

"That's what I thought, too. But apparently not. If we are claiming the body as her employers, or place of employment, we'll have to do the paperwork, produce a work permit."

"Hasan, don't be ridiculous! Since when have transvestite hookers working a clip joint been registered on any employment rolls?"

"That's what I said," he replied.

"You did well to! Well, at least find out who it is."

"I will," he said. He then added, "My battery's running out," and the line went dead. The shameless pantywaist.

Every time I was about to call off the whole Buse business, some new bit of information would pop up and I'd be strung along until I hit another dead end. And each time some new bait was dangled in front of me, off I'd go, imagining myself to be in hot pursuit of an important lead. Now someone with claims on Buse's body had materialized. Fine. It wasn't as though I had a thing for corpses. Whoever it was, they were welcome to her.

I'd put on my mourning best and simply attend the funeral. If it was held at a relatively convenient location, naturally.

I called Hasan back to tell him not to bother pursuing the funeral arrangements. There was no response. Either his battery really had gone dead or he'd switched off his phone.

I was exhausted. It was time to look after myself. I rummaged through the beauty treatments I had on hand. Clay masks, collagen creams, rejuvenating mud and creams I'd picked up in Ölüdeniz. There was also a selection of soothing lotions and aromatherapy oils. I was all set to pamper myself, but suddenly I started to dread the mess I'd make. The salon would be best. I called, and was told they had a cancellation. Abandoning my own beauty treatments, I was out the door. My home was getting messier by the day.

The technicians at the salon know me well and treat me with respect. I decided on a deep-cleaning steam facial, firming massage, and a full-body solarium séance.

As I waited for the facial, the lady friend who had come to the club with Belkıs, the journalist whose name I couldn't remember, emerged from the steam treatment room. Just as I was asking myself if she'd recognize me in my comparatively male state, she stopped right in front of me.

"*Merhaba,* what a coincidence. How are you, darling?"

"Darling" was of course me. I thanked her for her interest. I still couldn't remember her name. She leaned over to kiss me, but then remembered her newly opened pores. She contented herself with retaining both of my hands as we continued our conversation.

"Thank you so much for the other night. I spent the next two days telling my friends about what a riot we had. And about what a beauty you are."

I thanked her again. And then, on some sort of strange impulse, flattered her with, "But the real beauty is yours."

Encouraged, she instantly sat down beside me. She smoothed the skirts of her bathrobe and curled one foot under it. Then she turned her attention to me.

"So tell me, what's next?"

I must have looked slightly taken aback at the rather oblique question, for she added, "After the steam treatment, sweetie," then let loose a phony chuckle. Next, she placed a hand on my knee. And off we went. She was going to hit on me; I was going to pretend to be oblivious to it. The one with the most patience and determination wins.

I could have given her a tongue-lashing, but my business sense forced me to hold back. After all, she was a customer at the club. That said, her efforts at becoming a client of a more intimate nature went nowhere.

It was my turn. They called me into the room. I sailed off on winged steps, and floated into the steam room flushed with the unbearable lightness of the newly liberated. Naturally, I did not neglect to toss one last flirtatious glance over my shoulder. One for the road, so to speak. How was I to know what this would lead to? It all started so innocently.

Despite being able to breathe only with difficulty, I endured the steam for the appointed time. When it was over, my face glowed with the radiant pinkness of a newborn's bottom.

I thought I'd have a lemon soda in the lounge before moving on to the solarium. On my way there, I nearly fell straight into the lap of the waiting journalist. She gestured to the chaise longue beside her, so I reclined there.

"I was so sorry to hear about your friend," she began. "It happens all the time, doesn't it?"

"Murder, you mean? Unfortunately, yes," I replied.

Buse's fame seemed to have a taken an upturn now that she was dead.

"And the police aren't of much help, are they?" she continued.

"That's right . . ."

All I wanted to do was concentrate on my soda.

"Tell me a little about it," she persisted.

The tone of professional sweetness was unmistakable. It made my skin crawl.

"Are you trying to interview me?"

"No, not at all." She backtracked. "It's my fault, I've given you the wrong idea. Do forgive me. I was just curious—I suppose it's an occupational hazard. The moment I begin asking questions I'm somehow transformed into a pesky reporter."

"It doesn't matter."

I redirected my attention to my soda, stirring the ice with my straw. I was in no mood to answer questions.

I admit I have a weak spot for considerate women, but she wasn't one of them. Instead of leaning back and shutting up, she kept her eyes fixed on me. Without even blinking.

Disturbed by the stare, I glanced over at her.

"You've got a lovely nose. And those thick eyelashes . . ." she said.

When pronouncing the word "thick" she seemed to lick her lips. I supposed—hoped, even—that it was natural for anyone saying the word.

"When I was at the club I didn't realize how handsome you are," she continued. "It was so dark . . ."

She was most definitely hitting on me now.

"Now that I have the chance to get a good look at you, I can't tear my eyes away. You're really far more attractive without makeup. Some strange sort of charisma. You could have any woman you want."

As though I fretted over my skills in how to attract women. If I hadn't been a regular at the salon, I would have given her a real piece of my mind, but I didn't want to make a scene.

"When did you begin?" she asked.

I pretended not to hear.

"I mean, how did it all begin?"

Her face managed to arrange itself into an expression that was both cunning and curious. As though she would be able to produce an instant "cure" if she could just ascertain how it had all started. I scowled.

She realized she had gone too far. At least she retained that much decency. We both sat silently for a moment, her eyes still on me. She began breathing more quickly. That golden moment of silence was clearly coming to an end. But I was still unprepared for what came next.

"Did you know that I interviewed Buse a few months ago?" she casually remarked. "It never made it into print. I'm considering having at least some of it published now."

She certainly knew how to pique my interest.

"What did she talk about?"

"Her experiences as a transvestite, mainly, as well her relationships, the kind of men she liked, that sort of thing. She told me a secret or two as well."

My antennae were fully extended. Signals were being received.

"She drank quite a bit during the interview, even smoked a joint at one point. When she offered me a puff I refused on principle. The work ethic, you know. She must have been pretty stoned considering all she told me. About herself, and others. A long list of names. Celebrities, businessmen, politicians, performers of all kinds. Some of them famous, others rather obscure . . . You wouldn't believe it. We're not supposed to name names without confirmation of some kind, but I did anyway. It would have been quite a story. The exclusive of the year. I was all ready to collect my awards. But somehow, for some reason, it never got published. I was told off by my editor-in-chief, asked if it was my intention to 'have this newspaper banned.' He also said we'd be bumped off one by one even if it wasn't banned. The things Buse told me. I suppose I couldn't really have expected to see it in print."

I was all ears.

"Have you told anyone else about this?"

She continued examining my face and pretended not to hear me.

"She told me about her childhood, her teen years. All she went through. The hardships."

"I'd really love to listen to a tape of that interview. In fact, I'd like to have it as a sort of memento . . ." I ventured.

"Why, of course. Let's leave together. You can come over to my place. We'll have a drink together while we copy it."

I was in luck. I was onto something big. Yes, she was still after me, but she wouldn't be the first woman I'd had to fend off. When dressed like this, I get attention from the ladies; when dressed as a lady, from the men. I hoped she wouldn't misinterpret the smile that was spreading across my face. I didn't want any hassles. While I'd be happy to indulge in some harmless game-playing, I wouldn't go any further. And I didn't even know her name. I had no intention of sleeping with a woman whose name I didn't know.

My solarium séance was scheduled to last for twelve minutes. She was already done, but she'd have to wait.

I skipped off to the solarium.

Chapter 18

❖

$\mathscr{W}$e drove to her house. Each shift of the gears meant a chance for her to fondle me. I said nothing—in fact, I may even have encouraged her a bit. All bets were off until the cassette was produced. She talked about herself the entire way. She was a graduate of Notre Dame Scion; when she had divorced her diplomat husband she'd returned to Istanbul and begun a career as a journalist. No, I hadn't the slightest idea what it must be like to be abandoned for a chocolate-colored Portuguese girl. And the girl apparently wasn't even ethnic Portuguese, she added, although she did produce the same "vujt vujt" sounds. Our lady journalist had been destroyed. The fact that it had come out of the blue only made it that much more devastating. She seemed to assume that one could become slowly accustomed to betrayal and deceit. My eyes on the prize, I remained tight-lipped in the face of her lapses of logic and roving hands.

We walked up to the third floor, with her leading the way. I scrutinized her legs all the way up the narrow staircase. Her left foot was landing at an odd angle. The heel of her shoe was badly worn.

A cat greeted us at the door. It didn't like me. We entered an amazingly untidy living room. The PC had been left on, coffee cups crusted a deep brown were scattered about. She was clearly a chain smoker. The flat reeked of stale smoke, and the ashtrays hadn't been emptied for days. I silently nodded in solidarity with the ex-husband. Real ladies and their gentlemen husbands do not live in such squalor. She was no lady.

The expression on my face must have given me away.

"Excuse the mess, darling. It's a bit untidy, I know. Would you believe I just never have the time to clean up? You understand. It's the price we all pay for living alone."

I thought of my own flat. At the moment, it wasn't all that much different from hers.

At some point on the way here I had become *sen*. It was something else to be endured for the sake of the cassette.

"And there's no cleaning lady at the moment," she said. "The last one ran away. I asked the super's wife to find a new one. I can't be bothered with that kind of thing."

But she could be bothered with trying to get me into bed.

Straightaway, she plugged the portable tape player into the stereo.

"You'll be amazed when you hear it. She dropped so many names I thought she was lying at first. When I checked later, I found out that half of them are known for that sort of thing. But like I said, they never get written about. The self-censorship of the press. Or perhaps it's a form of self-defense."

She rummaged through a small basket on the floor full of tapes, many not in their cases, and CDs. I gave her credit for being able to find anything in that mess, but kept my thoughts to myself. I just stood and waited. I hadn't spotted a suitable place to sit.

"You'll have a glass of wine, won't you?"

"I don't really drink." Now, if I'd only left out the "really," that sentence would have had the desired result. It was too late.

"You'll join me, then."

So that was the game plan, to get me drunk. Well, I'm not that kind of girl. Or boy, even. There would be no passing out after a single glass, allowing myself to be ravaged. And I'm very experienced when it comes to the subject of overzealous ladies.

She returned with the wine. Both glasses were the size of vases. We would be sharing an entire bottle.

She didn't shrink from caressing my cheek as she handed me my wine. I waited for her to sit down, then chose a seat across from rather than next to her.

Without waiting for a response, she continued talking. If that was how she conducted her interviews, she must have had next to no material to work with.

She polished off her first glass and moved on to her second. Mine was still full to the brim. Half an hour had passed. My copy of the tape hadn't been recorded yet. I could hear the whir of the cogs. She'd begun slurring her words. Sentences were being abandoned so she could gaze meaningfully at me. And there I sat, the proverbial Cheshire Cat.

In short, I was not having the time of my life. I began resenting the tape and what I was forced to put up with to get it. I thought for a moment of blaming Buse. The whole thing had started because of her. On second thoughts, I abandoned the notion. I had only my curiosity to blame. That's right, it's always been my great weakness.

Like the proverb goes, pricks or prying . . . Even now I should have been able to get up and go—but my curiosity kept getting the better of me.

Finally, I took another glance at my Swatch. It was nearly half past five. I immediately interrupted her, as though it had only just occurred to me.

"I have an appointment at six, I almost forgot."

"With whom?"

"With a man," I said. It was the first lie that came to mind, and sufficiently searing.

"But we were having such a good time."

She had no intention of getting up to see me off. I rose to my feet.

"Don't trouble yourself, I'll get it," I said, taking the original cassette from the tape player. You can never be too careful. I had no intention of subjecting myself to this woman once again.

The expected protest was duly uttered.

I firmly responded, "It's of personal value to me. I'd like to keep the cleanest copy."

After I'd placed the cassette in my jacket pocket, I went over and placed a kiss on her cheek. That much I could, and should, do.

"Thank you so much," I added.

I raced out of the house, down the stairs, and into the first taxi I spotted. I still couldn't remember her name. It was either unusual or common. But what was it? I decided not to give it a second thought. One way or another, she had been of assistance, whether I knew her name or not.

I couldn't wait to get home and listen to the tape.

Chapter 19

✜

$\mathcal{M}$y sweet, if messy, home was waiting for me. I had so much to do before heading out for the club that night. I wasn't all that optimistic when it came to the usefulness of the tape, but it was going to demand a lot of my time either way.

It was hard to imagine Buse the introvert suddenly deciding to confide all her secrets, the details of her past life, to some so-called journalist. That is, unless she'd been drugged. If she had been doped up, she may well have talked at length, but it would have been a garbled mix of fact and fiction.

It's impossible to predict what someone on drugs will do. There are those who, after a few joints, find themselves in the embrace of their fantasy lover—and do nothing but nod off to sleep.

Cocaine can transform a macho man into an unbelievably sinuous sissy. A few snorts, and even the most irreproachable caveman can suddenly bend over and grab his ankles. I know. I've seen it. When the drug wears off they act like nothing's happened.

When one of the girls from the club got stoned she would engage in a late-night cleaning frenzy, washing her windows well after midnight. In fact, she once fell three stories while doing it.

These thoughts ran through my mind all the way home, a stupid smile plastered on my face.

It was nearly dark by the time I got there. The summer days

were getting shorter. The corridor light of the apartment building was off. I cursed—the electricity was cut. I cursed again a split second later when it occurred to me that I wouldn't be able to listen to the cassette. My stereo wouldn't play the tiny tape, but I'd hoped to use my answering machine. And now there was no electricity. I entered my flat damning the municipality to hell, along with the utility company, the Ministry of Energy and Resources, not forgetting the minister himself and his entire staff, as well as the government, Parliament, and every other organization and individual who shared the blame for the darkness. Fumbling my way up the stairs in the blackness, I had plenty of time to condemn them all.

Although it wasn't yet completely dark outside, it was pitch-black in the hallway. I even had trouble finding the keyhole.

The electricity was off in my flat as well. I took the tape out of my pocket and put it on the table, then removed my sweat-soaked clothes. I hung them on the balcony to dry. Stepping out onto the back balcony totally nude didn't seem a problem to me, a little exhibitionism is healthy. I splashed water onto my face and hair. The effect was refreshing.

Of course, now the TV wouldn't work, right when I needed a game-show fix. I prepared a large glass of iced tea and stretched out naked on the sofa. Staring at me from the table was the tape, its outline growing clearer as my eyes got used to the darkness. My heart beat faster at the thought of what it might contain. If Buse really had gotten stoned and gone on to reveal the identities of everyone she had slept with, I would have any number of important new clues.

My body was tense. I knew exactly what I needed, but I tried not to think about it. The windows were open. A cool breeze lapped at my naked skin.

I waited for the sound of the fridge, the first sign that electricity had been restored. There was a knock on the door.

The bell wasn't working, of course, but I was certain I had heard a tap. Who could it be at this hour? Hüseyin was the first person to come to mind. I decided to have a peek through the keyhole and tiptoed silently to the door. There's nothing like gracefully swaying one's way to one's front door. I am not without my talents. I didn't bend my knees, like those who cannot manage the art of walking in high heels, but stalked my way *en pointe*, as it were.

The corridor was too dark for me to see much. I did however detect a shadow, the outline of what was most definitely a man. My curiosity was whetted. The sudden appearance of a man at my door was not a common occurrence. Particularly when I was so desperately in need of one. It was a simple case of kismet. Normally, whenever I'm so completely in the mood, something goes wrong. The man I've set my sights on makes his excuses and the whole thing is called off. Who could it be? I'm ashamed to say that I gave in to my physical desires and curiosity.

I couldn't exactly open the door stark naked.

"Who is it?" I asked.

"It's me, Kenan, the policeman."

He lowered his voice when he said "policeman." Good for him, there was no sense in letting the entire building know.

"Just a second!" I cried out.

I was excited. I tingled. It was definitely my lucky day. I looked for something to cover myself with. The pashmina from the previous night was the first thing I found, and I arranged it as invitingly as possible.

I opened the door a crack. My head and naked shoulder were the only things visible to my visitor.

"How can I help you?"

"Uh, you said I could stop by when I finished my shift."

He was dressed in civilian clothing. He smelled of shampoo and deodorant. As he stared at what was visible of my body there was no mistaking the hopeful look in his eyes. I was as ready as I could ever be, but a bit of coquetry was required first. I opened the door a bit more, exposing my entire body. Like a vamp from a golden age, one hand clutched the door handle, the other clasped the pashmina. It could only cover so much. Much more than was entirely appropriate was spread before his eyes.

His expression changed. If anyone had entered the building or opened their front door at that point, I would have been disgraced. Kenan stared at me as he adjusted the lump in his trousers. There was no need for words. His intentions were clear. Nearly naked, I could resist him no more. I welcomed him in and we headed straight for the bedroom.

Frankly, it was just what I needed. Yes, it would have been better had it lasted for more than ten minutes. It is true that no more than fifteen minutes passed between his setting foot inside and his getting dressed and leaving. But as the saying goes, a priest doesn't eat pilaf every day, nor could I expect haute cuisine every day. Kismet only goes so far. There was no need for ingratitude, it was better than nothing. Compared to the lady journalist whose clutches I'd barely escaped it was a veritable feast. It was over in the shortest time possible, and though he was neither skilled nor playful in bed, there was no denying that he had what it takes where it counts. And the electricity was still cut. What could be better at a time like this?

I'd have preferred a bit more lovemaking, being kissed with full, rather than pursed lips. Who wouldn't have? But no matter.

He still made it into my top twenty, if not my top ten. His physique alone earned him that much. In terms of performance, though, he'd be somewhere near the bottom.

Kenan had helped my tensions to evaporate, if only superficially. Before he'd made it down the stairs, I was already in the shower. That's when the lights came on.

Chapter 20

❖

$\mathcal{T}$aking the taped interview with Buse, I went to the answering machine. The machine informed me I had five messages, but I decided to listen to them later. For now, all my curiosity was focused on the tape. To avoid any interruptions, I unplugged the phone. If there was a persistent caller, I could always answer using the cordless one. I began listening intently. The interview started with an exchange of pleasantries. Buse referred to the nymphomaniac lady journalist as *efendim*.

She summarized the changes she'd gone through, how she'd developed over the years. In excruciating detail. The pain of getting one's face depilated, not to mention the expense. The swelling and the resulting inability to work with a disfigured face. How much it stung when her cheek was so much as touched, et cetera.

She began talking about her family. She'd lost her father when still a child. He was much older than her mother: It was only natural that he had made an earlier departure. The way she had acted as her mother's "eyes" from a young age. She believed in any case that male children raised solely by their mothers were likely to turn out homosexual. Her own story seemed to corroborate that theory.

Her mother's blindness allowed her more freedom for sexual experimentation than was available to most of her peers. The first trysts were innocent, the sort everyone has: peeking at other boys in the toilet, playing doctor, falling in love with her chemistry teacher. As she passed through adolescence, however, they took a more serious turn. At age sixteen, she lost her virginity.

And the first name was uttered. Yusuf, one of the older boys in her class, was screwing her on a regular basis. Our girl immediately fell in love and began dreaming of marriage. The boy, however, entertained no such thoughts. In fact, because Fevzi regularly showed up at his house to harass him, he would beat her.

So was this "Yusuf" the person I was looking for? Had that skinny, penniless schoolboy developed into a paunchy, middle-aged power broker with a determination to cleanse his past of any unsavory elements? It was entirely possible. There's no shortage of respectable businessmen with humble backgrounds. He may have rashly jotted down his feelings for Fevzi in a diary of the sort kept in those days primarily by girls and queers. At that age, no distinction is made between carnal attraction and romantic passion. The two are often confused. Many unhappy marriages can trace their downfall to the point at which passion ends without being replaced by true affection and friendship. Those who cave in to social pressures and remain married are terminating their own prospects for personal happiness.

The journalist jumped in here, emotionally declaring how well she knew that to be true. The slight slurring of her words revealed how far through the bottle she had got. In the background, Buse could be heard drawing deeply on her marijuana cigarette.

Following this "catastrophe," Fevzi started sleeping with anyone who crossed her path. Having accepted that life was shit, she was determined to revel in all its filth, wilfully soiling and debasing herself in the process.

The dramatic tremor in her voice gave Buse away. Those

last few lines had been rehearsed and painstakingly polished in order to produce the desired effect on the listener. We all produce pretty-sounding accounts to explain our past behavior, particularly the more sordid bits.

From that point onward, Buse's speech became so slurred as to be almost unintelligible. The joint she had been smoking had woven its spell, and she was high as a kite. Like I said earlier, I'm completely inflexible on the subject of drugs. I don't like them one bit. Not only do I not use them, I keep my distance from those who do.

By the time she graduated from high school Buse considered herself adequately experienced and practiced. In fact, the actor Semih had even taken her to a film set.

Semih was a second-rate thespian with a well-known soft spot for young boys. Buse couldn't possibly add much to his already shady past. There would be no reason for him to resort to blackmail.

The young Fevzi had a walk-on role in that film. Later, Semih handed her along to the hardened, alcoholic leading man, Atilla Erkan. While that particular side of him was a well-kept secret, he, too, was fond of hairless youths. He took Fevzi to a back room during filming and, without undressing, just unzipping his fly, took her. Then he slapped an autographed photograph into her hand. She claimed to still have it as a memory of that day, that particular screwing. In his time, after all, Erkan had been a minor celebrity.

That's right, I dimly remembered an actor by that name. He was as untalented as he was handsome. There'd been no sign of him for years. He had married and divorced a series of beauty queens. He beat one of them so badly he finally appeared again on the tabloid front pages he had missed so much. The abuse of his wife was probably an expression of his suppressed homosexuality. Women very often catch their husbands in compromising situations. Often they don't fully understand, or they refuse to understand, the implications. They make a scene without taking into consideration the ramifications. That may have been what triggered the savage beating. Thanks to Fevzi, yet another tabloid riddle had been solved.

Whatever happened to Atilla Erkan? If he had been reduced to playing in third-rate television series I wouldn't have known. Considering my general lack of curiosity about him, it was unlikely anyone else cared. Were someone to attempt to blackmail him, he'd have nothing to lose. I struck him off the list of suspects. There'd be no point in kicking someone who had already sunk so low.

Semih and Atilla were followed by a succession of middle -aged men. In fact, one of Semih's cronies, a film extra, had begun peddling Buse. When the customer was finished, he'd pronounce her "nice and slippery," have a go, and then pay her.

One night, she was taken to a party at the mansion of journalist Korhan Türker, where she was one of a bevy of young men in ladies' underwear circulating among the guests. Korhan Türker and his cronies were playing poker. Fevzi had been instructed to wear a flesh-colored pair of lace panties. Another boy wore only a garter belt, his bits flapping as he sashayed about. The boys were occasionally pulled onto laps, pinched, fondled, and screwed. Then the card game would resume. The stakes were suitably high for such an illustrious group of men. Fevzi was pulled under the table. She gave them all blow jobs, for which she received generous tips. As she returned home early that morning her bottom was purple from all the pinching.

At this point in the tape, the lady journalist was boiling over with rage toward her editor. I was impressed by her range of colorful curses. She said she would do all she could to expose Korhan Türker, one of her paper's most illustrious contributors. She had him by the balls now. In any case, he was a total turncoat. She hadn't known anything about his interest in boys. He had a wealthy wife many years older than himself, and would stage stag parties when he sent her away on holiday. If confronted with his past parties, he would absolutely dismiss it all as fantasy. He was that shameless. It wasn't as though there were any credible witnesses to the debauchery. The contents of the tape wouldn't stand up in a court of law. The other men at the party would naturally not come forward. In any case, well -known journalists had achieved a certain degree of immunity and protection in the form of mutual censorship.

I didn't agree with the lady journalist here. The name I was looking for could well turn out to be Korhan Türker. Buse had mentioned letters and photographs. Even if they hadn't had a relationship per se, a single revealing photograph from the party that night would suffice. Letters would be icing on the cake.

Meanwhile, Buse found herself earning more and more, and climbed the social ladder accordingly. There was no hot spot, no fashionable holiday destination, she hadn't visited. Women, as well as men, occasionally required her services. Lesbian lyricist Suat had taken her to Bodrum, then on a "blue voyage" cruise of the Aegean. Buse enjoyed a fling with the cabin boy, but was unable to escape the clutches of singer-pianist Mahmut Gürsel. That "character"—the term was meant to be derogatory—was as ugly as can be, but hung like King Kong. He'd screw her at every opportunity. It'd hurt like hell each time, but pock-faced Mahmut would ignore her cries. "No one can hear you out here," he'd mock Fevzi, as he climbed onto her again. An exhibitionist, he'd usually have sex on the deck. In front of everyone. A glass of whiskey on the rocks in one hand, Suat would laugh raucously while she looked on, smoking.

Our lady journalist interrupted to confirm that the singer -pianist was a well-known exhibitionist. In a voice trembling with emotion, she pointed out that even onstage he would remove his shirt, citing the risk of heat exhaustion, in order to treat the audience to the sight of his muscular hairy chest and bulging biceps. She had heard the rumors about his penis. And yes, she had been intrigued, even fantasized about him a bit. But God, he was ugly.

Intimidated by the fame of these men, Buse/Fevzi said nothing. But each time was a painful ordeal. The cabin boy with the heart of gold—who was clearly a latent homosexual—would comfort her afterward, alleviating her suffering with caresses and massages.

"It's not the size, it's the way it's used," said the lady journalist sagely. Oh, really? Of course size is important. I mean, who'd compare an eggplant to an okra?

Thus ended the first side of the tape. Next came a great deal of idle chatter and homespun philosophizing on sex, the sordidness of women, and the treachery of men. Both the interviewer and interviewee were unable to speak clearly. Buse made little sense as she wandered aimlessly from subject to subject. She would certainly have found it expedient to later deny all she had said.

Then Buse/Fevzi launched into a diatribe about her determination to establish a brave new life. She started focusing on her body and the journey to full-fledged womanhood. Any progress would be expensive. Just as she set off on this transformation, she met Süreyya. He was young—in his late thirties—but still much older than Buse. A real lion of a man. Not exactly handsome, but strangely compelling. Buse asked if he wasn't still as charismatic as ever.

The voice of the lady journalist was barely audible, as she was quite far from the microphone. Using the answering machine as cassette player made it even more difficult to hear her. While I couldn't understand what she said word for word, the gist of it was connected to Süreyya. She was incredulous. She just couldn't believe it.

Who was this person by the name of Süreyya that both Buse and the interviewer seemed to know? I continued listening.

The affair had lasted for years, kept a total and complete secret. Buse would make an appointment to meet him at his house, where he lived alone, and would sometimes have to wait for hours to see him. She would then spend the night. If Süreyya had meetings to attend, or business out of town, he would sometimes be gone for days. He was very much involved in the party at that time. He would tell Buse not to see anyone else, to stay at home and wait for him. He was extremely jealous.

Party? What party was that? Who on earth was this Süreyya and what was his involvement with a party? I found the answer before my mind had even completed asking the series of questions: The second-ranking man at the Hedef Party, Süreyya Eronat! I switched off the answering machine. I needed a moment to let it sink in: the Hedef Party and Süreyya Eronat. The words ran in circles through my head. It couldn't be! I realized my jaw had literally dropped; my mouth was wide open. I went to the bathroom to splash cold water onto my face. It didn't do the trick. I drank a glass of ice water.

Hedef was one of the leading conservative parties. Its principles and platform were based on the role of the nuclear family, and it would not budge an inch on the question of the man's traditional role as head of that family. While it wasn't official policy, the party was associated with manly men at their best. It was anti- just about everything. Queers were at the top of the list of the abominable, no more than bugs to be squashed. Indeed, if the Hedef Party had its way they would all be executed.

Such is the enormous gulf between theory and practice. The second in command of that same party was a full-blown pederast.

Most of the members of the party were men. While there may have been women in symbolic positions, I had never heard of them.

The least likely element of their "macho man" image was homosexual relations. And Süreyya Eronat, the vice chairman of the party, was a homosexual! With that knowledge came the risk of death. Evidence would make a fatal end that much more certain and swift. The hairs rose on the back of my neck as I thought about it. Sofya was right, even just knowing about it was dangerous.

Using this evidence for blackmail! It was an act of suicide. Surely it wasn't possible that our girl Buse had stooped to such a thing. It was far more likely that in a fit of nostalgia Süreyya Eronat had recollected the photos and decided to retrieve them. Either that or he sent his men. The emergence of the pictures and letters could spell the death of the party. Their chairman hadn't been seen in public for quite some time. Although it wasn't spoken of openly, everyone knew that Süreyya Eronat was in control. He was the real power behind the throne.

Eronat's private life was of considerable interest to the press. He had married young, but lost his wife in a terrible car accident a few years later. It was hard to believe that he remained in mourning for the rest of his life, but everyone went along with it.

Of his two children, one was married. They lived very private lives out of the public eye. His son had moved to either Canada or America. The daughter had married, produced grandchildren, and quietly maintained her role as efficient housewife and self-sacrificing mother.

It was said that Eronat lived with his widowed mother and aunt. He went on nature walks and rode horses in his spare time. Holidays were spent at the hot springs with his mother and aunt. He was never photographed in shorts, a swimming costume, or *peştemal*. I couldn't remember ever seeing a photo of him when he wasn't wearing a tie. There was never any mention of a relationship. In fact, there was never so much as a suggestion that he may have had a love life. It was as though there were no evidence of any kind that Süreyya Eronat had ever been involved with anyone, either as a young widower or at present.

Because he was so feared, no one dared to indulge in gossip on the matter.

And my poor Buse, that dignified girl, had ended up his victim. And her blind mother may have been his victim as well.

My curiosity had been rewarded, but I just hoped I wouldn't have to pay too steep a price for it.

I couldn't decide whether or not to listen to the rest of the tape. Additional information would just put me more at risk. The more I knew, the greater the likelihood I would one day let something slip. Could I be certain that one day, in the arms of a lover, perhaps, or in a general rage over something, I wouldn't lose control and reveal all I knew about these extortionist pimps? We're all such unpredictable creatures! There's no knowing what I'll blurt out. Even if I weren't so outspoken, I'd surely wish to share my secret with someone one day—I couldn't possibly keep something that juicy to myself. I'd lose all sense of self-respect. My self-assurance would be shattered. I wouldn't be me.

I pushed the play button. I was in too deep to stop now. Buse's voice continued:

"But he was always so jealous. Especially when it came to me. Don't do this, don't visit there, don't go out at night. After a while he began helping to cover my living expenses. There was no way I could have survived on my mother's pension. Do you know how little she gets? I really pity old folks, they're barely able to stay alive.

"Anyway, thanks to Süreyya we were comfortable. Anything and everything, even *kuş sütü*, bird's milk, was mine for the asking. He was always so gracious about it. A real gentleman. After a while he started visiting me at home. He adored my mother, and she was fond of him as well. He always made a point of kissing her hand and chatting for a bit. She appreciated it. In the beginning she didn't really understand my relationship with him, but after seven years she must have had some idea. You see, we were like a family. I was crushed when we separated. She comforted me. How many mothers would do that?"

Hmmm, now, that was interesting. Süreyya Bey and his male lover's mother. A typical relationship between a mother-in-law and her groom. I'd never met Sabiha Hanım, but I could visualize the scene. The blind mother, a rather vacant smile on her face, sits in her favorite rocking chair. Her blank eyes stare at the ceiling. Right in front of her, in the throes of passion, are her son and Süreyya. They make love in absolute silence. The mother's eyes are lowered, unseeingly looking straight in their direction. They bite their lips and continue, not making a sound. When they're finished, Süreyya kisses the old lady's hand and thanks her for her hospitality. The scene is straight out of a film, but I can't remember which one. If asked to identify it on a game show, I'd be eliminated.

Yuck! It was so difficult to imagine Süreyya Eronat having sex. From what I'd seen of him in the media, he was the type who had seemingly gone beyond the carnal, who had either transcended sexuality or had been of an asexual nature from the start. There are few men that I would identify that way, but he was one of them. His behavior, speech, mannerisms, gestures, clothing . . . everything. There was not a trace of anything even remotely sexual about him.

I searched through some old newspapers to find a photograph of him. He wasn't particularly media-friendly, and was well known for his scathing indictments of the press. He certainly wasn't given much coverage in my own favorite paper. After a thorough search, though, I was able to find a photo. I examined it. Just imagining him with one of our girls would be an insult to the dear things.

Many more names were named in the remainder of the tape. I recognized some, while others were strangers. None of them were particularly dangerous types, as far as I knew. At least half had been the subject of so much gossip there was really nothing to add. Blackmail may have been undertaken, but a retaliation as drastic as murder would have been extremely unlikely.

I couldn't decide what to do with the tape. The most entertaining alternative was to leak it to the media. But then again, it had reached me through the media, by way of the lady journalist. If they'd failed to recognize how newsworthy it was, that was their problem.

Another option was to try to get the tape to Süreyya Eronat. That would be dangerous. If I posted it, it would be impossible to trace the sender. There was the risk, however, that they would identify the voice of the lady journalist, and somehow reach me through her. That would be a real mess, like sorting through rice to find a pebble. They'd get me in the end.

The only other choice was either to destroy the tape or hide it. Which would be preferable? Even if I destroyed it, how could I prove that I had? Let's say they came after me. Would they believe me? How would I persuade them? As long as the lady journalist kept her mouth shut, no one would know I had a copy. I decided to keep it.

And now for the bonus question, one that carried no cash prize: Where would I hide it? And once it was hidden, what good would it do me? But that was yet another riddle.

Chapter 21

✤

I needed to stop thinking about the tape and get ready for the night. Otherwise I'd be late getting to the club. As always on the weekends, it would be packed—a real circus. I thought about the people I would have to bar at the door.

The lady journalist, whatever her name was, would not be admitted. I had a ready excuse: women were not allowed on the weekends.

Ferruh, the husband of Belkıs, the boutique owner, would not be let in if he arrived on his own. I had already made that mistake the previous night. If he had left with one of the girls, Belkıs would have raised hell yet again. And I didn't appreciate his flirting with me.

As for the so-called "gays" who only came on weekends when they had had no luck at their own bars, staying until dawn in order to spare the expense of staying at a hotel, they would also not be allowed to pass through my doors. They were the sort who made a great show of friendship when it suited them, but had nothing but the worst insults for us at other times. I will not stand for such class consciousness.

And the penniless merrymakers, those who nursed a single beer the entire night, would also be barred. On weeknights I tolerated them, but the club was just too full on Friday and Saturday nights. Cüneyt had a special ability for spotting them. A natural-born talent.

As for the nerve-wracking Sofya—who probably wouldn't deign to come in any case—she would be politely refused.

The decrepit actor Ahmet Kuyu regularly beat up his dates so badly they would be out of commission for a week. He was to be barred as well. It would be no trouble to keep him out since he always arrived in a drunken stupor.

Nalan and Mehtap were two girls who had grown rather too fond of drugs lately, and would not be permitted to enter. I didn't want any trouble.

Dumper Beyza had picked a fight with Sırma the previous week, and she was out. The size of the party she arrived with would make no difference.

Serap's skinny little lover would be barred. Cüneyt could find a reason to do so. I couldn't be expected to justify all of my decisions myself.

Even as I busied myself with the list, my mind was occupied with another gnawing question. Why was it that Buse had revealed so much to the lady journalist in the course of the interview? When she told me she never had, and never would, betray an old lover, what exactly had she meant? It appeared that at the first opportunity she had freely divulged every detail of her adventures with Süreyya Eronat, and to a reporter, no less.

It just didn't make sense. I kept turning it over in my head. Yes, she had smoked a joint and downed a few drinks during the interview. That explanation wouldn't satisfy me, though. Not completely. Buse was no stranger to dope. She had gone from keeping a well-guarded secret for years to singing like a canary. A few tokes wouldn't create that kind of transformation.

I ran through some highly unlikely explanations for her suddenly loose tongue. Perhaps the reporter—now, what was her name?—had administered sodium pentothal, some kind of truth serum. No, that was ridiculous. How would she have suspected in advance that a middle-aged transvestite harbored such explosive secrets?

Then there was the possibility that Buse had formed some sort of romantic attachment to the journalist, that their closeness made it possible for her to confide without fear. That was impossible. Buse was extremely picky when it came to sex with women. Also, there was no indication that the reporter had lesbian tendencies. The fact that she had hit on me meant nothing. After all, it was my male side she was attracted to—I didn't even have breasts, like Buse. And the reporter seemed completely unfazed by Buse's death. She hadn't seemed the slightest bit upset, even considering that Buse was an acquaintance of sorts.

Another possibility was the opening of old wounds. That is, Süreyya Eronat may have caused her suffering just before the interview. Buse claimed that they had stayed in touch as close friends, and that she would never betray him. But the saying "Hell hath no fury like a woman scorned" would certainly hold true for Buse, too. The desire for revenge may have surged to the forefront, especially after a drink and a few joints had loosened her tongue. It couldn't be ruled out. But it didn't wash when I remembered her ladylike airs the night we talked in my office.

Finally, the possibility of hypnosis popped into my head. I'd been doing some reading up on the subject recently. At least in theory, hypnosis can induce anyone to say anything. As a plot device, the technique had become fairly common in the crime novels I read. Why couldn't that be the case in real life, as well? But the obvious question would then be: Who hypnotized her? I couldn't rule out the possibility that the lady journalist possessed such skills. But why would she have decided to practice her arts on Buse?

Despite my reservations, I decided to consult a hypnotherapist whose number I have in my phone book. The person in question claims to be the foremost authority on the practice, proclaiming as much in large type on the front and back covers of his books. When we met, he presented me with autographed copies of all three. He'd asked me to help him set up a website on hypnosis, and I worked with him for a few weeks. While involved in the project, I would call him every morning, afternoon, and night to ask him how business was going. It is my habit to cultivate close relations with my clients—at least until I have collected my fee. That isn't to say that I answered his phone calls once our business was concluded.

I called the hypnotist twice. There was no reply either time. He must not have been at home. I hesitated over whether or not to leave a message, then decided to do so when I recalled how infuriated I am when people hang up without leaving a message on my machine. I would telephone again later if he didn't return my call.

I really had to put all thoughts of Buse out of my mind so I could concentrate on getting dressed. While I may not wear an entirely original outfit every single night, I do at least select accessories that help me stand out from the crowd. As the boss, I also felt it was my duty to deserve such an honor, and to set an example for the girls. I am of course beautifully groomed at all times, and expect no less from my employees.

I take as my main inspiration the film stars of yesteryear. Nowadays, there's no one worth impersonating, with the possible exception of Cher and Madonna. But Cher is like a transvestite herself. What's there to imitate? As for Madonna, she's taken to cultivating an image of unstudied simplicity, a laid-back look that seems to have been thrown on without a thought. That simply won't do. Now, back in the days when she sported a bustier . . . that was different. We'd all copy her costumes. These days, we content ourselves with her music. I mean, really, can you imagine one of our girls in a pair of low-slung dungarees and a ten-gallon cowboy hat? Studied showiness is the name of our game.

I decided to model myself on Audrey Hepburn. Something elegant and understated. While it's true that I'm not all that subtle, the illusion can be created with the right clothing and makeup. No one would confuse me with the real Audrey, but my source of inspiration is obvious. I have to admit that I learned the finer points of maquillage from Sofya. I have since refined them over the years, and my technique is now superior to hers.

In the winter, I favor a chic adaptation of the outfit worn by Audrey in *Funny Face*, the one in the dance scene in the underground club in Paris. A tight black sweater and tapered trousers with a pair of unadorned black loafers. And my hair drawn back into a tight ponytail. Thank God for hair extensions, wigs, and hairpieces! In the summer heat, such a costume would be entirely inappropriate, not to mention uncomfortable. Instead, I opted for a dress similar to the one she wore starring opposite Gary Cooper in *Love in the Afternoon*. I slipped into a baby-blue collarless, sleeveless frock that extended to just below the knee and had a matching cloth belt. It fit like a dream. In deference to Audrey's rather bony chest, I decided to forgo my padded bra. Applying liberal amounts of gel, I achieved the desired hairstyle. Around my neck, I flung a fluttery white chiffon scarf. The outfit was completed with a pair of white kid gloves and white loafers. But then again, the gloves may be a bit much. Our girls just wouldn't get it. They'd think I was trying to hide my hands. I'd have to deal with silly gossip about a breakout of eczema or warts. I took them off and tucked them into my belt. I examined myself approvingly in the full-length mirror: nine points out of a possible ten. An honest judge, I was forced to deduct a full point for wearing daywear at night.

I rang for a taxi, requesting that Hüseyin not be sent. He wasn't there in any case. I wondered where he was. What's the fun in refusing his services if he's not even aware he's not wanted?

As I left the flat I noticed that one of the pictures was slightly askew. It's a photograph I had taken with RuPaul at Gay Pride Day in London. We see RuPaul as our patron saint. Those who don't view him that way are quickly encouraged by me to do so.

As I sorted out the picture frame I was hit by a sense of déjà vu. I recently did the same thing. But where, and when?

I suddenly remembered: It was at Chubby Cheeks's, the framed photograph on the living room wall! And in that photograph, her husband was shaking hands with . . . Süreyya Eronat. Damn it!

Chapter 22

✤

There was a huge crowd at the door. I felt a surge of pride when I swept past. However, the pinches and pats I was subjected to as I forced my way through the bodies did nothing to heighten my sense of superiority. As a blond guy reached over to feel me up I caught him, pulling his arm behind his back. A bit more pressure and I could have dislocated his shoulder, but I decided it would be heartless to take such drastic measures. The night was young, after all.

Hearing the guy's cries, Cüneyt emerged from the crowd and escorted me to the door.

"Hello, boss. I see you're as beautiful as ever."

"Thanks, sweetie," I replied. Then I pulled him to one side to recite tonight's list of undesirables. He leaned forward, listening intently.

"Which one is Mehtap?" he asked. "The tall one, or the one who always wears a red wig?"

"What difference does it make?" I snapped. "One's Nalan, the other's Mehtap."

"I really should be able to tell them apart. Customers appreciate being addressed by name. You know what we always say about customer satisfaction . . ."

The boy really did make me laugh. He's absolutely devoted to his work and asked his question in all seriousness, but that sort of solemnity always cracks me up. After all, we're talking about a third-rate tranny club. Who gives a hoot about our customers?

"Out of my way!" I said, chuckling. Our boys know that any show of anger on my part is usually a joke.

"Oh, and before I forget, boss, it seems to be your lucky night. Two men have asked about you separately. I looked them over real good. They seemed like regular, good-looking men, so I let them both in. One arrived only about ten minutes ago. The choice is all yours."

Cüneyt concluded with a mischievous wink and held the door open for me. As I entered, he gave me a military salute. He's quite the comedian.

The moment I set foot through the door I was swept up in the pulsating dance music. I found myself walking in time to the beat. My frock glowed phosphorescent under the club's black light. I was, as always, a sight to behold.

I immediately bumped into Refik Altın, the gay writer. He's a regular at the club, but usually arrives much later, to pick up the men not interested in the girls. Because he doesn't charge for his services, he's a hit at that hour with smashed boys from impoverished neighborhoods. Refik is a bit arrogant and aggressive. Although he doesn't pay me a commission like the girls do, he spends a lot on drinks and is a big tipper. His latest sensation had him very much in the public eye at the moment: He recently announced, to those who didn't already know, that he's a homosexual. On television, as well as in newspaper and magazine interviews, he described in detail the sort of men he likes. The uproar seemed to have given his self-esteem a boost, and he was more arrogant than ever.

"*Ayol*, what's that getup of yours? You look like a young wallflower at a wedding hall, the type who eventually dances with her big sister."

As an introductory line, it did not offer much hope for a warm conversation. Being compared to a girlish wallflower the moment I arrived in my Audrey Hepburn finery could have been rather dispiriting. A counterattack was always an option, but I decided it was unnecessary.

"That's exactly the effect I was after," I said, flashing a fake smile. He responded with an equally unconvincing cackle that exposed all his teeth.

"Aren't you the comedienne," he said.

As I walked past, he grabbed my arm again.

"Have you found what you're after?" he asked.

At first I didn't understand. He'd stopped laughing. He was completely serious.

"Buse's pictures," he clarified.

He was still clutching my arm.

"Whatever do you mean?"

"Come on, sweetie," he said. "I know all about it. You don't need to hide anything from me."

What was going on here? How did he know about Buse's pictures? Was that the reason he had come to the club early tonight?

"I'm not looking for anything. If I were, I'd have found it."

"Cut out the 'poor dumb thing from a bad neighborhood' routine," he said. "It doesn't suit you. If you find anything, let me know. I'll help you sell it. I know the market. I've got contacts."

The filthy bastard! So Refik Altın was also after the pictures, for reasons of his own. I wondered if he knew who they belonged to. But I wasn't about to mention the name Süreyya Eronat.

From now on, I'd have to keep an eye on Refik as well.

"Good luck, *abla*," were his parting words.

I do not appreciate being addressed as "big sister." And when gays use the expression it's even worse. The girls can say it as a sign of solidarity, but not people like him!

Added to my list of possible suspects, along with the innocent-looking Apple Cheeks, whose husband had been photographed with Süreyya Eronat, was that bastard Refik Altın.

In order to avoid further irritation, I decided to have nothing more to do with him. I headed for the bar to greet the boys and get my drink. Şükrü was busy. He muttered to himself as he prepared a drink, without looking up.

A cool hand touched my arm. I turned. It was a man in a dark suit. He was fairly young.

"Good evening," he said in a dry voice.

"Good evening," I responded. I looked him up and down. He must have been one of the two men asking after me. I tried to place his face. No, I didn't know him. He seemed respectable enough. Other than those cold hands, there was nothing objectionable about him. His hand remained on my arm. That was a good sign.

His suit was well tailored; his face clean-shaven; his white shirt pressed. His dark tie was fastened snugly. He was well groomed, smelled good, and was taller than me. His greenish blue eyes were a bit small for his face, but went well with his light brown hair. His chin was strong, his neck thick. Although he was no John Pruitt, he was most definitely what is conventionally known as handsome.

I ran through the men I'd slept with. Even if I don't recognize them at first sight, if I look a bit more closely, or hear them speak, I always remember them. But he was not on the list. He must have come to the club one night, seen me, and returned to meet me. But why hadn't I noticed him? He had the sort of face that would have caught my eye.

I leaned slightly over the bar and greeted Şükrü. He reached down to get my waiting Virgin Mary. Putting his face close to mine, he said quietly so no one else would hear:

"He's been waiting for you ever since we opened. He hasn't looked at anyone else. Vuslat was all over him, but he didn't respond. He rejected Aylin too. He's been asking about you all night."

I turned around and glanced at the man in the suit. In one hand he held a soda with lemon, in the other a cell phone. He smiled at me shyly.

Considering how long he had been waiting to see me, he could have been a bit more forward. I wanted to be seduced. With that bashful smile, he seemed to have been cast in the role of Gary Cooper.

While it's true that Gary Cooper seduced Audrey Hepburn with that smile in *Love in the Afternoon,* I am no Audrey Hepburn, and he was no Gary Cooper. I wanted more. And men his age don't even know who Gary Cooper was.

I flashed him a look of acknowledgment, but intended to proceed into the main room. After all, there was apparently another gentleman waiting for me. The suit was standing directly in my path. It would be difficult to get by unless he stood aside. I raised my eyes and looked directly into his.

"Excuse me please."

"Can we sit down and chat for a moment?" he asked.

"This really isn't the place for conversation."

A look of concern flickered across his face. It wouldn't do to frighten me off right at the start.

"I wouldn't mind talking to you later, perhaps, but there are some people I need to see now," I told him.

"We've got to talk. I've been waiting for you all night."

That was better. But certainly not enough for me. I had to see who else was looking for me. Competition is always fun. And we'd long since been spoiled for choice, from game shows and universities, to television channels and the products lining market shelves . . . The same principle applied to men.

"No, please . . ." he insisted. The look I gave him was unmistakable in its meaning. He stepped aside. Behind me, I heard:

"I expect you to come back."

I felt his eyes on me. Kissing the girls I encountered along the way, I was lost in the crowd.

The dance floor was full. Some of the young men were showing off the steps they had practiced at home. Even though no one paid much attention, they doggedly continued their little show throughout the night. They'd started the trend of stripping on summer nights. Off would come sweat-soaked T-shirts, revealing what were mostly rather puny bodies. Every so often, a fine muscular specimen would join their ranks, and he would be approvingly admired by us all. The rugged ones who were able to dance as well were immediately offered steep discounts. In fact, some of the girls would even go off for free.

One of those, by the name of Yavuz, was on the floor. The boy was fine. He didn't have puffed-up gym muscles. His strapping body had a rippling stomach, ridged like a tray of baklava. There wasn't an ounce of fat on his whole frame. His skin was flawless and bronze. It gleamed with sweat, making him even more irresistible. It was the kind of body that begs to be caressed. Fully aware of the effect he was having on the crowd, Yavuz danced alone, not even bothering to look around. His jeans hung loosely around his narrow hips, a trail of hair leading from his navel to disappear in his crotch. Occasionally there would be a glimpse of the waistband of his boxer shorts. Some of the girls are left weak-kneed by the sight of boxers, others turn to jelly over white socks. "Ay, what a sparkling-clean boy," they cry. And if a pair of white briefs turn out to be spotless they talk of nothing else for days.

I sensed the presence of Gary Cooper just behind me. I fought the urge to turn around. I talked to the girls right next to me.

I looked across the dance floor at the tables on the other side of the room. Customers who are middle-aged and older don't dance. They just watch. In the tradition of the old-style dance halls, they watch the girls and make their selection for the night. They order bowls of nuts and plates of fruit, spending a tidy sum, as least as far as they're concerned. In other words, they're the big spenders. I suddenly noticed Hüseyin sitting among them. Our eyes met. He grinned. I ignored him. Fixing my eyes on the same general area where he was sitting, I stared blankly, as though into space. He waved. Sitting at his table was one of our girls, Müjde. She'd adopted the name back when Müjde Ar was all the rage. Her long, dark hair had since been dyed red. She had a weight problem and was forever dieting. For the love of God, have you ever heard of a fat transvestite? Well, Müjde most definitely was. Of course, she'd claim that she was merely "shapely."

So Hüseyin was here at the club. Instead of being at his post at the taxi stand, he was here! I was filled with an indefinable sensation that was not unlike rage. Never before had anyone from the taxi stand, or even the neighborhood, come to the club. Now he was here as a customer. There was really no reason for me to object, but I didn't like it one bit. I could understand his having come here for me. But after all the attentions paid to me, here he was sitting next to porky Müjde. It was unforgivable. No one who admired me could possibly like her as well. It was such an insult. The ill-mannered thug!

If it was Hüseyin who was the other man that had been asking after me, he'd blown it! No, that would be impossible. Cüneyt knew Hüseyin. He'd have told me his name at the door. Hüseyin had often dropped me off at the club, and Cüneyt sees him all the time. They've even exchanged greetings. Which meant that, somewhere in the crowd, I had another admirer.

I undid my scarf and let it float freely around my neck. If he was trying to spite me by sitting with Müjde, I'd give him a run for his money. And with someone far superior to her. There was no time to waste. Unless I acted immediately, it would have no impact. My other fan could wait. I had to make a choice between Yavuz and Gary Cooper.

It was unlikely Yavuz would respond. He'd approached me when he first started coming to the club. However, unlike the other girls, I wasn't about to offer my services for free to customers. Were I to meet someone outside, there was no problem. I'd do it for my own pleasure. That was different. But I was the boss here and I didn't want to set a bad example. It was a simple question of principles.

Gary Cooper was standing right behind me. I could turn, take him by the arm and gracefully sway my way across the dance floor to a table. He was tall, handsome, and the only young man in a suit. He would certainly catch everyone's attention. What's more, I couldn't be bothered meeting someone new. After all, he was ready and waiting.

I decided to go for him. As I anticipated, he was right behind me.

"Would you like to dance?" I asked.

He hesitated. I don't relish rejection. Particularly in my own club.

"I'd rather we sit at a table," he said.

He took my arm, intending to lead me around the dance floor. I'd wanted to walk right across it, so everyone would see us.

"What's your name?" I asked.

"Süleyman."

"Pleased to meet you."

I dragged him to the dance floor. He seemed tense. I told myself that if it was really his first time at the club, and he wanted me, his attitude was only normal. With slow graceful steps, Süleyman's arm around me, I passed across the dance floor. His white shirt was phosphorescent, just like my dress. It glowed. I was certain Hüseyin was watching us. I didn't look in his direction, focusing all my attention on Süleyman as we settled at a table in the most secluded corner.

The corner tables are not very popular because it's difficult to see the dance floor or to be seen. For that reason, they're relatively quiet, generally used only for bargaining, inspection of the goods, or necking. Since the dance floor was full, we were able to find seats.

Süleyman pulled my chair back for me. I was impressed— most men have completely forgotten their manners. They don't even open car doors. I blame the feminists and lesbians.

Süleyman sat down across from me. My suspicions were aroused. *Ayol,* this sort of thing is best done sitting side by side. As he slid into his seat he unbuttoned his jacket and hitched his trouser cuffs up slightly. He sat ramrod-straight. He was not exactly forthcoming and certainly not at all talkative. I got no more than an intense stare. Following his lead, I sat up straight, not leaning back into my chair. If it kept up like this, anyone watching us would think we were conducting a serious business meeting, or that someone had arrived from the tax office. I glanced over toward Hüseyin. He seemed to be taking great interest in Müjde. He sensed my gaze and looked over at me. Our eyes met. I took a long sip of my drink and fastened my eyes flirtatiously on Süleyman.

"Is this the first time I've seen you here?" I began.

"Yes."

I waited for more. I wanted him to tell me where he'd seen me, what it was about me that had attracted him. Nothing. We just sat, staring at each other in silence. But there was nothing in his eyes that answered my questions. I have such a weakness for the strong, silent type.

"You're not very talkative."

"So?"

"I don't know if anyone has ever told you this before, but you bear a striking resemblance to Gary Cooper," I said. Just in case he had no idea who I was referring to, I threw in, "The old film star."

"I know," he said. "That's what my grandmother always said."

Not even his mother, his grandmother!

"My grandfather looked like him too," he added.

Once again, that delightfully bashful expression spread across his face. Either it was really his first time or he was a practiced ladies' man. He played the role of self-conscious lover to perfection.

"So what would you like to do?" I asked.

Without answering, he raised his hand and scratched his forehead. He smiled. His teeth were even and gleaming.

"I'd like to leave, to take you somewhere."

He was clearly embarrassed by having said so much. Despite the darkness, I could tell that he'd blushed. He avoided my eyes. I found his second smile even more charming than the first.

He was fast. But I'm no easy morsel. At the very least, I expect a bit more seduction and passion when I'm invited to leave the club.

"But it's still early. I've only just arrived."

"I've been waiting for you for two hours."

He did have a point. And he waited only for me, not the other girls.

"It's just getting lively here. I don't want to leave now," I said.

"But I do," he insisted.

At long last, the hand, which had seemed strangely homeless, landed on my knee. It was motionless.

He hadn't said "please." An oversight I found more attractive than irksome.

There was something strangely compelling about the way

he had waited for me for two hours, his determination to take me somewhere, and his unflappable coolness. There was none of that messy pawing. He wasn't at all vulgar. As the glossies would put it, this seemed like the start of a beautiful friendship.

I am nothing if not coy. It's my way. Knowing that Hüseyin was watching only encouraged me.

"If you really want me, you'll have to be patient and wait. I came here to have a good time."

"I'll bring you back," he offered.

"But where are we going?"

"Home," he said.

"Not to mine. I won't travel long distances and any hotel expenses are to be covered."

He smiled. "It's not very far."

I should have noted the modifying "very," but my feelings toward Hüseyin spurred me to unthinking action. I needed to make a point, and the sooner, the better. What's more, the guy wasn't half bad.

As always, Hasan arrived to save the day. He wore his usual low-slung jeans. Hasan was every bit as macho as one would expect of a waiter who bared his butt crack in a transvestite bar. I apologized to Süleyman and turned to Hasan. As I did so, I kept my arms slightly extended, placing my hands one atop the other on my lap. My legs were parallel and my feet side by side. In other words, I was the picture of Audrey Hepburn perfection. Had I worn my gloves the effect would have been better still. But perfection is elusive. I lightly batted my false eyelashes, then raised my eyebrows as I opened my eyes wide, confronting Hasan with a questioning look that also contained a hint of a smile.

"I didn't see you come in," he said. "Sofya called you twice. She said it's important."

I thanked him.

Hasan squeezed my shoulder lightly, murmuring, "Don't forget to call," and walked off. Then I remembered Refik Altın's proposal, and apologized to Süleyman once again as I rose to my feet. Catching up to Hasan, I grabbed him by the waistband of his sagging jeans.

"How does Refik know about Buse?" I asked.

"How should I know?" he replied.

He wasn't at all convincing. I let him go. He hitched his jeans up slightly.

"Look," I said, "don't mess with me! I know what a chatterbox you are. But some things aren't to be repeated. It's not safe to tell Refik even what you had for lunch. He is real scum."

Hasan looked at me, astonished. "But I didn't tell him anything."

I wouldn't keep Gary Cooper waiting while I wasted time with Hasan. So he'd decided to deny it. That was his business. He'd come to regret this when the time was ripe. He'd do best to watch his step.

"I'm warning you, be careful," was all I said.

"His ass was showing," was Süleyman's comment when I returned to our table.

"It's fashionable nowadays," I said.

"Not for me, it isn't."

"What's the matter? Aren't you proud of your bottom?" I needled him playfully.

My little joke fell on deaf ears. Süleyman didn't even smile.

"What's that supposed to mean?" he asked. "Do I have to exhibit everything I'm proud of?"

I could have prodded, *So tell me what you're most proud of,* but I'd leave that sort of common behavior to the other girls. It's not my style.

Süleyman's hand had begun to show signs of life as it rested on my knee. Hüseyin looked on from afar. When he realized I'd looked at him, he turned to Müjde. He must have been imagining he was provoking me. The fool.

"Look, sweetie," I said, "it's still early. I won't be able to stay for long. But seeing as you've waited for me . . ."

Süleyman had already risen to his feet. He looked even taller.

"I'll get the car. I couldn't find a parking spot. I'll pick you up at the door in fifteen minutes."

"Look, sweetie," I began again, "if you've got any kinky plans, forget it."

He placed a hand on my shoulder. "I don't," he said.

It's funny, but those who do usually say so straightaway. *I want it like this, I'll do it like that*, and so on. He wasn't one of those.

"I won't wait at the door. Send word when you arrive. The doorman is named Cüneyt."

"All right," he said. Planting a halfhearted kiss on my cheek, he left. That's right, on my cheek. I remained seated.

I decided to call Sofya while I waited. Who knows what she'd say to rattle me this time? I found Hasan and got her number. He had memorized it, which struck me as odd. It was only yesterday that he had claimed not to know exactly where she lived; now he knew her number by heart. I went to my office on the top floor, where I closed the observation window looking out over the entrance and dance floor. Otherwise the pounding music would make it impossible to hear myself speak.

I dialed the number. Sofya answered.

"*Merhaba*, Sofya, it's me," I said. "You rang?"

"I know what you're up to." She was off and running. "I told you not to get involved. But you've jumped in with both feet." Again, she spoke in distinct syllables.

"Jumped into what? What is it you think you know?"

"That you went to Buse's house, that you poked around. What you found . . ."

I wondered how she could have learned so much about me, but it really made no difference. The stout neighbor may have told her, or the apartment may have been under surveillance. I wouldn't even put it past Sofya to have me followed. Each alternative was worth a full point. Besides, how could she possibly know what I'd found?

"And what exactly is it I supposedly found?" I asked. The distance between us did no end of good in terms of my self-confidence. While even her voice was unsettling, Sofya had to be physically present for me to become completely unnerved.

A synthetic snort rattled out from the receiver.

"You surely know best. You're the one out hunting." Then her voice became more serious. "As soon as you find what you're looking for, you'd better hand it over to me. If not, the whole thing will explode in your face. Give it to me, and I'll be able to protect you. It's the only way."

"But I haven't got anything," I protested.

"You'll end up destroying yourself and me, too. You're acting like a fool. Don't. This is serious. Give me whatever it is you've found. They already know you have it."

"I told you, I haven't got a thing," I said. "The flat had been totally ransacked by the time I got in. Every last corner had been searched."

"Don't try to play games with that flea brain of yours!" That last bit was said in her most masculine voice. It was almost unrecognizable. It'd been years since I'd heard her talk like that. She instantly regained her self-possession and returned to her diva-like diction.

"They know where you were last night."

"Who are 'they'?"

"Full of questions, aren't you? I don't like it. Not one bit."

"But who are they?" I insisted.

"If you go on like this there will be nothing I can do," she warned.

"You know best," were my parting words as I hung up.

I'm not totally unskilled in the art of self-defense. Furthermore, I really didn't have anything, neither the letters nor the photos. The only thing in my possession was a taped interview in which both participants were drunk or drugged out. It wouldn't stand up in court. Technology had made it possible to reproduce anyone's voice. Failing that, recordings could be snipped apart and edited into the desired sentences.

Sofya had rattled me yet again. There was something about her that put me off balance.

I went down to the club. Hasan approached me at the base of the stairs.

"Have you spoken to Sofya?" he asked.

"Yes! What's it to you?"

"She's on the phone again. She said you were cut off. She's waiting on the line. What should I tell her?"

"I've got nothing to say."

"Are you going to speak to her?"

"Tell her I left."

"She won't believe me." As he said it, Hasan reproduced a facial expression often used by the girls. A pout involving distended lips—it didn't suit him. Though it was employed to good effect by the girls, it was inappropriate on the face of a man, nominal though he might be.

"Cut the coquetry, Hasan," I snapped. "Make something up. I won't speak to her."

"Okay, fine. But why are you taking it out on me?"

He turned, hitching up his trousers as he walked off.

I'd have to give the question of Sofya a great deal of thought once I'd finished my business with Süleyman and returned to the club. Hasan's attitude also begged a few questions. What was happening to him? Had I pressed a viper to my bosom? Why did he seem to side with Sofya? Why the interest in Buse?

If even Sofya was spooked, the situation was certainly critical. My knowingly being led into their trap was just asking for trouble.

I glanced over toward the commotion at the door. A group of five or six were entering the club. In front was Suat with her new girlfriend, a fashion model. They looked like Laurel and Hardy together. Next came the exhibitionist piano singer Mahmut Gürsel, who had screwed Buse on the deck of the boat. This was just great. It seemed everyone who had been mentioned in the tape was converging on my club.

Mahmut never came to the club. There had to be a reason for him to do so now. Suat wouldn't have dragged him along for no reason. But they couldn't know I'd listened to the cassette. When had they found out? How had they found out?

He seemed tense, even more so than would be accounted for by his first visit to a tranny club. Hasan met them at the door. His overly warm handshakes and kisses with Mahmut and Suat were annoying. Hasan was up to something. I didn't know what it was exactly, but I would find out. The model was shockingly beautiful, and icy.

I didn't know the other two members of the party. While I couldn't say for certain, they didn't seem like the sort I'd want around.

Cüneyt waved to me from the now-empty doorway. Süleyman must have arrived. I didn't want to encounter Mahmut and Suat. I was in no shape to withstand their questions and meaningful glances. The club, which had seemed so spacious, shrank to the size of a small pen. There was no escape.

I went directly to their sides. First I embraced and kissed

Suat. She congratulated me on my outfit. Some do appreciate the effort. Although I had never been introduced to Mahmut, as the club manageress I couldn't exactly ignore him. He was too well known for me to feign ignorance.

"Welcome," I greeted him. "It's such an honor to see you here."

He took my hand and pulled me toward him as he squeezed it. He looked as though he were preparing to devour me.

"The honor is all mine."

As he breathed in, he seemed to be inhaling and retaining my scent. He hadn't released my hand. In a word, the man was pure smut. Repulsive, even.

"Do forgive me, I really must go," I said, reclaiming my hand. "I'm late for a rendezvous. I do hope to see you later."

Suat protested unconvincingly, but Mahmut appeared truly outraged. Like a child deprived of its newest toy. He'd missed his chance.

I couldn't hear what Suat said about me as I left, but I could well imagine the gist of it. I sashayed my way through the crowd to the door.

Chapter 23

✛

*I*n front of the door was a black Volkswagen Passat with tinted windows. Cüneyt held the door as I inserted myself, Audrey Hepburn–style, into the waiting vehicle. First I elegantly slid my bottom onto the seat, then I drew in my legs, keeping my knees and ankles together. As he shut the door, Cüneyt winked at me. He always does that. It's his way to confirm that he's memorized the license plate. A simple precaution taken for all the girls. The only difference is that there are so many girls these days, he has to jot the numbers down. It's a tiny safeguard I've developed.

Süleyman got behind the wheel. We were off.

"You're late," he said flatly.

"I ran into some important guests on my way out. I had to speak to them," I apologized. "Forgive me. I hope I haven't kept you waiting for too long."

"No, not for that long. After waiting inside for two hours, what's a few more minutes?"

He kept his eyes on the road. With a press of his finger, the doors were locked.

"Why'd you lock the doors?" I asked.

"It's safer."

I wondered who or what we would be safe from, but I said nothing. Seeing as he didn't like talking, I sat in silence and thought. His hand was on the gearshift. I placed my hand on top of it. He turned and smiled at me. He was attractive, and I was on my way to a brief tryst with him. There was also the question of payback for that thug of a taxi driver, Hüseyin. The girls and my employees know that under normal circumstances I won't easily leave the club for this sort of thing.

He hadn't turned on any music, despite the car's expensive stereo. The air conditioner hummed quietly. After the hot taxis I'd endured all day, I luxuriated in the coolness. I enjoyed traveling in a style I believed I deserved. I dispensed with the erect Hepburn pose and settled back into my seat.

I raised my hand from his and placed it on his leg. After seeming slightly startled, he once again fixed me with that bold flirtatious stare.

"Not now," he said.

I respected that. With traffic accidents so common these days it's important to concentrate on driving. I removed my hand.

He was a practiced driver. There was no hard braking or sudden acceleration. We flowed along through Dolapdere to the ring road.

"Where are we going, anyway?" I asked.

"There's someone who wants to talk to you."

This is what they call a bombshell.

"Excuse me?"

"Someone wants to talk to you. That's where I'm taking you." Süleyman's eyes remained fixed on the road, his hands on the steering wheel.

"Stop this instant!" I shouted. "Who is this person? Why doesn't he come to me himself?"

"That would be impossible. It wouldn't be appropriate. That's why I was sent."

It wasn't difficult to guess the identity of the mystery man. There were two alternatives. It was either Süreyya Eronat or one of Sofya's blackmailing Mafia friends. I didn't want to name any names in the car. But whichever person it was, it was bad news. Both alternatives could mean my elimination from the game of life.

"Who are you taking me to?" I demanded. "Who wants to meet me?"

"My boss."

That much was clear. But I had no clue about the identity of his boss. We had exited the ring road and were now cruising through the darkness of Kemerburgaz.

"That much I understood. Who is your boss?"

"You'll see when we get there. It's not my place to tell you."

"Well, what does he want to talk about?"

"Like I told you, it's not my place to say anything. You'll get all the explanations you need. My job is to get you there as quickly and safely as possible."

My thoughts were lightning-quick, my speech thunderous.

"I'm not going anywhere. Stop now!"

As in any book or movie, he did not stop. His lips did form a half smile, however. He was no doubt saying to himself, I won't be bossed around by some sad tranny. Even if he had stopped, I was really in no shape to get out. It was pitch-black and we were driving through the countryside.

"Stop!" I repeated. "Take me straight back to the club!"

"Calm down," he said.

"I told you to stop right now."

Again, he just kept driving. Instead of stopping the car he reached down and withdrew a gun. Now I had no choice but to act. Paying no mind to the speed with which we were careening down the highway, I grabbed his right arm and twisted it behind his back.

Despite his look of astonishment, he didn't make a sound. Without giving him time to comprehend the situation, I delivered a sharp chop with the back of my hand to the patch of forehead just above the nose and below the eyebrows. With a low "Arrrgh," he released his foot from the gas pedal. We began racing faster down the hill nevertheless. After stunning him with a second chop, this time behind his ear, I made to grab the gun. His hand clasped my wrist. He was strong. A lesser man would have been writhing in pain by now. I tried opening the door with my free hand, but it was locked. I would have to press one of the buttons on the glowing panel between us. But which one? And how?

In order to buy time, I poked him hard in the right eye. Even if it didn't blind him, it would be days before he could painlessly rotate that eye. He bellowed. Naturally, he would shout—that sort of thing hurts. He instinctively covered his right eye with his right hand, thus releasing me.

"You goddamn faggot!" he hissed.

I began pressing every button on the control panel. Well, actually, I began banging my left hand on the panel as I tried to open the door with my right one.

He grabbed me again, this time seizing my left arm with his left hand. He had a viselike grip. The lock on my door popped up. I delivered a blow to the back of his neck, and his head smashed into the steering wheel. My arm was finally released.

The car was still moving. My mighty gorilla, Süleyman Bey, had not yet recovered from the blow to his head. I had to admit, he was unusually resilient. But there was no point in thought. I leaped out of the car. I had practiced similar moves in one of the martial arts classes I'd attended. I was no stranger to the technique. Real life, however, is not quite the same. It hurt. There was a vast difference between the application of a well-thought-out and planned roll in sports shoes and a sweat suit, and the same sudden move with bare legs and a thin dress.

The side of the road—the first thing I hit—was covered in gravel. From there, I rolled down a slope into a thicket of thorny bushes. The Passat screeched to a halt a mere ten yards down the road.

He was after me. It was unrealistic to have expected him to proceed merrily along his way as if having totally forgotten about me. My baby-blue frock shone like a flashlight under the moonlit sky. There was no point in trying to hide. I'd be his match in an open space, just as I had been inside the car. That is, if he didn't draw his gun!

He stepped out of the car. Lurching slightly, he headed straight for me, gun drawn.

Not a single vehicle passed. Where was Istanbul traffic when you needed it? Where were all those drivers clogging up the highways and byways? I'd settle for a single car, a minibus, a bus, even a truck. Now the situation could only deteriorate further, and I could expect no help. I would have to handle it on my own.

"Don't shoot!" I cried out, raising my hands over my head as I rose from a crouch.

"You're nuts!" he shouted. "You could have blinded me."

"I'm sorry," I said. I'd have to play nice until I was better positioned to topple him.

"Come here!" he ordered.

I could claim injury, draw him into the bushes by pleading for help. But it would be too difficult to fight in the close confines of the thorny scrub. I preferred a fair fight on the level asphalt. And that's exactly what I intended to have. Hitching up my frock, I was on the road in two jumps. He gestured toward the car with his gun.

"Get in like a man, and let's go."

He pointed the gun at me, in case I needed further persuasion. I would have to proceed with caution. Pretending I'd sprained my ankle, I slowly limped toward him. He was still rubbing his eye with his free hand.

"Did it hurt?" I asked.

"Real men don't feel pain!" he rumbled.

The distance between us was too great for me to reach him with a single flying leap. I had no way of gauging his skills as a marksman. It wasn't worth the risk. If he shot the split second I left my feet, that would be it. I'd have to relieve him of the gun first. For that, I would have to get nearly as close as I am tall, except for the length of my arm. Dragging my feet, I took two small steps toward him. Yes, that would do.

"I think I sprained my ankle," I said, bending over. I could jump farther from a crouching position. He didn't suspect anything.

"You asked for it," he said.

Before the words were out of his mouth, my right foot had connected with the middle of his face. I quickly let loose two more kicks. He was now sufficiently dazed.

Changing feet in midair, I dealt a heavy blow to his left kneecap. Then I booted him right between the legs. He doubled over. Clasping my hands together, I clubbed the base of his skull, then seized the hand wielding the gun. By bringing my knee up sharply against his extended arm, twice, I forced him to drop it. Then I kneed him in the face. He collapsed spread-eagled onto the ground.

I bent over to pick up the gun. That was a mistake. He was lying on the ground, but not quite unconscious. A hand suddenly gripped my right ankle, and I lost my balance. No big deal. I had the gun. I placed it against his nose. Raising his head slightly from the ground, he gazed at it, with his good eye, and fainted.

Süleyman's having fainted was a mixed blessing. It would enable me to get away, but it also meant I wouldn't be able to get him to talk. And I had so looked forward to conducting an interrogation at gunpoint and getting to the bottom of the whole business.

I could keep the gun trained on his head and wait until he

came to. A real bull of a man, he'd regain consciousness in no time. I could then proceed with the question-and-answer session.

Or I could leave him there. But that would only mean even more thugs chasing after me. This time one person had come to get me. Next time it would be an army.

I was still on an asphalt road on a black night. It wasn't the most suitable place to sit and have a good think. What's more, exhaust was sputtering out of the tailpipe and straight into my face. I felt nauseated.

There was no need to subject myself to more. In order to make sure Süleyman remained out cold, I gave a cursory kick to the back of his neck. He seemed to become even more sprawled and lifeless. Like someone finally relaxing after numerous days of hard labor.

I thrust the gun into my cloth belt and quickly searched him. He wasn't packing any other weapons, but I felt a cell phone in his jacket pocket. Perhaps I would be able to search through his phone book, find out who he had last called. I pulled out the phone. It was switched off, and I didn't know the PIN code. There was nothing I could do here. At home I'd crack the code in no time. I stuck the phone into my thick belt.

Next, I took his wallet. His name was Süleyman Bahattin Aydın. He must have been named after both grandfathers. He was twenty-seven years old. Born in Istanbul. His driver's license was registered under the same name. It featured a baby-faced youth doing his best to look tough. The wallet also contained a thick wad of cash and two credit cards, one of them gold, issued by two different banks. I felt like I deserved all of this money. It would barely compensate me for my dress, which was made of fine Italian cotton, but it would have to do.

When he rustled slightly, I hit him again. Naturally. He seemed to relax into the deep slumber of a moment earlier. It's so important to allow the muscles and joints to fully relax. By doing so, we wake up refreshed from even a short nap. Many aches and pains, as well as some illnesses, are the result of the failure to stretch out. As I remembered his tense posture and swaggering at the club, I decided I had in fact done him a favor, thus assuaging any guilt I may have felt.

As a final precaution, I removed his belt, tying his hands behind his back with it. Most people would pass out cold for at least twenty minutes after a sharp chop to the base of the skull, but this guy was extraordinarily tough. The lid of his good eye was flickering even now, and his back arched slightly. Such amazing resilience and ability to recover so quickly could only be the result of years of training. I silently applauded him.

Leaving him lying on the ground behind the car, I quickly riffled through the glove compartment. His registration and insurance documents were in order. And registered in his own name. In short, I had discovered nothing to reveal the identity of his employer. Finding a packet of condoms, I laughed softly. With the door open, and my eyes on Süleyman, I sat in the car, gun in hand. I inspected myself for damage: the skirt of my dress was torn. There were scratches and cuts on my naked arms and legs. At the sight of each one, I felt the stinging. Until I'd actually looked, I hadn't felt a thing. That I was filthy seemed even more important. I was covered in dirt and dust. Over this I cursed long and lustily.

There was no point in waiting around. Süleyman didn't seem like the sort I'd be able to break, no matter how long I held a gun to his head. He knew as well as I did that I wouldn't actually kill him. At most, I could only dare to shoot him in the arms or legs, just to frighten him.

I looked at the gun in my hand. It was covered with my fingerprints. I wiped it thoroughly with my skirt, then stuck it in the glove compartment.

I switched off the engine and took the keys. Just to be on

the safe side, I wiped any possible fingerprints off the steering wheel, glove compartment handle, and car doors.

Then I returned to Süleyman. He was still lying face down on the road, fast asleep. A thread of blood and spit drooled out of his mouth and onto the pavement. Lips parted slightly, he was bestowing a kiss on the asphalt. I nudged him in the ribs with my foot. He didn't respond. There's no way I had killed him, but I leaned over to check his jugular vein, just in case. It was pulsing at regular intervals. He was tough enough to recover fully in a few days.

I ran through the alternatives facing me: (A) Wait for him to come to and interrogate him—which I had already decided against; (B) Take the car, leaving him behind; (C) Leave him and the car, and find some way to get home on my own. I tried, and failed, to come up with an alternative (D).

There was nothing to prevent me from taking the car and going. But what would I do with the car later? Also, I didn't have my driver's license with me. Traffic checks and police barricades were common at this time of night, especially on the weekend. If I abandoned the car somewhere, someone might see me and identify me later.

Just striding off into the night, leaving the whole mess behind me, seemed an attractive option at first. Particularly in terms of cinematography: In my tattered Audrey Hepburn finery I would haughtily toss the keys into the bushes so he couldn't follow me, then stride off into the night along the highway. But that would take far too much effort. Although close to Istanbul, we were out in what passed as the wilds, and hitchhiking on a nearly deserted road would not be easy. It would take some time to walk to the motorway. I was in no shape for that. My ill-timed fall had injured me.

Even if I did manage to reach the motorway, hitchhiking at this hour could result in some unpleasant surprises. I might find that the driver wouldn't let me go until I'd returned the favor. And I wasn't in the mood for another brawl.

I poked Süleyman in the ribs again. He turned his head slightly. So he was regaining consciousness. I decided to ask him for advice.

"What do you think I should do?" I asked. "Should I take the car and go, or should I leave the car and go?"

His good eye opened. "Huh?"

I repeated my question.

"Go fuck your mother!" he suggested. Or at least that's what he tried to say. His lips were still plastered to the asphalt and my right foot rested on the back of his neck. I don't appreciate references to my mother, particularly those of a crude nature. And my mother's privates are certainly no one else's business. I pressed down hard with my foot. His cheek was crushed. His lips reminded me of a guppy's.

"You certainly have no manners!" I scolded. "You asked for this," I added, with a graceful kick to his head. He passed out again.

Pulling the white kid gloves from my belt, I put them on. I placed my scarf on my head, tying it under my chin. I got into the car, started the engine, and drove off.

Chapter 24

✧

$\mathcal{I}$ was in no shape to return to the club. I would have to abandon the car somewhere and go home. The road was empty. I drove straight to Taksim Square, where I could leave the car in the Atatürk Cultural Center parking lot. It would stay there for days. Better still, there were so many customers on the weekends that the attendants would probably not remember me.

Rolling the window down just a crack, I took my ticket, parking the car right in the middle of the lot so it wouldn't attract undue attention. I couldn't decide whether or not to take the keys. I could leave it unlocked—someone might take it. That was it! A stolen car. Or Süleyman's bunch could trace it here. Assuming they'd have an extra set, I took the keys, but left the doors unlocked.

I exited the front of the parking lot, hugging the wall of the cultural center so no one would see me. I hailed the first cab that came along.

The driver was young. He looked over my outfit as I got in.

"*Geçmiş olsun*, lady," he commiserated.

I was, of course, the "lady" to whom he referred.

"Thank you," I said. "It's nothing important. I'm afraid I had a little spill."

"That must have been quite a fall. Are you sure you're all right?"

"Yes. Thank you. I tore my dress."

"They say the fallen have no friends," he said, making an attempt at humor.

He even laughed at his own little joke. Uncomfortable with the ensuing silence, he then turned on the radio. I was in no mood to argue with him over what to play. As a result, all the way home I was forced to endure not only the pounding music, but his shouting into his cell phone to make himself heard over the racket.

I paid the driver from Süleyman's roll of bills. Racing into my apartment, without even turning on the lights I began stripping. Leaving a trail of filthy garments behind me, I reached the bathroom.

The shower did me good. My legs were more badly scratched than I'd realized, but not too deeply. There were no wounds worth worrying about. I would, however, be covered with bruises, judging from the extensive areas of reddened flesh. My left arm, which had been held in Süleyman's viselike grip, was an especially promising candidate.

I applied an ice pack. Then a dressing. My face had emerged from the ordeal entirely unscathed. That's all that was really important. The right clothing would conceal the rest.

I'd injured my right shoulder during either the fall or the fighting. I spread on a soothing balm I'd purchased in the Far East.

All in all, I was fine, and well enough to feel hungry. I discovered a bar of bitter chocolate in the fridge. I always keep my chocolate refrigerated. I began gnawing on it with gusto.

I should call the club. They'd best be careful, especially Cüneyt. He wasn't to give my address to anyone, even my father. I remembered that I'd unplugged the phone jack while I listened to the tape, so the answering machine wouldn't have been working while I was away. I plugged it in. There were still five messages I hadn't listened to. That's right, I'd ignored them in my haste to play the tape. First I'd better phone the club, though.

Hasan answered. Without even waiting for me to begin he launched in. The idiot.

"Sofya has been calling every five minutes. She keeps asking whether or not you've returned. She hasn't been able to reach you at home. It's all been too much for me! What a stubborn woman. I've had it, I tell you."

"You deserve it," I said. "You brought it on yourself. Now listen, and listen good."

Whatever the relationship was between Sofya and Hasan, it had gone too far. Without going into detail, I told him what had happened. I decided that I couldn't reveal too much to Hasan until I'd given him a good dressing down. I'd have to cross-examine him, too, but I just wasn't up to it tonight.

I concluded by saying I might stop by the club later that night, but that it was highly unlikely.

"*Geçmiş olsun*. Is there anything you need? Shall I come right over? Or do you want me to send anything with one of the girls?"

No, the last thing I needed was nosy Hasan. We hung up.

I began listening to my messages. The first caller hung up without speaking, which is unforgivable in my book. If you have no intention of speaking, why wait for the tone? It isn't as though I expect a detailed explanation; name and reason for calling will do. I mean, really. If it's too personal or confidential to say on the message, tell me as much and hang up.

The second message was from Hasan. He had researched the people claiming Buse's corpse: they were relatives. No documentation is required when claiming a body, so he had been unable to find out exactly who they were. In other words, there was nothing new.

The third message was from Ali. He was bombarding me

with detailed questions. I would have to hit the pause button and take notes. And that's exactly what I did. The time allotted for Ali's message had been insufficient, so the fourth message was also him. I jotted it all down, filling an entire sheet of paper. At the end, he wished me a good—and horny—night.

The fifth, and final, message was another non-talker. I erased all five.

I was wide awake, and feeling fed up with the whole business of the mysterious letters. Why was it any of my concern? Why not just let whoever it was find whatever it was? If that meant a scandal, so be it. It'd blow over quickly enough. Some would get snuffed out, others would go on living. Before the year was out, it'd all be forgotten.

What did the blind mother's problems matter to me? She'd managed to disappear without a trace. Even the neighbor, who had claimed to know each time she stepped out the door, who heard the slightest peep, who was unable to sleep without knowing every detail of what went on in her building and neighborhood, hadn't heard a thing. Well, good for her!

What's more, she appeared to have taken the letters and photos with her. I tipped my hat to her, especially considering her affliction.

If she'd been abducted, rather than fled on her own, then I congratulated her captors. They deserved a big bonus for managing to spirit her away right under the nose of the busybody neighbor. Naturally, they'd also taken the letters and photos. Anyone would have done the same, whether it was the Mafia or Süreyya Eronat's henchmen. What difference did it make to me?

I also found my trust in Chubby Cheeks waning by the second. A photograph of Süreyya Eronat with her husband hung in pride of place right in the living room. She hadn't heard the murder upstairs. She'd seemed sincere enough, but it could all have been a big act. Either that or the husband was deeply involved without his wife's knowledge.

There had been two murders: Buse and the elderly upstairs neighbor. The possible cast of suspects included a gang intent on blackmail, Süreyya Eronat, whose very name chilled the bones, self-censoring journalists, and a bunch of celebrities, some minor, some major, desperate to conceal their past relationships. As if that weren't enough, I had to deal with Sofya, who was doing all in her power to intimidate me. I'd had it.

Hasan was another thorn in my side. He seemed determined to poke his nose into everything, and had far exceeded what I would consider the normal interest in high society gossip. There was no excuse for his having revealed so much to so many, filling in the blanks as he pleased. His loose lips had only succeeded in getting that filthy Refik involved. The fact that he was collaborating with Sofya made it that much more unacceptable.

I could forget all about Refik Altın. He was truly pathetic. But that didn't mean his time wouldn't come, that I wouldn't make him pay.

To do anything further would mean asking for trouble, making a fool of myself. Clearly, someone had been provoked and that blockhead Süleyman had been sent to attack me. Someone wished to meet with me. I was sick and tired of the whole thing. It was a convoluted puzzle no matter how you looked at it.

I had lost all desire to crack Süleyman's mobile code or struggle with anything similar. Once I experience actual pain, the movie is over, as far as I'm concerned. Even if I'm starring opposite John Pruitt, that's it. And I was in pain. The End.

My thoughts returned to my arms and legs. What a waste of time and expense, trouble and inconvenience, at the beauty salon that same day. My belief in fate was reinforced. I intended to rub in some restorative lotion and play with my computer.

First I'd put on some Bach. My hand once again reached out to take the BWV 1060 double concerto from the shelf, but the late hour called for something more extravagant. I looked over the orchestra suites and Brandenburg concertos. Handel's Water Music caught my eye. Yes, that would do nicely. I have a finely honed appreciation for the Baroque, and an extensive collection. It's just the thing for working on the computer, or after lovemaking. Authentic performance instruments are played with lighter force, attaining a sound that is both full and soothing. The instruments have a less overpowering tone, so that the playing of one note interferes less with the hearing of simultaneous or neighboring notes. That is, it might help me relax enough to fall asleep. Modern orchestras lack the same transparency of musical texture and are more subject to the interpretation of the conductor.

I selected the modern, nearly experimental Pierre Boulez rendition. As a proponent of contemporary music, he was a true pioneer. As far as I knew, this was his only Baroque recording. The largo part of the first suite washed over me. I sat down in front of the computer.

There were a couple of minor tasks I needed to complete for the company. I set to work. I was halfway done when the CD ended. It would be good to finish tonight and send everything along to Ali the following morning. Because he's so swamped with visiting clients on weekdays that he doesn't get much work done, Ali always works at the office on Sundays after his morning exercise regime. The analyses and programs I was working on would be helpful to him.

I never send this kind of work over the Internet. It's not secure enough. I removed the CD and inserted Satie. "Gnossiennes" was an excellent choice, and I resumed work to it. The glassy tones floated through the house. I wanted coffee, and brought a cupful to my desk. When I had finished, I loaded everything onto a disc. For Ali's amusement, I added a photo of John Pruitt. I'm of the firm opinion that even the most hetero of men benefit from the occasional sight of handsome men. If nothing else, they'll have a source of inspiration. The pictures don't have to feature nudity, although I prefer it. I set the disc so that the first thing to pop up would be John Pruitt. Each time a new file was opened, the image would reappear.

Ali would be cross at first, then he'd come to appreciate my little joke. And since he didn't know how to erase the image, he wouldn't be able to share the contents of the disc with anyone else. I grinned evilly as I thought about it.

I placed the disc into a bubble envelope. Labeling it, I put it to one side. I'd have a driver from the taxi stand take it over in the morning. I was in no shape to do it myself. Ali was a workaholic, and would be in the office until sometime in the afternoon.

I'd started to get sleepy. With a feeling of peace from a job well done, I switched off the computer and stretched out on the bed. The pillow still smelled faintly of the policeman, Kenan. Or at least that's what I imagined. He was so good-looking, a real male beauty, and it had been such a disappointment for it to end so quickly. Maybe he was overexcited by being with me for the first time. I'd been too compliant, allowing him to have his way. Which he'd done, in record time. If he visited me again I'd take control, do it my way.

I'd read somewhere that having erotic thoughts just before falling asleep boosts sexual potency and libido. I was applying the technique.

Chapter 25

⁘

$\mathcal{W}$henever I fall asleep at dawn, I sleep until noon. Or I try to, at least. In order to ensure that my rest isn't interrupted, I unplug the phone in my bedroom and let the answering machine handle any callers. I also close my thick curtains all the way.

I couldn't have been asleep for long. In fact, I may not have even fallen fully asleep. Or I'd just nodded off, relaxed completely. No, I hadn't fallen asleep. The doorbell was ringing.

I wasn't expecting anyone. Whoever it is, they'll give up and go, I thought. But they didn't. Whoever was pressing the button clearly intended to remain doing so until the door was opened.

I was groggy with sleep. I ran through the possibilities of who the visitor could be:

(A) John Pruitt—my first choice—was not a possibility. There was no point in even fantasizing about it.

(B) A fan—Kenan, for example. I would hold him in my arms and fall back to sleep. If it was Hüseyin, and he was drunk, he would be roundly beaten. Chase after me, flirt with me, pull out all the stops, try to seduce me . . . then run off with the first girl you meet at the club! I wasn't having it! My pride, and the fatness of the transvestite in question, left me no choice but to pound Hüseyin.

(C) Mafia man. As I remembered this possibility, my eyes popped open. After Süleyman was sent after me the previous night, there could now be a gang of thugs at my door. Even if I didn't open the door they'd force their way in.

(D) Süreyya Eronat's henchmen. It would be easy enough to learn my address. They'd be no better than the Mafia men. That is, only divine intervention would save me.

I shuddered at the thought of alternatives (C) and (D). (A) and (B) were quickly eliminated. I threw on a robe and raced to the door.

I seemed to have lost my wits. I mean, was this really the time to imagine myself on a game show, to run through the list of possible alternatives facing me? The bell was ringing nonstop. By now my neighbors had probably been roused and would be waiting with ears pricked to see who had come.

"Coming!" I cried out. I tried to keep the volume down. Apartment buildings are a form of communal living, after all. Early morning screams are frowned upon.

When I reached the door, I said, "All right, I'm here!" I peered through the peephole. Confronting me was a highly disarranged Sofya. She hadn't even featured on my list of possibilities. I hesitated, wondering whether or not to open the door. If I didn't, she'd continue ringing the bell until she'd woken up all my neighbors. I'd called out; she knew I was at home and awake. I also feared her wrath. It was unclear what Sofya would do if she imagined herself provoked.

Without undoing the safety latch, I opened the door a crack. I blinked furiously, raising my eyebrows as high as possible in my best imitation of a person barely awake.

"Efendim—"

"Open that door. Now!" she barked.

I wilted before the authority in her voice.

I opened the door. She shoved me aside as she came in. It was her first visit to my apartment, and a rather rude entry under those circumstances. Her makeup was smeared, her carefully arranged coiffeur plastered to her head. While not a compete mess, she was close. Sofya is never totally wrecked. She maintains a regal air whatever the outfit. That didn't seem to be the case at the moment. She wore a pair of trousers fit only for scrubbing floors and a T-shirt that pinched her gel-filled breasts. I would have been shocked to see such garments in her wardrobe, let alone on her person.

"What do you want? What is it at this time of the morning?"

She glanced around the room mockingly, like an unimpressed buyer. She obviously didn't think much of my appearance, either.

"Go wash your face."

Confronting Sofya would be a waste of time. If she set her heart on something, she'd keep at it, like a wave crashing into a breaker, until she got her way. There'd be no silencing her, no sign of tiring. We all boast various skills, and that was one of hers. I obediently trotted off to the bathroom. It would also give me time to collect my thoughts and form a strategy. Behind me I heard:

"And put something on!"

I did as I was told. I had hit upon my best tactic: to remain unmoved. I wouldn't give Sofya the satisfaction of unsettling me. No matter how confused I became, no matter what role she adopted, I would grin and bear it. And I was sleepy. Failing all else, I'd nod off.

In contrast to her dishevelment, I put on a tight, sleeveless striped white T-shirt that highlighted my slim elegance to best effect. I also selected a pair of fire-red hot pants I'd picked up at a lingerie shop in Amsterdam. Not only do they lift and shape the buttocks, they barely cover them. I proceeded to the living room. Sofya hadn't been impressed by the armchairs. She was perched on a dining room chair.

"Sit down!" she said. "Are you awake yet?"

"Yes," I replied. I sat down in an armchair near her.

"Come here," she commanded.

She pointed to the table. The way to remain unfazed by Sofya was to follow her orders unthinkingly. When I did try to make sense of them, my head hurt. In line with my strategy, I rose and walked to the table.

She watched as I sat down in the chair next to hers. Roughly seizing my chin, she stared straight into my eyes. Through slits, she examined me. I treated her to my most innocent, sweetest smile.

"You're still asleep . . . Go get a strong cup of coffee!" she said. It was really a bit much.

"But I've just had one. Too much coffee causes cellulite," I lied. I'd barely finished my sentence when I received a stinging slap across the face. She's got a heavy hand, but it took a moment to sink in. I immediately assumed a defensive position.

She sniggered.

"That's better. Your eyes are sparkling now," she said.

She had mistaken a flash of lightning for a sparkle. Neither a borrower nor a lender be. I let her have one.

"Ayyy!" She clutched the cheek I'd struck. "You vicious little whore. See, you're wide awake."

Then she emitted a fake laugh.

I was surprised. The Sofya I knew wouldn't laugh off being hit. It must have been the early hour, the murder cases we'd become caught up in, or the heat that had worn her out. But I didn't give it any more thought. It wasn't worth it.

"What do you want?" I asked.

"Whatever it is you've found and taken, that's what."

"I told you, I haven't found anything—"

She grabbed my chin and looked into my eyes, this time even closer and more penetratingly. I wasn't happy about her face being so close to mine. I unclasped her hand. I could have grabbed her wrist and twisted her arm behind her back. If she'd resisted, it would have hurt. I had the impulse to do it. It seemed a good idea. But then again, it would be an unsatisfying gesture unless done in front of an audience.

"You're as stubborn as ever, as determined to do things your way. Most people mature as they get older—they get a bit blunter around the edges, they lose their childish whims. But I see you haven't changed a bit."

Sofya had begun speaking like a normal person. They say costumes have a powerful effect on people. That was definitely true. Dressed like a normal person—or even worse—she spoke just like everyone else.

"Maybe that's because I'm still young," I said.

The realization I'd hit a nerve pleased me.

"You're a fool," she said. "You're still playing childish games. You've got no idea who you're up against. The darkest of the dark. No one can beat them. There's nothing they won't do to get what they want. I'm just a go-between, an ambassador. I've only gotten involved to protect you, for your own sake. Otherwise, you'd be up against them, not me. You'd have met the same fate as Buse. She was a stubborn fool. She'd smoke a joint, tell everyone who she'd been with, and then deny it all when she was sober. Then she mentioned the photographs. Naturally, they went after her."

"And when she stood up to you, you killed her without mercy."

"Don't include me. I'm not like them. I'm just a pawn. An employee they get to do their dirty work, but I am rewarded handsomely. Just like you, I took it upon myself to recover the photos. I said I'd get them."

As she said this, she held my hand between her own. I don't think much of girl-chat, nor do I appreciate fatherly advice. I withdrew my hand.

"What are you going to get, what am I supposed to give you? I have nothing! I don't understand what you want from me. I know about the letters and photos, but I've never even seen them. That's all I know."

She looked at me suspiciously, and took a deep breath. She closed her eyes and waited. Then she emptied her lungs in my face. She was no longer perching on the chair, but had turned into a sack of potatoes. Sofya had lost her cool and her poise. I had never seen her looking so ordinary—there wasn't a trace of the diva I'd so admired. Who was this pathetic middle-aged man in women's clothing, who had apparently come to scrub the floor? Her voice softened.

"Let me start at the beginning," she said.

"All right, go ahead."

"We're not talking about four or five people. We're talking about an entire organization. They've got their feelers and their spies everywhere. They collect blackmail material on anyone who might be useful one day, then use them as puppets."

"Sounds profitable," I commented. What else could I say? And it was true. These people, whoever they were, had hit upon a great racket, and it had been ticking over nicely so far.

Sofya seemed to be telling a fairy tale, and I sat as though listening to one. I could have stopped paying attention, but I was fascinated and wanted to hear the ending. Not to mention the fact that my face still stung.

"We all have something to hide, a weak spot. Is there anyone who doesn't?"

"I suppose so. What do I know?" I said. "Still, there are plenty of people with nothing to be ashamed of. At least I think there are."

"If they couldn't find anything, they'd arrange material for blackmail. That's how I got involved. I was summoned to a luxurious house, one of our old customers. I didn't expect any trouble. They filmed everything that happened that night. Then they drugged me and took photographs in which I seemed to be shooting up heroin. Just think about it, me and drugs. If the police got hold of the pictures I'd spend the rest of my life in prison. That's how they reeled me in."

Sofya is terrified of the police. Her recurring nightmare involves being arrested and "rotting in jail." Like any middle-class child, she'd been raised to fear imprisonment. Once, a long time ago, she'd been arrested on the job and kept in police custody for two nights. She talked about it for years. While her experience was nothing like *Midnight Express,* she emerged totally petrified. From the way she talked about it, you'd have thought she'd suffered even more than the character in that film.

"So then what happened?"

"Whenever I was needed they'd call me to appear in photos and films. Politicians, businessmen, celebrities, civil servants, and bureaucrats. The old, the young, the ugly ... All sorts. They'd start by researching the sexual tastes of the victim: age preference, woman-girl-transvestite-homosexual-man. That pretty much covers everyone. A rendezvous would be arranged and I'd arrive. I'd make sure that the men were captured in the most compromising positions imaginable. There was always a hidden camera, of course. Rooms were kept reserved at even the most expensive hotels. All varieties of film were produced, from underage gay sex to heroin parties and orgies. The blackmail victims were then recruited to help entrap others."

"They certainly knew what they were doing."

"Yes, they did."

"But didn't anyone try to resist them? You mean, there wasn't a single person prepared to stand up and fight them, and damn the consequences?"

"Sweetie, we've all got our fears, something we'd hate to lose. The most basic example is the fear of being exposed to family, friends, spouses, and colleagues. Yes, of course there were those who refused to cooperate at first. At first they'd be all bluster and protests, but when the materials reached their family, they'd suddenly sing a different tune. No photos were ever leaked to the press. Well, maybe one or two. Their careers were over just like that, and they were replaced by newer, more pliable talent."

"I see," I said.

"Good. Now bring me everything you have on Süreyya Eronat."

I burst out laughing. It was the first time either of us had pronounced his name. He'd always been a mysterious presence, to which we alluded in the vaguest terms. Now, just like that, out popped his name from Sofya's lips.

"I swear I haven't got a thing," I said. "Someone broke into that flat before I got there. They must have taken whatever was there."

Her voice grew harsher and she sat up straight. "Let's not start playing games again. Don't you understand? I'm trying to save you."

"Why?"

"I still love you, even if you don't realize it. You're like my own child. I get cross, I tell you off, but I still have motherly feelings for you."

"Don't be ridiculous, Sofya! I've never known you to love anyone. Your whole life is a series of cold-blooded calculations."

"It's hard for you to understand, but that's the way I feel. I have no intention of trying to convince you. Believe what you will."

It was true that at one time she had acted like a rather oppressive mother. She had transformed me from an intellectual and naïve fag into a ravishing transvestite. Still, unless all the ingredients had been in place to begin with she'd never have managed it. She'd acted as my protectress and mentor for a while, advising me on everything from what to wear to which creams and lotions to apply. She'd even decided who I should sleep with.

Next came our adventures in Paris. It's true, there had been something maternal about her. But I ask you, which mother, no matter what the relationship with her child, would pimp her daughter to a string of men just to fatten her wallet? That's exactly what Sofya had done.

She'd have me believe that her maternal instincts had led her to handpick my gentleman callers. Accepting that she had acted out of love was as attractive an option as lapping up a puddle of vomit.

We stared at each other. She had aged. She looked terrible without makeup. Without false lashes, there was nothing striking about her bleary green eyes; she had bags under them and a wattle developing under her chin.

"So, you're saying that unless I hand over the photos and letters they'll kill me, too?" I asked.

"It's possible . . . anything is possible. They think you have them."

"Is that why you sent Süleyman after me? He tried to kidnap me. He was taking me to talk to someone. Of course, I got out of it, he was such a blockhead. Tell your friends that they should consider hiring more professional help."

Now she looked stunned.

"I don't know a thing about that," she said. "They'd never tolerate amateurs."

With her index finger, she traced a line across her throat.

"Do let them know. I kind of feel sorry for the poor guy."

"I didn't know anything about it. Mind you, there's a lot going on I know nothing about. But they'd given me full responsibility for the photos. This is a surprise. I should have been informed.

They must be running out of patience. They've been pushing me up against the wall . . . They've tortured me."

Suddenly, she was wracked with sobs. It wasn't an act. Blubbering and snot mixed with her tears. After each word she'd bawl, or at least whimper messily.

"If I don't get you to hand it all over they'll blame me. They expected me to get it from Buse, but I failed. I'm in a tight spot. First they accused me of holding on to it, of keeping something that lucrative for myself. They came after me . . . came down on me hard . . . tortured me . . ."

"Are you telling me it's up to you and you alone to recover the pictures?"

"Yes . . . I was given the job right from the start, and I'm expected to finish it. But how much power have I really got? How much influence do I have? Compared to them, what can I be expected to do? Who am I? I'm just a washed-up poor old transvestite."

This was hard to swallow. It's true that she'd aged, and I agreed that she no longer worked her old magic, but the last word I expected to be used in connection with Sofya was "poor." If that was true of Sofya, what could be said about the other girls, the ones who were truly hard up?

"Just look at me!" she said, rising, turning around and lifting up her T-shirt. She was badly bruised.

"I'm so sorry," I murmured. *It'll pass, no one stays bruised forever,* was what I said to myself.

"If I manage to locate and hand over the pictures and letters I'll be back in their good books. They won't regard me as just another low-level foot soldier. I could become one of them, a real part of the system. And I've always dreamed about a big payment, a comfortable retirement. The chance to travel around the world a couple of times, to go on a cruise . . . If I don't find those photos, I'm afraid they'll kill me."

She let out a great sob to punctuate that final sentence.

"You mean the way they killed that old lady upstairs?" I had to ask.

"Look, that whole thing's a bit complicated. One of our men went to the wrong floor, as you know. When the lady made trouble . . . it was unfortunate but necessary."

She illustrated her point with a finger cocked at her head.

"It's terribly sad, of course, but it was too late by the time they realized they'd entered the wrong flat. Naturally, the person responsible was punished. When they went down to the floor below they were unable to find either the blind woman or a single piece of paper."

"So where is Sabiha, then?" I asked.

"We didn't do a thing. We're asking the same question."

"Well, if you didn't take her off somewhere, who did?"

Now it was time for both of us to be astonished. I was suddenly wide awake.

Chapter 26

❖

Sofya and I just sat there staring at each other. She scrutinized me suspiciously; I did the same to her. The minutes passed.

"I might as well make some coffee," I said, breaking the silence. "It looks like we could both use a cup."

"That'd be great," she said.

"A little fat wouldn't do me any harm, I suppose. Look, I'm still thin as a whip." I stood up and ran my hands up and down my body as I said this. A girl has got to retain her sense of poise under all circumstances.

I went to the kitchen. Before I'd even filled the machine, she was at my side.

"If Buse's mother took the pictures and ran—" she began.

"She's a sharper woman than we thought," I said. I threw in an extra measure of coffee.

"But that's totally impossible," Sofya protested. "The woman's blind. How would she understand what was going on?"

"I don't get it, either," I admitted. "What's more, Buse told me her mother didn't know a thing about what she got up to. That it was possible to get away with anything at her flat, or to hide anything she wished."

"This is ridiculous," she said.

It was getting light. I felt the morning chill, and shivered.

"I'll go and put something on."

"You'd better," she said. "Running around like a third-rate

porn star, half your ass showing. A real woman retains an air of mystery."

"Weren't you the one who advised me to show off my assets?" I asked. "Well, that's exactly what I'm doing. And it's hard as a rock, crisp and fresh."

In view of the fact that our lives were possibly in danger and we had no idea how to proceed, our dialogue was beyond belief. I put on my long-suffering pashmina. I'd been wrapping it around myself at every opportunity for the last two days. I returned to the kitchen.

"Sofya," I said, "you didn't kidnap Sabiha Hanım, I saw no sign of her, even the nosy neighbor didn't notice a thing. So how did she manage to just up and disappear without a trace, especially being blind and all?"

"Good question. I suspected you. I even had you followed for a while."

"I don't believe it, Sofya! You had me followed?"

"What's the big deal, sweetie? How else was I supposed to know what you were up to?"

"So you're saying you sent a man after me?"

Sofya was totally unpredictable. Her moral code inclined her to view as fair and square absolutely anything she chose to do. In that sense, she was a completely unfettered person. She'd do whatever she had to in order to get her way. I shouldn't have been surprised.

"It would be more accurate to say 'men' rather than 'man.' I'd hoped you'd lead us to Sabiha, but instead you foolishly wasted all your time in that building."

"But I had no idea she was missing."

The coffee was ready. I handed her a mug. She could pour it herself.

We sipped our coffees in silence. Sofya lit a cigarette. One of those thin More cigarettes that so beautifully accent her long, tapering fingers. By the time we finished, the sun had come up. My flat was filling with the morning light I love so much. I got up and turned off the lamp. Sofya's makeup-free face looked even worse under the natural light. I was getting sleepy.

"I'm not sure whether or not to believe you," she said. She fixed that piercing stare on me again.

"Do whatever you want," I said. "I'm tired. I've had it. Just when I thought I was free of those thugs you'd sent after me I found myself leaping out of a moving car. I couldn't care less anymore. All I want to do is sleep."

"So you're telling me to go."

"Implying you should go, yes. Of course, you can stay here if you like. I'll put you in the guest room, last slept in by Buse. You'll be comfortable. God knows I stayed at your place often enough."

"Do you realize that if I leave here empty-handed there's no saying what'll happen to me? I can't bear the thought of it. It'll be a lot more difficult for me to convince them than it was for you to convince me. They expect me to come up with those pictures."

"So are you saying there's someone waiting outside the door even as we speak?"

"I don't know. There shouldn't be. I didn't plant anyone outside. But there's no way for me to know for sure. I'm not in on everything. If someone else is now involved I have no way of knowing what they'll do."

We exchanged a long look.

"Sweetie," she said, "no one gives a damn about the blind lady, but if you have the letters or photos and you hand them over, it'll make your life a whole lot easier. They might even make you a handsome payment. You wouldn't have to hang out at the club all night. If there's some guy you fancy, just tell me his name. You can keep him at home, use him all you like. Whatever your heart desires."

"Sofya, you really don't believe me, do you?"

"I can't decide. I don't know anything anymore. I want to believe you, but I can't. My instincts are sending mixed signals. Something tells me you haven't been completely open with me. I've got no idea what it is; it's just intuition. So I just can't decide whether or not to believe you."

"Maybe it's because of what we went through together all those years ago."

"It could be," she admitted. "Whatever. At the moment, I believe you. But that could change later. That's why I'd better get going. I don't know how to handle them. I'm sure I'll find a way. Or at least I'll try. I suggest you use your head, keep your ears pricked, and call me the second you hear anything."

She stood up and walked toward the door. When she caught herself in the mirror, she stood up straight, pulled back her shoulders, and ran her hand through her hair. It would take a lot more to bring back the old Sofya, but that bit of effort did her good. She took a pair of sunglasses from the little basket next to the door and put them on. Then she examined herself in the mirror once again. It was most definitely an improvement.

"It's light outside. I can't go out like this. Lend me the glasses. I'll return them."

In order to get rid of her as soon as possible I'd have been prepared to throw in my favorite dress with the sunglasses.

"But of course. You're welcome to them."

Blowing kisses over each other's shoulders, we said our farewells. She turned and left.

I took a deep breath. It had been an eventful and tense night, but it had ended calmly and easily. Handling Sofya had been as easy as pulling a hair out of soft butter. That was strange. I was too tired to ponder it. It was nearly seven.

Not even bothering to take the mugs to the kitchen, I headed straight for the bedroom. The flat was a mess in any case. I'd sort it out later. After all, some people lived like the lady journalist. Two mugs and a Napolitano coffeemaker were no big deal.

On the way to the bedroom, I noticed the envelope I'd prepared for Ali. If I went to bed now, there was no telling how late in the afternoon I'd get up. It would be best to call the taxi stand now and arrange for the envelope to be dropped off at about ten.

Using my final ounce of strength, I called the stand, explaining what I wanted. I asked for someone to be sent over immediately. I would, of course, tip them extra for their courier services. Hanging up the phone, I proceeded to the bedroom, where I drew the heavy curtains. I heard the taxi honk in front of the building.

I decided against my usual practice of tossing the envelope from the living room window with shouted instructions. If I was really being followed, as Sofya claimed, it might cause a misunderstanding. I didn't want the driver to get into trouble. Sleepy or not, I had apparently retained my faculties. But I hadn't asked for the driver to come to my door. He'd honk the horn until I appeared at the window.

I was just about to call the taxi stand again, praying my phone wasn't bugged, when I heard a rustling at the door. It was the silly boy from the corner market delivering my morning newspapers. I raced to the door and caught him. He seemed frightened by the sight of me, even taking a step backward.

He was right to do so. I was an unusual sight. The poor boy had never seen me in all my finery. It was unlikely he'd ever seen anyone like me at all. He was still quite young. If he liked what he saw, he'd dream about it for a night or two, that was all. Contrary to the folk wisdom of old school psychologists, a glimpse of a man in women's clothing does not mean a certain future as a homosexual. I've never known it to have that effect.

I told him what to do, pressing some change into his hand.

He listened, eyes fixed on me. After asking him to repeat what I'd told him, I sent him off. I decided not to watch from the window, in case I was being observed. I waited patiently until I heard the taxi drive off.

I waited a few minutes, then called the taxi stand. Yes, they had the envelope. The boy had told them not to deliver it before ten, "under any circumstances." They knew the address, having delivered there before.

I took off my shorts, which pinched like a corset, especially around the waist. I kept on the T-shirt as a precaution against the morning chill. I could now sleep in peace. As the reward for a hectic, exciting day, that's all I asked for.

Chapter 27

✣

It was well after noon by the time I woke up. I'd had a short, troubled sleep. While I don't need much rest, I needed more than I'd got. I'd been bombarded with film images, struggling with a blackmail operation just like the evil SPECTRE organization in the James Bond movies. The faces of the company chairmen, whoever they were, didn't appear in my dream. But I could hear their perverted, growling voices as they made death threats to their victims.

Sofya appeared as a diabolical woman based on the role played by Lotte Lenya in *From Russia with Love*. The wife of composer Kurt Weill in real life, in the film she played a Russian agent working for SPECTRE. Daggers would pop out of the tips of her shoes, and she fought to the death with Bond. Lenya's homeliness didn't really mesh with Sofya's beauty, but so be it, it was just a dream. Sofya would have been much more appropriate as Pussy Galore, the character played by Honor Blackman in *Goldfinger,* or perhaps as Luciana Paluzzi in *Thunderball*.

Anyway, in my dream Lotte Lenya-Sofya and Süleyman, played by whomever, were standing in front of their boss, dejected at having failed to recover Buse's letters and photos. Their fastidious boss was stroking a fluffy white cat as he listened to them. The more they tried to explain themselves, the more frantic they got, and they started accusing each other and begging for forgiveness. They asked for one last chance.

Süleyman was ready to admit to anything as he sank to his knees and pleaded for his life. He was a sorry creature indeed. He'd lost any and all shreds of dignity and breeding. It was a moving scene, but I was unable to feel any pity for him. The boss pressed a button under his desk. As Sofya looked on with eyes widened in terror, Süleyman writhed as though fried by an electrical current. And died.

Speechless and terrified, Sofya received a set of new orders. I didn't hear what they were. My dream had ended.

I ran through the images in my head as I prepared my coffee. The conclusions I reached were highly unpleasant: Someone thought I had the blackmail materials. Yes, they were mistaken. But they didn't know that. And they weren't satisfied with my explanations. And now they were out to get me.

As I scanned the papers, I listened to my answering machine. Hasan had left a message informing me that the funeral would be held the following day after noon prayers. It was to take place in Samatya at a mosque I'd never even heard of. The service had been arranged by whoever the family members were who had claimed the body. It'd be a good idea to stop by the funeral if I had failed by noon the following day to sort everything out. It would give me a chance to see who was attending the funeral, or at least find out who had claimed the body.

There were two more messages in which the caller hadn't bothered to speak. Of course, it infuriated me. I was tense enough as it was, and, after the nightmares, this was the final straw.

If it hadn't been so hot, I would have gone to the gym to work off some toxins and stress. I suppose I could always go to an air-conditioned gym. I'd exercise and look over my fellow enthusiasts.

And the showers are always a mine of titillation. Some look

down their noses at me at first, but when they see that I'm every bit as fit as them, if not more, their attitude changes and they approach me one by one. All that's left for me to do is choose between them. If I time my exit to the showers just right, I'm flooded with offers to lather up my back. What follows is limited only by their imaginations and my inclinations.

But it really was a hot day. Air-conditioned or not, I didn't feel like going to a fitness center. Neither the desire to maintain my figure nor the thought of shower play was enough to entice me from my home.

I thought it best to sit lazily where I was. I'd watch TV or pick a DVD from off my shelf.

I took a shower to wake up more fully. The cool spray brought me to my senses. As I stepped out, the phone rang. I was soaking wet, and didn't want to drip water everywhere as I ran to the phone. I listened carefully as I dried myself off, close enough to the answering machine to hear any messages.

It was Turkey's first and only certified hypnotherapist, Cem Yeğenoğlu. He wished me a good Sunday in his brightest voice. I raced to the phone just in time to catch him. After the usual pleasantries, I asked him for his professional opinion: Could someone be hypnotized without realizing it? If hypnotized, how much would a person reveal? Can you trust what someone says under hypnosis?

He listened carefully without interrupting.

"The answer to all your questions is yes!" he announced. "Although we don't advise it, hypnosis of the kind you mention is done. Looking directly into the patient's eyes can be enough to set off a hypnotic trance. In fact, by simply ordering the patient to 'look at me, look at me,' followed by a sharp jab with a single finger in the center of the forehead, a hypnotic trance can be initiated. As I told you, however, this is not something we advise or implement."

His use of the third-person plural "we" would imply that there were others, like himself, who had been certified in America. Considering his claim to be the first and only certified hypnotherapist in Turkey, I wondered who they were. If they existed, I'd never heard of them. No, I think this was simply a case of using the royal "we."

"Statements made by patients under hypnosis are generally accurate. That is, unless the patient is induced to tell a falsehood. The wishes of the patient are also important. We do not consider it ethical to hypnotize anyone without his permission and full knowledge."

He'd answered all my questions. Buse could have spoken under hypnosis. The question of who would have hypnotized her, and under what conditions, was one I could not answer.

"So is just anyone able to hypnotize others?" I asked.

"It's not that simple," the doctor replied. "Technically, the answer is yes, anyone can do it. A little information, a course, would suffice. In fact, some do it as a hobby. But it only works if the subject is open to being hypnotized. Technically speaking, there is little chance of success otherwise. In order to be a truly effective hypnotist, however, years of training are required."

"I know that. You told me earlier. What I'd really like to know is, would it be possible for someone to hypnotize someone else just for the fun of it? Without being certified or anything."

"Of course it would be. And there are those who do, particularly these days. A woman from Portugal even offers them some sort of so-called training. She's been churning out hypnotists left and right. My website and I are both bombarded with questions. There's so much they don't know . . . Sometimes they find themselves in a bind and panic. Then they come to me. Oh, by the way, the site could do with updating. It wouldn't be a major project, just adding some links and some of my more recent photographs. You'll be able to help me, won't you?"

It was no time to refuse, or to demand payment. He'd been of use and had immediately demanded payment in kind. He was prompt about settling all debts. The answering machine was still on. It announced with a piercingly unpleasant tone that the message was full, and switched itself off.

Mimicking the sound, I said, "Of course."

"Come by today if it suits you. I'm free. It's summer. Everyone's on holiday; I have few clients for therapy."

Now, that was a bit too prompt. I couldn't be expected to be free just because he was. I saw no need for such immediate repayment.

"I won't be available," I said. "Unless it's urgent, I'll give you a call soon and we'll sort something out. I'm a bit weighed down with work at the moment."

"I'll be going on holiday next Saturday. It'd be nice to be finished by then."

I was at his command. As if I didn't have enough on my plate, I'd now have to update his website.

"I don't think I'll be able to," I said. "I've taken on so much. And next week will be even busier. Maybe later. Let me finish what I've got and I'll give you a call."

His reaction was far more reasonable than I'd expected, thankfully. We hung up, promising to speak again as soon as possible.

There was no reason to leave the conversation recorded on my answering machine. I pushed the erase button. I began spreading lotion on my body, my conversation with Cem playing in the background. I started with my shoulders, working my way down. My skin became beautifully slick; I nearly started desiring myself.

One word that Cem had said suddenly caught my attention: "Portugal." I hadn't noted it when we were talking, but now I remembered that he had specifically mentioned a hypnotist from Portugal. The lady journalist whose name I'd never learned was also from Portugal. It could be a coincidence. But then again, it might not be.

Excited, I sloshed lotion onto my legs. I wanted to visit the journalist as soon as possible. I threw on some clothes.

As I was going out the door the phone rang, but I didn't answer. As I locked the door, Ali's voice floated out. Good—I assumed he'd received the package and had called to chat.

Chapter 28

✤

$\mathcal{I}$ gave the waiting taxi driver the address. It was one of the older drivers. Given the slightest encouragement, he'd hold forth on any subject.

As we drove up the ramp to the main motorway, he began:

"I was just about to deliver your package this morning when a customer came. Hüseyin handled it instead. That young friend of yours."

So Hüseyin was back in action. For whatever that was worth. Strange, the way he seemed to show up whenever there was a crisis.

"Good," I said.

My tone of voice suggested I was not interested in further conversation. The driver interpreted it correctly.

It suddenly hit me. I'd sent the envelope early in the morning, but hadn't gone to the window to see who the driver was. I'd also warned them to make sure it wasn't delivered before ten a.m. Hüseyin had been at the club the previous night, flirting with tubby Müjde. If he'd arrived at work by ten, then nothing much could have happened between them. I wondered how much Müjde had cost him. Or had she serviced him for free, on account of his good looks and youth?

Some of the girls do that. If they run into someone they like, they'll say, "This one's on the house," and off they go. Although I don't think much of him, Hüseyin is actually a good-looking guy. Müjde could well have been attracted to him. It's not like anyone decent ever approaches her. We called her our "country gal." Because of her plumpness, only those with a predilection for some extra cushioning—that is, country men visiting the big city, mostly middle-aged and older—prefer her. During those rare periods when she adheres to her diet she bargains ferociously, but when her figure is at its fullest, she'll go for the first bidder, not playing hard to get.

The motorway was riddled with road works, as it always is in summer. And as always on a Sunday, everyone in Istanbul takes their family out sightseeing. Any bit of grass, or area shaded by a tree, was a potential picnic spot. The nauseating smell of grilling meat wafted into the open window of the taxi from all directions.

"Just look at this; everyone's dumped their cars in the middle of the road. What if there was an emergency? There's no way we'd get through!" I complained. I said all this without thinking. Otherwise, I had no intention of encouraging the driver.

"Isn't that the truth, sir," he began, leaping at the chance to make conversation. "Traffic is the worst on Sundays. The roads are pretty clear until noon, but after that it's a nightmare. If we'd tried to go to the Bosphorus we wouldn't have made it. That's how packed it is. I went last week. As if getting there wasn't bad enough, it took me two hours to get back. As you can imagine, it meant I was out of pocket. It's because of the coast road, Bağdat Caddesi. Take Hüseyin, for example. Off he went all those hours ago and he still hadn't returned by the time you called. He may have picked up a fare on the way back, but even so . . ."

So Hüseyin hadn't returned from his trip to the office. Ali had called me just as I left. I didn't know what he had said, but the fact that he called surely meant the envelope had been delivered. Traffic on the way to Maslak could be heavy, thanks to the day-trippers heading to Belgrade Forest and the beach in Kilyos, but Hüseyin had left at ten, and should have avoided the worst of it. Maybe he was so tired from the previous night he'd pulled over for a nap.

"Just come out and say it: that delivery is going to cost me a fortune."

"That's not what I meant, sir. You'll only pay what the meter says. It's not like you're a stranger. I was just letting you know how bad the traffic must be."

"Yes," I said. My one-word reply meant it was time to shut up again. He understood.

We'd arrived in any case. I paid him and got out.

As I entered the apartment building, someone else was coming down the stairs. I don't normally look at strangers, preferring to maintain a certain aloofness, but something told me to look up, so I did. I suppose what really made me look closely was the dark suit. I mean, who wears a suit on a hot Sunday afternoon? As we passed each other on the stairs I recognized him: It was the man with the high-pitched voice who'd been standing guard in Sabiha Hanım's flat. A chill ran up my spine. He recognized me as well, and spun around on his heel as he reached the landing, taking a long look at me. On his right cheekbone was a huge bandage. His colored eyes flickered coldly. He had the look of a natural-born killer.

We exchanged glances for a split second, then he quickly exited the apartment building. I considered chasing after him. If he wasn't armed, I could catch and interrogate him. In other words, despite my vows of the previous night, I was prepared to dive right back into this.

Either he wasn't after me or he'd decided that this wasn't the place to dispose of me. And if he wasn't after me, he must have come for the lady journalist. One thing was clear, they now knew exactly where I was.

I raced up to the third floor. I'd expected an open door, even a body inside, but the door to the flat was firmly shut.

I rang the bell. Shortly afterward, the door swung open. More accurately, the head of the journalist poked out from the partly opened door. She was one of those rare people who look really bad in light blue. In her blouse of that color, she looked like a corpse.

"*Merhaba*," I greeted her. "I'd like to speak to you, if you have a moment."

She was clearly displeased to see me. You'd have thought that the woman who'd hit on me, who'd pinched and prodded me, was a distant relation of hers. She looked tense.

"I'm not really free. I have a guest."

Her hair was in disarray. Had I caught her at a delicate moment? Considering how sex-mad she had been the previous day, it was highly likely she'd have resumed the hunt once she woke up sober and alone.

"It won't take long. Please, it's very important," I pleaded.

She looked surprised. I realized that she wasn't listening to me. She was barely aware of my presence at all.

"All right, then, but I really am busy at the moment. I'm discussing something urgent with a friend," she said.

My insistence must have done the trick. She stepped aside to let me in.

Occupying my spot of the previous day was none other than—surprise—that pansy of a reporter, Ahmet. With his two-day stubble, messy hair, and swollen eyes he looked to be well over forty. It was hard to believe that a nancy boy like him could be up to anything erotic with the journalist, but you can't underestimate the powers of a driven woman. Bedding a man like Ahmet was a test of wills some couldn't resist.

He shook my hand without rising from his seat. His hand was greasy and moist. I found him repulsive, and knew no one who felt otherwise, but there's no telling what becomes desirable once hormones reach a certain level. My presence clearly disturbed him.

Moving closer to the lady journalist, I asked, "Can we speak in private?"

"Certainly, that'd be better. Let's go to the kitchen," she agreed, preparing to lead the way. Her phone rang before she'd advanced two steps. She apologized, returning to the living room to answer it.

In rapid succession, she said hello, opened her eyes wide, and looked directly at me. Naturally, my suspicions were aroused. I listened intently to her end of the conversation.

"Yes," she said, her eyes still on me. "All right, then, we'll handle it," she interjected, before listening to the caller for a considerable time.

As she listened, she kept her eyes trained on me, glancing away only when I caught her eye. I was sure she was talking about me, probably with the thug I'd encountered in the stairwell. I was the one to be "handled" and "we" referred to herself and Ahmet. This is what is known as "falling into their lap." So the lady journalist was involved, and Ahmet was also in on it. It seemed everyone I knew was working for these people.

I needed to formulate a strategic plan—and quickly. I smiled at her, as though I had no idea what was going on. She responded with a tense smile of her own, then hung up the phone.

We went to the kitchen. It was even filthier than the rest of the flat. On a piece of newspaper on the floor were watermelon rinds several days old.

"Would you mind waiting just a second? I need to tell Ahmet something, so he can continue working while we talk," she said.

Leaving me on my own in the kitchen, she left, closing the door securely behind her. So that was it; she'd come up with a plan and was briefing Ahmet on their course of action. He didn't seem particularly strong, but there was no knowing what he'd do if cornered. I panicked.

The huge knife used earlier to carve the watermelon rested on the table. Its steel blade was dull with rust and dried juice. I grabbed it. As a precaution, I carefully kept the hand holding the knife behind my back as I sat at the table.

The door opened, and she came back in. My grip tightened on the concealed knife. She leaned on the table and pulled a pack of cigarettes out of her pocket.

"All right, I'm listening. What is it you want?"

She blew smoke in my face. Scrutinizing me carefully, then looking me straight in the eye, she began doing something strange with her eyes, narrowing and widening them. She may have been trying to hypnotize me.

"Did you study hypnosis in Portugal?"

"Yes," she answered, instantly abandoning the odd winking game.

"You continued after you returned to Turkey?"

"Well, of course I did. It's not like journalists get paid that much. I mean, some do, but most earn what I do. There's a lot I do for a bit of spare income. Why do you ask? Are you interested in the subject?"

"You could say that," I said. "Did you hypnotize Buse? To get her to talk?"

I'd adopted the tactic of being short and sweet. She looked a bit shaken. She took a deep drag on her cigarette. First she glanced at the floor, then the ceiling, and at last right at me. A guttural "Yes" emerged in a cloud of smoke.

"I suspected as much," I said. "That will be all. Thank you. I really don't want to disturb you further."

I knew all I needed to. Buse had been under hypnosis when she revealed everything. There was no reason for me to remain in this filthy, foul-smelling flat. The sooner I got out, the better. I casually eased the knife onto the floor, on top of the newspaper, and got up from the table. She stopped me.

"Is that it?"

"Yes," I said. "You were expecting more? That's all I was interested in."

I was prepared to answer no to whatever her next question was. I wanted out. She laughed softly.

"Come on, let's not play games," she said.

"Fine."

I regretted having given up the knife. Squatting quickly, I retrieved it, then stepped back, leaning against the wall.

"What do you want?" I asked.

"What do *you* want?" she countered. "Leave me out of this. I swear I didn't do anything. Ahmet's the one who's mixed up in it."

I had no doubt of that last statement, but knew that the journalist couldn't be entirely innocent, either. She looked like she was hiding something.

"What is going on here?"

She was clearly hesitating over whether or not to speak. "Things got out of hand," she said. "Maybe you can help."

Help? I was out to save my own ass.

"Listen," she continued, "Buse asked me to use hypnosis to help kick her drug habit. That's why she came to me. I later realized how sensitive she was to suggestion. When we'd finished her therapy, I tried again. It was easy, and she began talking about her past, her life. Believe me, I wasn't expecting anything or plotting anything. All I cared about was an exclusive, a five-page spread, maybe even a front-page headline."

She sat in the chair I'd vacated, the only one in the kitchen. She stubbed out her cigarette on a dirty plate. Looking at me, she continued:

"Then, like I told you, my story was censored. I was so pissed off. That's when Ahmet came in. When he saw how upset I was, he comforted me, and I told him everything."

So that was it. Queer or not, Ahmet was screwing her when he could. So that's how he maintained his manhood. The business about comforting her was just an excuse.

"He's the one who had the idea of selling the information. I was angry at the newspaper. It seemed like a reasonable proposition, so I agreed. We tried to get into Buse's house, but failed. That's when Ahmet arranged Kayhan."

"That icy number I ran into on the stairs?" I asked.

"That's him. He recognized you, too."

"He's the one who called, isn't he?"

"That's right," she said, suddenly laughing hysterically. She covered her mouth with a hand, fumbled for another cigarette.

"But you just put one out," I said, pointing to the butt on the plate.

She shrugged and lit another. Then she once again stubbed out the butt on the plate, which was still smoking.

"Kayhan is a professional thief. There's not a door he can't open. But when he arrived to break into Buse's flat, someone else was already inside. Someone had broken in before us."

"Bad timing," I commented.

"We were shocked to hear Buse was dead. When we learned it was murder, we were terrified. All we had in mind was a simple case of blackmail. And maybe theft. That's all. We were scared, so we gave up on the whole idea."

"Really?" I said. "Then what was iceman Kayhan doing in Sabiha Hanım's flat?"

"Ahmet got the address from the mortuary correspondent. He thought we should give it another try, said we had nothing to lose. Maybe the photos and letters were still there. That's when you and the neighbor found Kayhan."

"The poor boy doesn't seem to have much luck."

What I really meant was that he was a hopeless failure, but I held my tongue.

"You're right. We've all been pretty unlucky."

She hesitated. She was about to say something else, but couldn't for some reason. So these two had also been after the photos and letters. We had Süreyya Eronat and his men, Sofya and the Mafia, and a couple of amateur reporters. It was amazing. If Buse were alive, she'd be thrilled.

"Now," she continued, "they think we have the photos. They're after us. They nabbed Kayhan, threatened him."

"So the bandage on his cheek . . ."

"They beat him. He gave them Ahmet's name, and now Ahmet is beside himself. So am I. What are we supposed to do? We haven't got a thing. All I have is the tape, but you have the original. Please, try to understand . . ."

"But what can I do?"

"You mean you aren't working with them?"

We exchanged surprised looks. Now it was my turn to laugh. How could anyone be so stupid? If I'd really been working with them—the Hedef Party's men or the Mafia—what on earth would I be doing in this flat right now? If I was one of them, why would I have needed the chubby-cheeked neighbor to get into the flat? Her husband was right to have left her. What woman could be so filthy and unkempt, live in such a messy flat, and be so stupid to boot?

That she had ever married at all was a miracle.

"I'm in the exact same situation that you are. Someone thinks I have the blackmail materials," I said.

She gasped.

"Let's go in and tell Ahmet. We thought you'd come here to threaten us. Kayhan was especially nervous after seeing the men waiting downstairs."

"Men waiting downstairs?"

It was my turn to gasp.

We joined Ahmet in the living room. As she filled him in, I peered out the window. On the street below waited two men in a dark car. They saw me. I gave a halfhearted wave. It was silly, but it was the only thing that came to mind. At least I didn't smile.

So Sofya's little helpers had been following me. I hadn't taken any precautions when I woke up. And now I'd been tracked to this flat. This was just great!

Ahmet had gone from looking edgy to looking rather sheepish.

"Believe me, I had no idea this was going to turn out to be such a mess," he said. "Otherwise I'd never have got involved. I mean, if I was really into this sort of thing, why would I bother running around the city with my camera for a living?"

He may have been telling the truth, but he was still the one who'd arranged the inept burglar, Kayhan. There was still something dark about Ahmet.

There was no reason for me to spend any more time with the panicked journalist and Ahmet. At most, we could wring our hands and try to console each other. There was no need for that.

I wondered where to go when I left them: If I went home, the men would follow me, and I'd be under observation. I had to shake them off somehow. But where could I go?

The one place I'd always considered safe, my refuge, was my home. If something went wrong, if I was at all troubled, that's where I'd go. And now the Mafia was posted just outside my building. My most personal spot in the whole world, no longer safe. It was a distressing thought.

Ahmet and the journalist had opened a bottle of wine and were snuggled up together on the sofa, comforting each other.

They told each other that things would turn out all right. That must have been what they were doing when I interrupted. At this rate, they wouldn't get to first base. Both lacked any fervor. Passionless sex is not for me. I disapprove.

As I looked at them I also felt pity. They kept asking each other what they should do next. It was pathetic.

"Why don't you just hand over the cassette, then? Save your skins!" I suggested.

"But they wouldn't believe that the tape is all we have," said the journalist.

"Tell them exactly what you told me," I advised. "You never know, they might believe you."

I didn't find my own advice particularly credible, but I was fed up with their whining. No one is truly desperate; it's just a question of taking unpalatable actions.

"Do you really think so?" she asked.

"We could try," said Ahmet. "Let's go down and hand it over."

"They'll suddenly be faced with a cassette they know nothing about. And a copy, at that. We'll just end up making things worse," she argued.

She had a point.

"You still have the original, don't you?" she asked.

"Yes, at home."

"What about handing that over? We could go down and talk to them. You could take them to your flat, give it to them. This whole nightmare would be over! What do you say?"

The journalist obviously believed that this would be the best solution and wanted it done as soon as possible.

The cassette could never be used as evidence; what's more, any gossip could make the same claims. Without proof, words had no importance. The source was a dead transvestite, as unreliable a source as any. The cassette wouldn't do us any good.

We'd heard all we needed to and even had a copy. There was no reason not to hand over the original.

"Fine," I said. They brightened.

Taking the copy as a precaution, the three of us trooped down the stairs. We headed straight for the car.

Two men were eating *dürüm* inside. They couldn't be expected to go without eating as they followed me around all day. They, too, had needs, got hungry and thirsty. They were drinking cans of cola. As we approached, they straightened. The window was open. I was hit by the smell of raw onions.

I began making our case, but the journalist and photographer kept interrupting. So I shut up and stepped to one side. After all, they were reporters.

The men in the car listened expressionlessly. They were third-rate henchmen. I suspected they hadn't even been briefed. They'd just been instructed to follow me and phone their boss, whoever he was, to report my moves. The idiot reporters started from the beginning, with Buse's murder, and mentioned Süreyya Eronat numerous times. When his name was mentioned the men in the car seemed to shift slightly, smiling oddly. My stomach turned.

The long-winded explanation took ages, but eventually they finished.

"Give us the tape, then," said the man in the passenger seat.

"We can't. It's at his flat."

Ahmet pointed to me as he said this.

"Let's go there, then," ordered the driver.

He was clearly stupid. The three of us got into the back seat. Mixed with the stench of *dürüm* and onions was the tang of sweat. If we'd intended to attack them, the two in the front were completely defenseless. As it was, we had no intention of making trouble.

I didn't have to give them directions. They knew the way.

Chapter 29

✥

I handed over the tape and the four of them left.

It couldn't be this quick and easy. Here I was again, at home. Home, sweet home. I was probably still under surveillance. After all, the only thing they'd been able to get their hands on was a cassette, not the letters or photos.

I was just about to get in the shower when the phone rang. It was Sofya.

"What's this cassette? What's this all about?"

It was impossible for the cassette to have reached her so quickly. And it was beyond impossible for her to have listened to it.

"It's an interview Buse gave before she died. In it she talks about everyone she's ever slept with."

"Even him?"

"Yes," I confirmed.

"Why didn't you give it to me? You've had it all along." She'd reverted to her ill-tempered self.

"I didn't think it was of any use. Tapes can't be used as evidence."

"We'll decide that."

And she hung up.

They were astonishingly quick. Amazing.

After showering I got into bed, still wet. I'd scrubbed off the filth of the journalist's flat. There was still no news of Buse's killers. The police must have relegated her case to the unsolved murders file. I'd failed at everything I'd set out to do. I hadn't found the letters and photos, rescued Buse's blind mother, or discovered who'd murdered her. I'd been kidnapped and threatened, and torn my favorite cotton dress. All for nothing. The scratches and bruises were an added bonus.

If they were satisfied with the tape, and I doubted that, I wanted to wash my hands of the whole affair. I felt thoroughly exhausted, but I couldn't sleep. I decided to settle in front of the TV with a cup of fennel tea. I filled the kettle with just enough water.

While waiting for it to boil, I went over to the answering machine and pushed the button. There would be the message Ali had left just as I was leaving the apartment. From the kitchen, where I'd returned to make my tea, I heard Ali's voice:

"Happy Sunday, it's me, Ali. I'm in the office, working. I'd expected you to send me something. It's going on two o'clock. I'll be leaving soon. I just wondered how you were. Call me when you can. Good-bye."

I couldn't believe my ears. He hadn't received the envelope I'd sent. I'd told the men at the stand to deliver it after ten, and from what the other driver had told me, that's exactly what Hüseyin did. But the envelope had never reached Ali. There was something funny going on.

I called Ali immediately. He always carries his cell phone. He answered on the second ring.

"Oooo, *merhaba,* or should I say good morning, maybe even good evening," he began.

"Ali, did you get the envelope I sent?"

"No," he said. "I left you a message telling you I was about to leave the office. I stayed for about another hour but I never got an envelope."

"Something has gone wrong here. I gave the envelope to the

taxi stand early this morning and told them to deliver it after ten. A driver who knows where the office is took it and went off to deliver it to you."

"He may have left it with the doorman, but I never got it. You know, I saw Nevzat Efendi on the way out, and he didn't say a word."

So Nevzat Efendi was the doorman as well as the gardener.

After I hung up, I tried to put my thoughts in order. I'd given the envelope to the corner-market boy with instructions to hand it on to the driver waiting in front of the building. The man at the taxi stand later confirmed having received it. Then the old, chatty driver told me that Hüseyin had left at about ten with the envelope, but hadn't yet returned, well after noon. So the envelope had set off for Ali's office, but hadn't made it.

I'd had my doubts about Hüseyin all along. He seemed to pop up at the most opportune times. He might have wondered what was in the envelope and opened it up. He could have thought it was something personal. But I had even worse suspicions. What if Hüseyin had been in on it all along? If so, whose side was he on? He couldn't have been one of Süreyya's men. They'd jump back three paces if you so much as mentioned the word "homosexual." But Hüseyin . . . he had no such aversion. He might be working with Sofya. Or even operating alone. He'd told me all about his dreams of being a proper detective, wanting to work with me. None of the thoughts running through my head seemed entirely unlikely.

Perhaps the building had been under surveillance when I sent off the envelope, just as it could be right now. They'd have noted the sending of a package. And if they'd seen Hüseyin out with me the first night, it was only natural they'd assume he was of importance, perhaps even tailing him as well. Hüseyin was certainly an attractive enough quarry for either the Hedef Party's men or the Mafia.

Just thinking about it gave me a terrible headache. I went to the bathroom and took two painkillers. From my eyebrows to my hairline, my entire forehead throbbed. It was a sensation closely resembling a guilty conscience. In fact, there was no reason for me to blame myself, or to hold myself responsible in any way. But such reasoned thinking did nothing to alleviate my aching head.

Part of me even thought Hüseyin fully deserved whatever he got. There were his airs, his clumsy, hopeless attempts at seducing me, the fact that he'd come to the club two nights in a row, no doubt using my name at the door to get in, and then the way he'd ended up with that tub of lard, Müjde. But despite my wounded pride and desire for revenge, I still couldn't talk myself into wishing harm to Hüseyin. I have a heart of gold, maybe even platinum—at the very least diamond-encrusted. It was distressing indeed to imagine Hüseyin getting into trouble because he'd been sent on an errand of mine.

I rang the taxi stand and calmly asked if Hüseyin was there. The person who answered was, I think, a friend of Hüseyin's, a guy with a shaved head and tattoos on his hand. "He hasn't come back yet. I'll send him along when he does," he said in an unpleasantly cloying voice.

My serenity only recently restored, I felt a surge of anger. A little voice told me to run to the stand, grab the guy by the throat, and beat the crap out of him. That'd be one way to vent my frustration!

I often ignore that little voice, and that's what I did this time too. Settling into my favorite chair, I removed from its plastic wrapper a computer magazine delivered three days earlier. But I hadn't forgotten the offensive friend, and would get him one day. I leafed through the magazine, my mind on the future drubbing. If I'd felt like reading, there was page after page of mostly useless information. I had more pressing things to focus on, however. Finishing my tea, I got up.

I began pacing through the flat. It's what I most often do when I need to concentrate on a certain subject. I clean, throw out whatever I don't need, sort through my possessions, even move the furniture sometimes. I tolerate the changes for a few days. Then, when the cleaning lady comes on Monday, everything goes back to its original spot and I feel better. The first task I faced was the heap of things spread across the sofa, everything from a pair of underwear and a single earring to old notebooks and photographs. I began quickly picking up and discarding things. Out of an old photo album fell a music hall photo, the kind they take at your table and sell to you that same night. Old black and white photographs were stapled onto the cardboard frame. As I looked through them, I suddenly had another realization. Buse had posed in Ferruh's arms one day when we went out together in a large group. Belkıs was not in the picture; she must not have been among us.

Now I understood why Ferruh kept trying to talk to me. When I'd left them that night at the club, Buse had been headed over to their table. I knew they'd once indulged in a ménage à trois, but I'd completely forgotten that Buse and Ferruh had once had a more "intimate" relationship by themselves. So Ferruh had also been spooked by news of the tape and was out to save his own ass.

Without wasting another second, I dialed Ferruh and Belkıs's number. Belkıs answered. We chatted about nothing in particular, while I tried to think of a reason to ask to speak to Ferruh. But I couldn't. No matter what I came up with, I knew that Belkıs would suffer a fit of jealousy.

Sending my best wishes to Ferruh, I hung up.

There hadn't been a peep from Sofya and her gang ever since they had gotten their hands on the cassette. I wondered if they'd found the Passat I'd left in the cultural center parking lot. Sofya hadn't mentioned anything about it. If they hadn't found it, then why hadn't they come after me? Süleyman knew where the club was, and could just as easily find my flat. At the very least, he should have shown up with a couple of heavies—knowing he couldn't handle me on his own—and forced me to tell him where it was. What was this Süleyman character after, anyway?

It was an unusually cool night, with an occasional breeze. Nothing like the usual humid, oppressive Istanbul nights. I hadn't turned on the TV or the CD player. The quiet seemed almost eerie.

The pills had done their magic; my headache was under control. I took a half-finished book from my nightstand. I was asleep before I'd finished the first page.

Chapter 30

❖

$\mathcal{T}$oday was Buse's funeral. That is, the day I'd at least find out who has claimed the body. I tried to suppress my curiosity; it was still early. Waiting around has never been my forte.

If I were to continue going to bed early at night and rising with the dawn, my lifestyle would be turned topsy-turvy. I am a lady of the night; a man by day. Assuming there was no unanticipated trouble, I'd have to rest for a few hours after the funeral. Otherwise, I'd be a mess at the club: bags under my eyes, dulled gaze, no coyness, no airs. Someone who lets loose a succession of synthetic cackles. Not my style!

I showered, prepared my breakfast, watched TV, dressed, changed my clothes . . . still not a single visitor or phone call.

Satı Hanım knew I normally rose late, and wouldn't come to clean until the afternoon. I don't like any movement in the flat while I'm sleeping, and will not tolerate the sound of a washing machine or vacuum cleaner. I usually leave the moment Satı Hanım arrives, and either go shopping, to the cinema, or spend the day at the office. It was still hours before she'd arrive.

I riffled through the day's papers, skimmed my favorite editorial columns. As I looked over the fashion pages I decided the outfit I was wearing was a bit much for a funeral. I'd have to change. But I couldn't decide whether to attend as a man or a woman.

If a crowd of our girls showed up, and that's what I

anticipated, I should appear as a chic but tastefully restrained lady; if the mourners were mainly from the neighborhood, I'd have to go as a man.

The showier alternative was the more attractive of the two. I put on a navy blue dress. It was sleeveless, collarless, zipped up at the back, and extended to midthigh. So far, so good. On my head, I placed a navy blue straw hat the size of an umbrella. Short satin gloves and black Gucci sunglasses finished off the demure effect. Just as I was trying to decide whether to wear a double strand of pearls or a fake corsage, Satı came. She has wonderful taste. I asked her opinion, and we decided on the pearls. Once I'd slipped into a pair of nearly heelless patent-leather buckled shoes, I was ready. I looked remarkably similar to the YSL models of the 1970s, and not unlike Catherine Deneuve in *Belle de Jour,* or perhaps Elsa Martinelli or Charlotte Rampling. I blew myself a kiss in the mirror. Yes! That was it: Once again, I'd managed to look just like Audrey, this time in *How to Steal a Million.*

"Well, don't you look wonderful, sir."

Satı Hanım is too polite not to address me as sir at every opportunity.

I was ready, although still a bit too early. There was no reason for me to hang out there ahead of time.

Thinking I might be required to say a prayer at the funeral, I began running through the *sure* I remembered. I hadn't practiced for a long while, so hadn't retained much. I was unable to recite the entire Fatiha. Only with Satı Hanım's assistance was I able to complete the entire opening chapter of the Koran.

The phone hadn't rung all day. It was strange—I had expected that at least a few of the girls would be planning to go to the funeral together. But no one had called me to make a plan! I lifted up the receiver and listened to make sure it was working. The dial tone buzzed out loud and clear. No, it wasn't broken and it hadn't been cut. But no one had called me. I began creating conspiracy theories: Perhaps my phone was being bugged.

I realized I was being silly. It'd be best to just call some of the girls myself.

I started with the ones living nearest to me. Melisa answered in her sleepiest, most male voice. I asked if she planned to attend the funeral. She drew out each word as she replied.

"*Abla*, but where is it? Let's not go out to some godforsaken spot on a morning like this," she said.

I told her it was in Samatya.

"Heaven help us, *ayol*, what business have we got way out there? Forgive me, won't you, I'm worn out in any case. Problems kept me up all night."

Because I didn't wonder what her troubles had been, I didn't ask.

"Go if you want to. If anything happens, let me know when you get back. It'll be just like I went myself," she said, hanging up.

Next I rang Ponpon and İpekten, both of whom wanted to go with me. The fact that it was in Samatya wasn't a problem. Ponpon would pick me up in her car, then we'd get İpekten on the way. Naturally, Ponpon asked what I was wearing.

"My navy blue dress," I said. "I didn't want civilian clothes."

"Well, of course, *ayol*, it's paying our last respects to her. I'm dressing up, too. I'd nearly decided to go civilian as well."

"Yes, but sweetie, from what I recall, all you've got are those fabulous costumes of yours. Will you be able to arrange a nice subdued outfit?"

"You bet," she assured me. "Why do you think I've been hanging on to my dear, late mother's tailored suits all these years? I've got them in mothballs and bring them out for weddings, funerals, court appearances—that sort of thing."

She'd be quite a sight in her mother's old-fashioned suits, but I didn't say a word.

While I waited, I copied onto another CD the programs I'd prepared for Ali. This time I didn't take any chances, and called one of those motorbike courier services. I handed the envelope over to Satı Hanım with my instructions.

As I was licking the envelope, Ponpon arrived. I put on my hat and went down to the car.

I got into the car and we looked each other up and down, then burst out laughing. She wore a smoke-gray headmistress's blazer with a matching skirt.

"How could you wear a woolen suit in this heat?"

"What could I do? The others didn't fit," she said. "You look like you're off to a fashion show, not a funeral."

"Ascot," I corrected her.

"What?"

"Ascot, the English horse races. Where everyone shows off their hats . . ."

"You mean the one in *My Fair Lady*?" she asked. She's a cultured girl and knows about such things. She also knows how much I adore Audrey.

We giggled all the way to İpekten's. Neither of us had mentioned our dress intentions, so she was in men's clothing.

"Just look at the two of you," she began. "They'll never let you perform *namaz* in those outfits. We'll all be stoned."

Ponpon asked, "Who's planning on performing *namaz*? I intend to stay to one side and get a good look at who's coming and going. Oh, and to accept condolences."

"As you can see, I have no intention of praying, either," I said.

"Well, I never," İpekten complained. "Why are we going, then? To provoke the public?"

"Look," I said, "if this is enough to provoke the public, so be it! In any case, we're far too lazy to go to this much trouble just to offend people."

"Maybe it will do them good," added Ponpon with a low, drawn-out laugh. "The time has come. Whatever will be, will be."

"Cut it out, *ayol*! We're going to a funeral, not a gay pride parade."

Asking directions along the way, we found the mosque in Samatya. It had a small garden, and there was a children's playground right next door. We parked the car in front of it, opening the doors and waiting inside. I lowered my long legs out of the car, keeping them parallel. But it was just too uncomfortable to maintain that pose for long, so I crossed them.

Two funerals were scheduled, with both parties waiting. It would be another half hour. I spotted a few of our girls. Most were dressed as men, with the others in fairly restrained costumes. I looked for Hasan, but didn't see him. The enormous flower wreath sent by the club had been placed near the coffin. I caught a glimpse of Cüneyt standing among the neighborhood mourners, and he also saw me. Without letting on to those around him, he nodded a greeting. I could tell he was embarrassed. He was reluctant to be seen with us, but loyal enough to come and pay his last respects to Buse.

The crowd was swelling. From where we sat, we could see those arriving from only one side, and the entrance to the mosque was blocked from view. If it went on like this, I would miss whoever it was I thought I was looking for. I decided to get out of the car and join everyone.

The first person I noticed was someone I'd expected to see, but had hoped wouldn't be the first person encountered. The moment she spotted us, Gönül lunged toward us. A head scarf tied securely under her chin, she also sported an enormous pair of sunglasses.

"You can really tell who your friends are at a time like this," she cried, attempting to embrace me.

She crashed into my hat. Its wide brim was a natural protective device against unwanted advances like hers. I introduced her to the girls. Perhaps mistaking her shabby outfit as a sign of a natural affinity, she familiarly took İpekten's arm. İpekten is impatient. She gets bored easily. I couldn't understand why she put up with this.

In her serpentine fashion, out popped the killer question from Ponpon's lips:

"And who is this person in the prayer shawl?"

I briefly explained who Gönül was. Her lower lip protruding, head shaking slightly, she listened to me.

"*İnşallah*, she won't be one of our party," she murmured, looking in the opposite direction and saying not another word.

The other mourners were looking at us a bit disapprovingly. I didn't give it a second thought. We had as much right to be there as anyone else.

I threw my arms around Dumper Beyza, who's famous for her bad temper. But as was always the case on days like this one, there was a general atmosphere of goodwill. Dumper had let her long black hair spill down over her shoulders. She was a mix of restraint and show: a sensible pair of jeans and a T-shirt, but full stage makeup. She asked me in low tones so that not everyone would hear:

"Do you think the imam will announce funeral services for a man or for a woman?"

I laughed, biting the insides of my cheeks like Ajda Pekkan to keep from exploding.

Hasan finally appeared, climbing out of a car. His jeans were slipping off his hips, as usual. As he extended a hand to the person he was assisting out of the car, his entire butt crack was exposed. My eyes traveled from Hasan's bottom to the person he was helping: Sofya!

I knew the two had met, but I never expected them to arrive at the funeral together. Hasan waved and grinned when he saw me.

Sofya had managed to get out of the car. Her sunglasses covered most of her face. One side of her mouth looked swollen. I went over.

Yes, the left side was definitely swollen. And her foundation failed to hide a dark bruise. With a crooked mouth and much difficulty, she spoke.

"It wasn't at all easy to persuade them about you," she said, pointing to her face.

I held my tongue. I mean, was it my fault she'd been beaten? She wrapped her arms around me.

"Whether you accept it or not, I love you in my own way."

I didn't know what to do. I felt not the slightest urge to throw my arms around her and weep gratefully. I checked my throat. No, no sign of a knot or obstructions of any kind. No emotional reaction at all. I slapped her on the shoulder in an easy, loutish way.

Despite my black Gucci glasses, Hasan was able to detect my withering glance. It would have been impossible not to. He seemed tense.

When he hugged me, I whispered, "You little snake!" into his ear. That was enough. He'd be off balance for the rest of the funeral. I didn't know what it was that bound him to Sofya, but, knowing her, it was something unsavory. Maybe Hasan was a part of her gang of blackmailers.

"I can explain," he said.

"I'm sure you can," I answered.

I looked away. I really didn't care to hear an explanation. It wouldn't be difficult to excise Hasan from the club and from my life.

I told myself a funeral wreath sent by a local market couldn't possibly be intended for Buse. Meanwhile, a group of militant girls arrived. They didn't know Buse, but whenever there was a funeral for a murdered transvestite they would show up in full force. Just like the other day at the morgue, they were on the verge of exploding. Their movements were short, swift, and menacing. They looked around restlessly, eyes blazing, hackles ready to be raised at the first sign of trouble. They were absolutely right to rebel, and my sympathies lay with them. In contrast to their apparent lack of organization, they managed to protest events in an incredibly systematic way. I can't say I appreciate their style, though. I'm more of a drawing room type, myself.

Noon prayers were read and the congregation began to enter the mosque to perform their *namaz*. Cüneyt and İpekten went in nearly side by side. I remembered Dumper Beyza's question, and wondered whether İpekten would pray with the women or the men.

While I busied myself with these thoughts, three dark luxury cars pulled up in a line. The crowd was stirring. As the murmuring grew louder, the crowd started to mill toward the cars.

I'm tall, but was unable to see exactly who got out of the cars. I think they were men in suits, and they carried two ostentatious funeral wreaths.

From somewhere behind me, I heard Gönül cry out, "Aha, it's my Sabiha Hanim!"

I immediately began shoving my way through the crowd toward the cars. It wasn't easy with my hat, but a few well-directed, discreet elbow jabs and one light kick cleared my path.

There was a large group in front of the middle car. It was surrounded by men in suits. The back door was open. Sitting in the back seat of the car, on the side nearest to me, with the blank unfocused stare of unseeing eyes, was Sabiha Hanım, in a state of dignified silence. Surprisingly, those eyes were not swollen with weeping, but she did look drained. She extended her hand, allowing those offering their condolences to kiss it. On that hand was a simple ring.

The bodyguards kept most of the crowd back, and the few well-wishers allowed to reach the old lady were permitted only to kiss her hand before being hustled off.

On the other side of the car was another small crowd. While a certain amount of shoving and pushing was going on, the crowd was silent, in deference to the funeral. Bending my legs slightly, I leaned down to get a look at the other occupant of the car.

What I saw was more of a shock to me than the simultaneous pinch on my bottom: Sitting in the back seat, next to Sabiha Hanım, was none other than Süreyya Eronat!

Ignoring the pinch, I quickly maneuvered around to the other side of the car. Upon seeing Süleyman sitting in the driver's seat, I was even more astonished. A sharp curse escaped my lips, and all heads turned in my direction. Momentarily, a space cleared between me and the car, which was two or three yards away, and I came eye to eye with Süreyya Eronat.

Just like in the photographs, he had a certain gravity. A faint smile played around the corners of his mouth as he looked at me.

Chapter 31

✤

$\mathcal{W}$e exchanged the briefest of glances. With his right hand, he gestured for me to come closer to the car. The bodyguards made way. Propelled forward by the crowd, and drawn by curiosity, I approached him.

"Reaching you proved to be more difficult than I'd hoped," he said.

The look he fixed on me was compelling. His face was free of expression, almost lifeless. But his eyes darted about like two little black bugs. I tore my eyes away from his and glanced around me. Gary Cooper Süleyman sat like a statue in the front seat. He didn't even turn to look at me. You would never have thought he was the one whose bashful airs had seduced me just two nights earlier. That sort of thing is a real blow to one's self-confidence.

"I wanted to meet with you. Süleyman was rather unsuccessful at arranging that." As he said this, he touched Süleyman lightly on the shoulder. "Please don't go right after the funeral. In fact, let's leave together if possible."

Despite the courteous phrasing, it was clearly not a casual invitation. I accepted without a second thought. Considering that Sabiha Hanım was with him, I believed he'd do me no harm.

"Now if you'll excuse me I'd like to join the *namaz*."

I'd stationed myself directly outside the car door, blocking his way. I moved over, he got out, and was immediately surrounded by bodyguards. From the courtyard of the mosque he called out:

"Wait for me in the car."

The authority in his voice was unmistakable. It must be part of what they call charisma. Otherwise, what were all these men doing at his beck and call? A path was cleared as he advanced, everyone stepping back to make way for him.

Süleyman said, "Please get in the car. Don't stand out in the sun."

I was amazed. It was as though I had no relation to the person he had tried to kidnap, the one who had knocked him out, tied his hands, and left him out in the middle of nowhere without a car. Yet he was determinedly civil. I thanked him, but didn't get in. I just leaned over to extend my condolences to Sabiha Hanım. I introduced myself as a friend of Fevzi's.

Buse was right when she told me that "the blind see with their hands." The elderly lady also had a keen sense of smell. She'd immediately understood that I was wearing ladies' perfume.

"You're Buse's friend, aren't you, my child? You don't have to call her Fevzi. Even I started calling her Buse toward the end."

I wanted to ask her what she was doing in Süreyya Eronat's car, where she'd been hiding all this time, how she had managed to disappear without a trace. But she placed her hand on my mouth so she'd be able to hear the imam. Closing her eyes, she began muttering a prayer, her lips twitching. When she closed her eyes I realized how full of pain her face was. The unseeing eyes masked a great deal when open. At the moment, though, the muscles around her eyes twitched, the corners of her mouth tightened, and her brow was furrowed. Each muscle told a separate tale of suffering.

I must have looked quite a sight with my upper body in the car, my bottom stuck outside. I accepted Süleyman's invitation for the moment and got in. Although the doors were open, the air conditioner was on. It didn't do much good, but the interior of the car was slightly cooler.

Sabiha Hanım ended her prayer with a nearly inaudible "Amen," and I remembered to pray. I pronounced the Fatiha I had practiced with Satı Hanım before leaving the house. I suspect I missed a few verses, but I believe the intention is more important than the words themselves. I mean, if prayer really does any good at all, my version would do just as well.

From the stirring of the crowd I realized that the funeral *namaz* had ended. Wondering if Süreyya Eronat would act as one of the pallbearers, I quickly got out of the car for a better view. Süleyman suddenly turned around as I got out. I silently gestured to him that it was all right, that there was no reason for alarm. He returned to his original position.

Yes, indeed, right there in front of everyone, a corner of Fevzi/Buse's coffin rested on the shoulder of Süreyya Eronat. What was most strange was the complete absence of the media, who usually followed his every move. Not a single photographer or TV camera. So the choice of a mosque in a secluded neighborhood of narrow streets hadn't been entirely coincidental. The media hadn't caught wind of it. Or they hadn't been permitted to approach. Perhaps the entire neighborhood had been sealed off.

Süreyya Eronat spent no more than a few seconds carrying the coffin. He turned his spot over to another mourner. After shaking hands with a few people, he then returned to the car, surrounded as before by bodyguards.

The bodyguards formed a protective shield around him, but even so, the wall of flesh wasn't enough to prevent a few people from shaking his hand, with one or two even managing to embrace and kiss him. I wasn't surprised to see that one of those kissing his hand was none other than the law clerk husband of

Aynur, the chubby-cheeked neighbor. That act of deference was to be expected from someone who hung a photograph of Süreyya Eronat in pride of place in the living room. Who knows what else the husband had done for him? It seemed that everyone I met was involved with either gangsters or the Hedef Party.

In order to allow Süreyya Eronat to slide into the car, the people were kept back. I, too, was pushed back into the watching crowd.

Once he was in the car, he looked out the window. When he saw me, his eyes remained fixed.

"If you please, we'll drop you off. And we'll have a talk on the way," he said.

Instructed by a motion of his hand, the bodyguards tugged me toward the car. He was sitting in the back seat with Sabiha Hanım, and my enormous hat alone was reason for him not to invite me to sit beside them.

"In the front, if you please," he said.

I did please. Now the bodyguards hustled me around to the other side of the car. The door opened. Removing my hat, I got in. A mini-convoy of three vehicles, off we drove.

I was holding the hat in my hand, unable to find anywhere to put it. I tried to place it on my lap, but it didn't fit. Nor was there room between Süleyman and me or under my legs on the floor.

"If you'll allow me, I'll put it in the back window," Süreyya Eronat offered. He was far more courteous and well spoken than I'd expected. I handed him my hat. Removing my dark glasses, I held them in one hand. Then I attempted to turn halfway around, so I could face him.

"Please fasten your seatbelt," said Süleyman.

I did as I was told. With the doors closed, the air conditioner made itself felt. Cool air spread through the car.

"I'm listening," I announced. Silence makes me edgy.

"First of all, I'd like to say that I appreciate all you've done," he began. "I had you tracked, and know everything. I know that you tried to help us, to protect Fevzi, may Allah rest her soul in peace, and to reach Sabiha Hanim."

So there had been hordes of spies following my every move for the past few days: Sofya's gangsters on the one hand, Hedef's henchmen on the other. And I hadn't noticed a thing. I put it down to the fine line separating an amateur from a professional.

"Be at ease. We have everything you were looking for. We had it all from the beginning. There was no danger. I destroyed it all. With my own two hands."

I wanted a more detailed explanation. Noting my look of surprise, he continued:

"The attachment I shared with Fevzi ended many years ago."

I was made uneasy by the apparent ease with which he talked of this queer incident from his past—and right in front of the mother of the boy in question. Again, he sensed my feelings.

"Süleyman knows everything about me. He's been at my side since he was a child, like an adopted son. I have nothing to hide from him."

So were these secret and forbidden sexual needs now met by Süleyman? Had a transvestite with breasts been replaced by a strapping bodyguard? I turned and looked at Süleyman again. Without taking his eyes from the road, my Gary Cooper was listening. He spoke.

"*Estağfurallah*, sir. You've always treated me like a son."

I wasn't sure whether or not I detected passion in his voice, but, even if it was only the result of profound respect, his voice quavered. And here I was thinking that beautiful friendships, the kind that one spoke of in trembling tones, belonged only to a bygone era.

"Thank you, Süleyman," he said. "If necessary, he'd lay his life on the line. Fortunately, that has not yet been Allah's will."

Sabiha appeared to have added deafness to her blindness, sitting without saying a word or reacting in any way. She fiddled with the wedding band on her left hand, turning it around and around on her finger. Süreyya placed a hand on hers.

"As for my dear *teyze,* she's known everything for years. Allah alone knows more than she does."

Sabiha shook her head and tears began streaming down her cheeks. Süreyya's well-manicured, gentlemanly hand took both of her hands in his. And squeezed. Harder than would seem necessary as an act of condolence. I'm not sure how much it hurt, but the tears started coming faster.

"It's no comfort to be told not to be upset. You're grieving. It's the will of God. There's no avoiding it," he said, his voice as icy as before.

Sabiha turned her face toward his voice. Süreyya pulled her onto his shoulder. They were like a mother and son, locked in an embrace. No, actually, they weren't. Their ages were too close for that. Sabiha withdrew a handkerchief secreted in her sleeve, wiping her eyes and nose. Then she bit the corner of the handkerchief as she wept silently.

"My relationship with Fevzi ended, but not with my Sabiha Hanim. I would call by to kiss her hand when possible, and would definitely phone on holidays and *kandil* days. She's like a mother to me. She has embraced me as a son, ever since the day we met. She also listened patiently to my troubles. I confided in her about everything. You know how Christians confess, rather like that. Whenever I was burdened with a problem, uncertain about how to proceed or weighed down by a guilty conscience, I would go to Sabiha. Tell her everything."

What he said was moving, but one thing was missing: emotion. He seemed totally devoid of feeling. His face remained impassive, and his dry voice was chilling. If I had read the words he was saying, I may have believed them; coming out of his mouth, they just weren't credible.

"From now on, she is to live with me, as a member of my family. That much I owe her. Being of assistance, even in this small way, is my duty."

I was being treated to a display of respect-affection-fear. It didn't last long. Süreyya Eronat was as annoyed by Sabiha's constant weeping as I was.

"That's enough!"

He pushed Sabiha off of his shoulder, suddenly hard and authoritative. The theater was over. Scolded and slightly roughed up, Sabiha was quiet. I wondered why she was willing to sit like this at his side, then my thoughts moved on to her living in his house, forever under his control and in his grip.

"Long before I rose to my present position I was well aware that the photographs taken so long ago could one day emerge, to damage me. However, Fevzi was fiercely devoted to her memories. She did not want them destroyed. They were her memories, as well as mine. I respected her wishes for a time."

We were now driving along the motorway. Through the tinted windows, it looked dark. It would be impossible to see us from outside. It was just what I'd expect of Süreyya Eronat. The windows were probably bulletproof as well.

"Later, Fevzi claimed to have destroyed the letters and photographs, but I didn't believe her. I had her flat searched. There was no trace of them."

Sabiha's fear registered clearly on her chalky white face.

"At first I accepted as truth what she had told me. But then I began hearing rumors. I had to do something. I had no idea where she was hiding them. When I asked her, she denied it, repeating that she'd destroyed them."

I congratulated her silently. Clearly, Buse—that is to say, Fevzi—had managed to string him along beautifully.

"I had been aware for some time that Fevzi was being harassed. But I didn't interfere. Then Fevzi informed you where he had hidden the photographs."

That's right, she'd told me at the club. In my little office on the top floor. But how did Süreyya Eronat know about that?

"Naturally, this comes as a surprise to you," he said. "Don't trouble yourself trying to understand. Hasan was listening."

So that was it. It was somewhat shocking: Hasan, my own Hasan! That's right. Hasan had come into the room while I was talking to Buse. So that's why Buse had seemed on edge.

"So is Hasan with you?" I asked, rather nervously.

It was hard to believe. What kind of relationship could Hasan have with the Hedef Party? He spent all his time sashaying around transvestites showing off his butt crack. And if he was involved with Hedef, what was he doing with Sofya?

I was answered with a courteous smile. That simple smile was expressive enough to earn an Oscar. The ability to convey so much with such a minimal amount of facial expression would have been the envy of any actor. The smile told me that Hasan was their informer, and a plant in Sofya's gang. As well as at my club. He would get his comeuppance, that much I vowed to myself.

Süreyya Eronat once again read my mind.

"Don't get the wrong idea, he has no direct links to us. Let's just refer to him as a friend," he suggested. "I'd like him to continue working for you. I think it would be more secure both for you and your club."

There you go! I was being openly threatened.

"Now let's move on to that fateful night. We were also informed only through the television news. Without hesitation, I went to visit my Sabiha Hanim. I knew she would need me."

I wasn't that gullible. He was after the photos and letters, of course. But I said nothing.

"In order to avoid any potential unpleasantness, I've kept her at my side from that point onwards."

"You also stripped the flat of any written or printed materials," I observed, unable to help myself.

"Exactly. We weren't prepared to leave anything to chance."

"How did you manage to keep things so quiet? That neighbor would notice a mosquito in the hallway, but she heard nothing."

"You're absolutely right," he said, ending with a difficult-to -decipher smile. I was certain it was another Oscar-winning performance. But this time I couldn't interpret it.

"The neighbors," I mused out loud. "Now, what was his name, the court clerk . . ."

"That's right," he said. "You see, you're very well informed. Brother Gökberk was most helpful. He took all necessary precautions in the apartment building."

"But how?" I asked. "Everyone there is so nosy . . ."

"How true. He arranged a minor distraction. While everyone was occupied, our plans were quietly executed."

I suddenly remembered the burned-out building on the same street as the Teksoy Apartment Building. I even recalled the acrid tang of smoke.

"A fire?" I asked.

Süreyya Eronat didn't answer, contenting himself with a small smile. The meaning was clear. The man wasn't required to give a stellar performance every other second.

For a short time we proceeded in silence. I hate sitting backward in moving vehicles. I get carsick. I was beginning to feel nauseated now. It wasn't just my position in the car that did it, though. The things I'd learned, the twisted relationships, the self-serving calculations, the stab in the back from Hasan, the surprisingly militant partisanship of Chubby Cheeks's husband, Gökberk . . . everything. I grimaced.

"Are you all right?" he asked.

"Yes, thank you," I said. "I'm just a little carsick from sitting backwards."

"Please make yourself comfortable. If you'd like, we'll stop for a moment. Get a breath of fresh air. Süleyman?"

Süleyman instantly slowed down and began swerving toward the far-right lane.

"There's really no need. I'm fine," I said.

"As you wish."

"I'd like to ask you something," I said.

"Please do. I'd be happy to assist your understanding on any subject . . ."

"Why did you have Süleyman try to seduce me?"

He smiled. This time it was completely sincere.

"He was merely under instructions to escort you to me. But he may well have appreciated your charms. He was not acting on orders on that account."

Süleyman blushed all the way up to his ears, but said nothing.

"There's no reason to be embarrassed, Süleyman," said Süreyya. "The charms and beauty of this young lady are obvious. If you like her, feel free to say so. We could arrange another invitation for her."

I felt even more nauseated.

"D–don't trouble yourself, sir . . ." stuttered Süleyman.

How blunt and discourteous! Did he mean to say that he had never been attracted to me? How right I was to have beaten him. Süreyya looked on, smiling.

"You gave him quite a pummeling, and injured his pride a bit. We weren't expecting that."

"I'm sorry if I hurt him," I lied. I knew I had. "But I wish he'd told me what it was all about."

"It wasn't my place to tell you anything," said Süleyman. He sounded like a wounded child. Because of the glare, when I looked over at his profile all I could see was his bobbing Adam's apple. His eyes remained on the road, as usual. He didn't so much as glance at me.

"I wish you'd have at least warned me with a note or a phone call. I got caught up with the blackmailers for no reason," I said.

"You're right, but your flat might have been under surveillance. I don't take risks."

Fair enough. It's true, my house was being watched. And I still didn't know whether or not I was being bugged.

Sabiha had stopped crying, but she'd turned her face toward the window to show she wasn't listening. She gazed out at the passing scenery with unseeing eyes.

"But the media is bound to find out about this. You participated in a public funeral. You've taken a transvestite into your car. You've also taken under your protection—forgive me, Sabiha—the mother of another one. I mean, you've suddenly displayed for all to see exactly what it is you've been concealing all these years."

"*Efendim*, an overly protected eye is inevitably pricked. We took all the necessary precautions. You're right, it all may still come out. But then again, the fact that I've taken under my wing the elderly, blind mother of a man I'll call my distant relative, will only reinforce my image. It only emphasizes that my party is prepared to embrace all sorts of people, the flexibility of our views. There's nothing to worry about, in fact. Everything is proceeding under our control."

"What about the people who saw me get into your car? What about when I get out?"

Naturally, I raised a single eyebrow as high as possible as I asked this. I also parted my lips slightly. It is a pose I've often practiced and admired in the mirror.

"Every family has certain members whose conduct is not approved of. That does not mean they are to be rejected. Especially during difficult times such as these. Our party embraces one and all. Our supporters are prepared to accept this as well."

It's true that he wouldn't have made a single move without carefully factoring in the possible ramifications. While his emotions may have played a part, his every action hinged on calculation.

"Do you plan to do anything about Buse's—I mean Fevzi's— murderers? That gang of blackmailers . . ."

When I mentioned Fevzi's name, Sabiha's eyes welled once more.

"We know who they are," he said. "As do you."

"They've got their tentacles everywhere," I observed.

Sabiha's sobs became audible. Her handkerchief was soaked. I couldn't stand it. I handed her the box of tissues that rested between me and Süleyman.

"Here you are. Use these," I said.

She nodded her thanks as she fumbled for a tissue.

"We have known all about them for some time. In fact, they've been of use to us on occasion. However, as you say, they've grown too strong. Their roots are too firmly entrenched. It would be impossible to wipe them out completely with one blow. We have determined the identity of those who killed Fevzi. For now they are our only targets. Don't worry, we've begun the procedure."

His mischievous wink as he said "Don't worry" was an unnerving sight on such an expressionless face.

"So far so good, but what about me? As you know, they're out to get me too. I'm being followed, my flat is being watched. They've got me by the throat. I don't have your power. My life wouldn't be long enough to knock them off one by one."

Looking me in the eye, he was silent for a moment.

"Sofya Hanım was sufficiently warned when she appeared at the funeral. We hope we persuaded her. It's important to realize when working with such elements that one should not necessarily remain always on the same side. It's critical to have a strong grip. An eye for an eye, a tooth for a tooth ... We laid out all our cards. It's obvious what they'll do next. Certain unwritten rules are in force in this community. The world we live in is without mercy. I must say, though, that the cassette you produced yesterday created complications."

"What do you mean?" I asked. "A tape can't be used as evidence. Unless I'm mistaken, the court of appeals has even ruled on that."

A smile flickered across his lips. "That's right, such a ruling has been made. But as you yourself know, evidence is not needed to produce gossip."

For some reason, I felt the need to defend myself. "But you know that it was all that woman journalist's doing."

"Ayşe Vidinli Hanım ..." he said, correcting my use of the word "woman."

That's right, her name was Ayşe. The name I couldn't remember was the common Ayşe. What's more, it's one of my favorite names.

"And she even handed over the interview to her newspaper," I continued.

"They would never have published it."

He said it with such authority it was impossible to claim otherwise.

"Forgive me for asking, but what exactly is the problem then?"

"A number of superfluous elements became aware of the existence of that tape of yours. Still more superfluous elements then became involved."

"They're just greedy," I said, springing to their defense.

He smiled as he looked at me. "Precisely. Greed. One of the seven deadly sins. But they'll be taken care of in due course."

He was as unruffled, as full of self-assurance, as ever. When it came to handling Ayşe Vidinli and her sidekick Ahmet, I wondered what he had planned. My curiosity did not mean I needed to ask him. The less I knew, the better.

"Fine," I said.

We were both silent. Süleyman and Sabiha appeared to have lost their tongues. I turned around, facing front. If the interior of the car hadn't been so cool, my churning stomach would have long since got the better of me. Air-conditioning is a wonderful thing.

"Where shall we drop you off?" he asked.

I had naturally expected to be taken to my flat. I was a bit miffed at his question, but I didn't let on.

"The first taxi stand will be fine," I said.

There was no need to give Süleyman directions. He took the next exit, driving toward Esenler. We approached the city bus terminal. I had no intention of getting out there.

"I'd really rather not get out at the bus terminal," I said, perhaps a bit sharply.

We continued on toward Davutpaşa. There was a taxi stand at the mouth of the road leading to the post office. We approached the first taxi and stopped.

"Thank you for your interest. We will not forget your actions," he said.

I shook the extended hand.

"And we would also appreciate your taking no further interest in these matters," he added.

That last bit was pronounced in bone-chilling tones. My hand was still in his; he was looking into my eyes. I understood once more why I had never been able to stand the man. Those dark eyes were terrifying.

I once again extended my condolences to Sabiha Hanım. She automatically extended her hand for me to kiss, which I did. Süreyya Eronat handed me my hat. Although he didn't deserve it, I wished Süleyman a good day as I got out of the car.

They drove off the second I got out. Fabulous hat in hand, dressed to the nines, I stood in the middle of the Topkapı Industrial Zone.

But before I even had a chance to find a taxi, a Corolla stopped in front of me.

Chapter 32

❖

$\mathscr{F}$rom the back window Sofya cried out, "Quick, get in!" Without thinking, I did. We drove off.

"Have you been following me?"

"Sweetie, don't play dumb with me. No, it's not a coincidence that we're here."

The car was being driven by an ill-tempered man I'd never seen before. Hasan sat in front, next to him, and said not a word. If Sofya had allowed him, he would no doubt have greeted me.

"Listen, sweetie," she said. "Things have gotten more out of hand than you can possibly imagine. I need you."

"I handed over the tape—"

"Don't start with me. You just got out of his car. I doubt you were playing doctor. I need to know everything he told you. While it's still fresh in your mind; before you forget a word. Otherwise, he won't believe me."

Outdoing herself, Sofya said all of this in a single breath.

"Please speak more slowly, one word at a time. You're overwhelming me."

The tentacles of the blackmail Mafia were fully extended. Sofya, perhaps Ferruh, maybe even that literary sensation Refik Altın, were all part of it somehow. Even I had become involved, with my name jotted down in a file somewhere.

The other set of powerful, far-reaching tentacles belonged to

Süreyya Eronat. It was a classic battle of wills. Süreyya Eronat now expected me to extract myself completely from the matter.

"He didn't ask me nicely. I had to go with them," I said.

"Naturally. So?" asked Sofya.

I had hoped she'd continue. She didn't.

"What do you mean, 'so'? The man threatened me. He implied that if I got mixed up in this any further he'd have to take measures himself."

Chatterbox Hasan couldn't hold his tongue any longer. He blurted out, "Didn't he tell you what they planned to do?"

"Idiots! Both of you. Do you think he'd tell me anything? He gave me no indication of their plans."

We sat in silence.

"Now," said Sofya, beginning again, "you're coming with me; you've got some explaining to do!"

"To whom?" I asked.

"To someone who no longer listens to me, who tells me at every opportunity that he doesn't trust me. Your dear friend Mehmet Sebil."

I swallowed hard. Mehmet Sebil was a businessman I'd known for years. He used to do business in the former Eastern Bloc countries. Occasionally, he'd require my services to provide some unusual entertainment for his guests. I'd send him the girls he requested. It was profitable for all concerned. Although I'd known him for years, we'd mostly only spoken on the phone.

"So he's at the head of all this?"

"No, dear . . . But he's responsible for me. Even he doesn't know who's at the top. I'm not sure there is such a person. It's all so complicated."

"What makes him a friend of mine?" I asked. "I've rarely met him in person."

"How do I know? That's what he told me."

"The pimp!"

Sofya cackled. "Really! You call him your friend, you provide him with your services. You see, sweetie, not everyone is as naïve as you. It's a dog-eat-dog world. Perhaps it's time for you to grow up."

It hadn't taken Sofya long to regain her former composure. She was as sharp-tongued, as haughty as ever.

"So what am I supposed to tell him?"

"Whatever you talked about with Süreyya Eronat. First I'll tell him, then you say the same thing. That way, we'll cover each other's backs. If necessary, this pansy can chime in, too."

The "pansy" was none other than Hasan.

"Why don't you just come out and say it? We'll vouch for each other's lies."

"I prefer not to put it like that," Sofya said, distancing herself. "It's a golden opportunity for both of us. It's the only chance we have to get them off our backs until we put all of this behind us. Do you understand what I'm saying?"

"What's there not to understand, *ayol*?"

"It's just that you're looking so vacant."

"I'm thinking."

She flashed me a look of scorn. Rather than using her eyes, she made economic use of her lips to get the message across. Meryl Streep would have been wracked with envy.

"And if I don't come with you?" I asked.

"This is no joke. It's not up for discussion. Pull yourself together and wise up. Your days as an amateur sleuth are over, sweetie. Now it's your ass on the line! Your life hangs in the balance. If you value it, you'll act accordingly. Won't you?"

Meanwhile, we had passed in succession Merter, Bakırköy, and Ataköy as we proceeded along the E-5 motorway. We exited at İkitelli. Because I don't consider the area to be part of Istanbul, it's a shock to me every time I see it. The city silhouette had completely changed since my last visit. I realized that I passed through the area so rarely that each visit represented the passage of a few more years.

The huge media holdings that had, one by one, cleverly moved out to the city outskirts now found themselves creeping back toward the city center. We turned onto a side road and bumped along a succession of smaller roads, each more badly paved than the previous one.

Once we had passed the sleek media towers, things became less orderly. Dotted here and there among the well-maintained modern headquarters were an increasing number of crumbling maintenance centers, iron foundries, and depots selling construction materials. The buildings became fewer and farther between. If anything happened, a quick escape, especially in the costume I wore, would be impossible. I was like a lamb blissfully heading for the slaughter.

I felt less and less confident that Sofya and Hasan could protect me.

"Here we are!"

We'd arrived at a place surrounded by high walls, the only entrance a sliding metal gate. As we approached, the door began to open. We drove through an inner courtyard covered with gravel. I dislike walking on such gravel and in the shoes I was wearing, I'd be unable to do so.

We parked in front of a new two-story building. There was no sign of life inside, or even in the vicinity.

As Hasan made to get out of the car, Sofya snapped, "Stay here! We'll call if we need you. We don't need to get you mixed up in this." Apparently, she still retained a trace of humanity.

Climbing three steps, we entered the building. Sofya led the way with her driven, resolute stride.

Our footsteps rang out as we crossed the imitation granite floor, echoing through the spacious, empty interior. The feeling of spookiness increased with each additional step.

"Are we the only ones here?" I asked, instinctively whispering to avoid any echoes. Sofya didn't even turn around to acknowledge my question.

Two large double doors swung open directly in front of us, and out walked a plump, round-faced, bespectacled man. He advanced toward us. As far as I remembered, he didn't look at all like Mehmet Sebil. He couldn't have changed this much since our last meeting.

Dispensing with the usual greetings, he moved to one side and said, "Go in, he's expecting you." The plump man's solemn face was belied by a pair of mischievous, darting eyes.

The room we entered had clearly been designed as an executive office, with the usual showy furnishings on display. A corner room, it afforded a view of both a green garden and the inner gravel courtyard through which we had arrived. In other words, our every step had been monitored.

Sitting in easy chairs in the section of the room reserved for meetings were Mehmet Sebil—my dear friend!—and a man I didn't recognize. Tension fairly radiated from them both. My pal gave no indication of any kind that he had any idea who I was. He didn't greet me at all, let alone rise to his feet.

Just like Lotte Lenya in *From Russia with Love*, Sofya adopted a pose that was as deferential as it was absurd: both knees slightly bent, a single foot pulled back a bit. I looked on in pity and surprise.

The plump man had followed us into the room. He sat stiffly on one of the uncomfortable chairs in the corner, demonstrating his relatively low ranking.

The voice of the man I didn't know was mechanical:

"Sit down, please."

That "please" was not of the variety used when making a request, presenting a gift, or displaying hospitality. From his airs, he was clearly top of the pecking order in the room. And he made certain everyone knew it. Perhaps that explained the hesitance of my old friend Mehmet Sebil to greet me.

"*Merhaba*, Mehmet Bey. It's been a long time," I said as I approached him and extended a hand.

"It has . . . really . . ." he mumbled as he shook it.

I turned to the other gentleman.

"I don't believe we've met," I said. "*Merhaba*."

"I know you well enough," was the scornful reply. My hand remained in midair.

Her eyes on my every move, Sofya flashed me a look that meant I should sit down.

"I spoke to Süreyya Eronat," she began. She implied that the little talk had been her idea, her achievement.

Süreyya Eronat had openly threatened our Sofya, warning her of the consequences if she didn't shape up. She pointed to me. "She witnessed the whole thing."

I contented myself with a stupid nod.

"So?" asked the smirking, antisocial creature.

"You know better than I do, sir. I'm merely conveying what I was told. Don't shoot the messenger."

"So you're suggesting that we shouldn't do anything? That's not the way things work."

"Two people have died," I interrupted. "Isn't that enough? And what's more, one of them was totally innocent."

He pretended not to have heard me. I didn't exist. I was invisible, inaudible. Frowning, he stared off into space. I supposed this was his thinking pose. We all watched him. I got goose bumps.

"Actually, Buse was innocent as well," I added. I couldn't understand how my voice had been reduced to a murmur. Again, no one heard me.

"I'm sure you had her killed." I didn't know if I said this out loud or just thought it. The man's icy stare suggested the former.

Sofya looked at me anxiously. Fabulous lips slightly pursed, eyes narrowed, she was telling me to shut up. The goose bumps were increasing in number, despite the warmth of the room.

I glanced over at Mehmet Sebil. The look he gave me was a masculine version of Sofya's. That is, I didn't mistake the pursed lips for a kiss blown in my direction. Sebil seemed to have grown somewhat slovenly—sluggish, even. Either that or I hadn't noticed it before.

I did as they wished. I was quiet. The menacing atmosphere seemed to have worked its spell on me, as well.

Frosty continued staring into space, apparently deep in thought. I, too, began thinking. Who knew the unsavory ways the girls I had arranged for Sebil had been used for blackmail purposes? Fortunately, most of them must have been blissfully unaware. Otherwise, I'd have heard about it by now. Never again would I send him one.

The thinking process completed, he spoke:

"We will evaluate what you've told us."

When Sofya immediately rose to her feet, I understood that we had been ordered to leave. I got up as well.

"As for you, watch your step. Stop popping up from under every stone. Just so you know, you got off easy this time. But your file is getting fatter with each passing day. Decide whose side you're on. We'll contact you if necessary."

For the second time that day, I was being instructed not to get involved. First, Süreyya Eronat had politely suggested as much, now this ox was openly threatening me.

"Sofya will keep you informed," he said.

I had learned not to shake his hand, and ignored Mehmet Sebil. I mutely followed Sofya, who quickly strode toward the door.

As Sparkly Eyes rose to open the door for us, the dictatorial voice of our antisocial host called after us:

"Who's in the car?"

We both froze. He must have seen Hasan.

"Why did you bring him?"

"We came here straight from the funeral. He's reliable, sir," said Sofya. "A close friend."

Silence.

"Don't let it happen again!"

I decided that one day I would laugh at the sight of Sofya, wind completely gone from her sails, as she quailed and cowered in the presence of overpowering authority.

The second we were outside I asked, "Who's the ox?"

"Shhh . . ." hissed Sofya.

We didn't talk all the way back to the car.

Chapter 33

✣

$\mathcal{M}$y spirits were low indeed when I got home. Even back in the car, while listening to Sofya, I'd decided to block out all she said. I wanted to flee, to be somewhere far from her reach, in another country, to assume a completely new identity and take up residence in Shangri-la or Panama.

But it seemed like the best thing to do was to follow the instructions that I'd received from two sources today: forget what had happened and stay out of it. I had solved the mystery of Buse's murder, and that was enough.

Satı Hanım was still hard at work cleaning.

"Welcome, *beyefendi*," she greeted me.

"Sir" strolled in wearing a short skirt. He wore a tray of a hat on his head. I asked if anyone had called.

"I didn't answer the phone, sir. There were some calls; they left massages," she said. "You'll have to listen."

"That's 'message,' not 'massage,'" I corrected her as I went into my bedroom.

I'd begun to perspire. I removed my dark dress before it became stained with sweat. A cool shower would be nice. If I stayed in long enough, I might even find my mind and soul becoming as cleansed as my body. But first I would listen to the messages.

Hasan was the first caller. He was suggesting that we go to the funeral together if I hadn't already left. I'd deal with him later.

We needed to talk. His behavior had been atrocious, especially considering his ability to look me straight in the eye the entire time. He was immature and far too eager to get mixed up in everything. I was sure he wasn't a bad person, but he was definitely a bit too green, and far too nosy. On top of all this, he even claimed he wasn't gay. No, Hasan was difficult to pin down or place. And what was all that prancing about with his ass exposed supposed to mean? Just thinking about it infuriated me.

Ali had left two messages, one after the other. In the first, he confirmed having received the envelope from the courier. He hadn't yet looked at it, and had not been treated to the sight of John Pruitt. The second message informed me that Wish & Fire had called and was interested in our proposal. As always when discussing the prospect of money, his voice was all blooming roses and fluttering butterfly wings.

The next message was total silence. After that came one impossible to make out. It was a male voice, calling from a noisy place on a cell phone with a weak signal. I decided it was a fan. I didn't recognize the voice, but judging from the odd comprehensible word we had once enjoyed intimate relations. I silently prayed Satı hadn't heard this one.

Then Kenan called. He said he had tried to leave a message and apologized for the noise. This time, the message he left was clear as a bell. He desired me, and told me so in the most graphic terms. Satı would have turned red as a beet if she had heard what he said.

Last of all was another nontalker. The phone must have been ringing the entire two hours I was gone.

"Satı Hanım, cut up the watermelon in the kitchen, would you? I'll be in the shower. Put a few slices in the freezer so it gets nice and cold by the time I get out," I instructed, heading for the bathroom.

.   .   .   .

The watermelon was ready. Satı was up to her usual tricks. When I'm at home, she draws her work out, meticulously dusting bric-a-brac she'd normally just ignore. I don't consider myself to be overly fastidious, but a clean house is my natural right. I suspect she sometimes does no more than iron a couple of shirts.

What I really needed was for her to sort out the accumulated magazines, cluttered CDs, and tangled cords and cables in the office. Oh, and wipe the keyboard. I mentioned what I had in mind. When I said "cable" she interrupted:

"But I'm afraid. Electric shocks and all . . ." she said. "Getting electrocuted on a summer's day like this!"

Would it be any more pleasant on a winter's day?

"Don't worry," I assured her. "Everything will be all right. We'll unplug them. Straighten them out and then I'll handle it."

"All right, then," she agreed. "If you'd like, I'll even connect the cables myself. Should I braid them for you?"

No, I really didn't see the need for braided computer cables.

"Get it done, then we'll see."

As she went into the office she called out, "Come and unplug everything so I can clean."

You'd have thought she'd never used a vacuum cleaner, iron, or food processor. I did as she asked. She disappeared under the desk, where she attacked the tangle of cords and cables. She even disconnected the keyboard. I told her to wipe it with a damp cloth, just a drop of detergent and not too wet.

I began sorting through the backlog of magazines and reading a bit, intending to do so until Satı finished her work and left. She wouldn't stay much longer. It was her habit to leave at four. And that's what she did.

"Would you like me to do anything else?" she asked, having already changed into her street clothes.

After she left I checked the keyboard. It was virtually

dripping. That was one way of getting the message across that such tasks were not to be assigned in the future. We were no strangers to each other. I knew her ways. I placed the keyboard upside down on a sunny windowsill, cursing Satı the whole time. If it didn't work when it dried out I'd have to buy a new one. Though that one would at least be clean.

She hadn't braided the cables, but had tied them with a thick red bow. It looked ridiculous. I'd leave it like that for a while.

I needed a nap before going out to the club. If Kenan called again, I'd consider his offer.

I had barely stretched out when the doorbell rang. The apparent link between my getting into bed and the ringing of the bell had started to get on my nerves. I rushed to the door anyway, on the chance that it was Kenan.

Crushing disappointment! Standing before me was Hüseyin, his face a wreck. I'd intended to give him a good scolding, but the sight of him stopped me cold. It wasn't difficult to guess what had happened. I invited him in.

"What happened to you?"

"Your gang did it." He looked at me plaintively, like a homeless kitten.

"And just who exactly is in 'my gang'?"

"You know, the ones who are trying to get whatever it is you're hiding. They took the envelope. When they couldn't figure out what it was, they beat me up."

"I'm sorry," I said.

"When they realized it wasn't what they were after, they let me go. At first I thought they were going to kill me. They turned out to be merciful."

"Did you go to the police?" I asked.

"What would the police do? I'm a taxi driver. Have you forgotten? If I was lucky enough to get a sympathetic cop he'd listen, say he was sorry, and send me on my way."

Hüseyin was the second person that day who had trouble speaking to me. Sofya had managed to mask the worst of the damage to her face. Hüseyin hadn't used any makeup.

"I've been getting thrashed for two days. There's not a single spot that doesn't ache."

I apologized again.

"It's not your fault," he said.

"I still feel responsible for all this," I said.

"No," he said. "I was an idiot. I'm the one who was after you. When I heard it was your package, I jumped at the chance to deliver it. Someone else from the stand was going to take it. I wanted to be able to stop by and tell you I'd dropped it off. I was itching for it."

My inner Florence Nightingale was awakened. His eyebrow was split open. I moved closer to him, lightly touching the wound. The blood had dried.

"Did you go to the doctor, at least?"

"No, I came straight to you."

The traces of iodine on his face told another story. He understood my look of disbelief.

"I went to the pharmacy. They dressed it."

"Good," I said. I withdrew my hand, pausing. Florence would have to wait.

He was looking deep into my eyes. Like a little kitten saying, *Take me.*

"It's my back that's bad; my face is nothing," he said.

He pulled off his shirt. They really had beat him good. I ran my hand along his back.

"Don't touch it! It hurts like hell," he said.

"You need a good alcohol dressing," I said.

"Would you mind doing it? I can't reach . . ." he said.

There wasn't a trace of a grin. Florence Nightingale was back with a vengeance.

"So what did you do with Müjde?" I asked.

I shouldn't have asked. But I couldn't help it.

"Nothing," he said. "What else? I just wanted to make you jealous. That's all. When you left the club I went home."

It was nice to believe him. A smile must have spread across my face. Otherwise, he wouldn't have dared to kiss me. Despite the swollen lip, he was a good kisser. I have to admit I enjoyed it. I responded. He then pulled me into his arms. A hand found a nipple, which hardened at his touch. As I caressed him, he gasped slightly and gritted his teeth from the pain. Then he let out a deep sigh. I withdrew my hand. He retrieved it in his, drawing it down to a more suitable spot.

It was early evening, but things were heating up.

Glossary

abi	elder brother
abla	elder sister
aman	oh! ah! mercy! for goodness' sake!
ayol/ay	exclamation favored by women; well!
bey	sir; used with first name, Mr
dürüm	sandwich wrap
efendi	gentleman, master
efendim	Yes (answer to call). I beg your pardon?
estağfurallah	phrase used in reply to an expression of thanks, exaggerated praise, or self-criticism
Fatiha	the opening chapter of the Koran
geçmiş olsun	expression of sympathy for a person who has had or is having an illness or misfortune
hanım	lady; used with first name, Mrs, Miss
inşallah	if God wills; hopefully
kandil	one of four Islamic feast nights
maşallah	what wonders God has willed; used to express admiration
mevlit	a religious meeting held in memory of a dead person
namaz	ritual worship, prayer
peştemal	waist cloth worn at a Turkish bath
rakı	an anise-flavored spirit
sen	you, second person singular; used in familiar address
siz	you, second person plural; used in formal address
teyze	aunt; also used to address older women
vallahi	by God; I swear it is so

Fiction
Crime
Noir

Culture
Music
Erotica

dare to read at serpentstail.com

Visit serpentstail.com today to browse and buy
our books, and to sign up for exclusive news and
previews of our books, interviews with our
authors and forthcoming events.

NEWS — cut to the literary chase with all the latest news about our books and authors

EVENTS — advance information on forthcoming events, author readings, exhibitions and book festivals

EXTRACTS — read the best of the outlaw voices – first chapters, short stories, bite-sized extracts

EXCLUSIVES — pre-publication offers, signed copies, discounted books, competitions

BROWSE AND BUY — browse our full catalogue, fill up a basket and proceed to our fully secure checkout – our website is your oyster

FREE POSTAGE & PACKING ON ALL ORDERS…
ANYWHERE!

---

sign up today – join our club